# We're all a little SCARED

you are enough

BOOK 3

A NOVEL BY

# TIFFANY ANDREA

Copyright © 2021 Tiffany Andrea. All rights reserved

No part of this book may be reproduced or stored in a retrieval system, or transmitted in any form or by any means, electronic, mechanical, photocopying, recording, or otherwise, without express written permission of the author.

The characters and events portrayed in this book are fictitious. Any similarity to real persons, living or dead, is coincidental and not intended by the author.

All brand names or product names used in this publication are trade names, service marks, trademarks, and registered trademarks of their respective owners. The publisher and the book are not associated with any product or vendor mentioned. None of the companies referenced within the book have endorsed the book. All product, business, or brand names remain intellectual property of their registered owners.

Paperback ISBN: 978-1-990724-15-2
Hardcover ISBN: 978-1-990724-16-9
eBook ISBN: 978-1-990724-17-6

Cover Design by: Burden of Proofreading Publishing featuring Graphics by JemStock via CanStockPhoto

Interior Graphics by Yupriamos

*My girls. When it comes to expressing my love for you both, words fail me.*

*Thank you for allowing me to be your mom and for teaching me more than I could ever teach you.*

*Always remember, "happiness doesn't just happen. Reach for it, work for it, and don't let it slip through your fingers when you find it."*

*I'm so glad I found you, forever my happiness.*

Table of
Contents

As you'd expect, if you've read the previous books in this series, Isla's story is an emotional roller coaster. Grab your tissues, buckle up, and enjoy the ride.

You'll notice a Taylor Swift theme throughout this book, and even if you don't like her music, I recommend you listen to her song "Eyes Open" before you start reading. You'll notice one of Isla's unrelenting thoughts is a lyric in that song, and it's more fun if you sing it. *Pretend there's a cry-laugh emoji here.*

If you don't want any spoilers, skip ahead to chapter one, because below I mention some sensitive topics the book addresses.

Like the other books in this series, this one tackles issues surrounding mental health, racism and discrimination, child abuse, alcoholism, and drug use. However, I don't feel any of the above topics are particularly triggering in this story. If you're sensitive to anything mentioned, please proceed with caution.

It's surprising what comes to your mind when you're watching someone you love cling to life. Their quirks and nuances that used to drive you nuts, their irritating habits, all the pointless arguments you wasted time on—none of them matter. You recall the smiles they brought to your face, the times they supported your wildest dreams, and the love they gave.

"Don't close your eyes, Rory. Help is coming. Stay awake!" I cry, watching my best friend struggle to stay conscious as she lies slumped in the driver's seat of her Chevy Cruz, which is no longer on the road, nor on its wheels. I want nothing more than to reach out and hold her, but my seatbelt is the only thing holding me in place and preventing me from tumbling on top of her as the car rests on its side partway down a snow-covered embankment. "Come on. Sing a song with me. We can sing *Bad Blood*."

I realize how stupid my song suggestion is when Rory groans a snort laugh, spewing blood from her mouth and nose. Tears are streaming down my face, but the centre console has my left arm pinned and my right arm clings to the handle over the door, so I can't wipe my eyes. My vision is blurring and while I wish I could see anything other than what I am right now, I don't want to take my eyes off of my best friend. Her dark-brown hair is caked in blood and her near-black eyes are only slits in her normally cheerful face. The dimples I've spent the last eight years treating as my goal when making her laugh are absent.

"Isla..."

"I'm here. I'm right here." The panic is evident in my voice despite me trying to keep calm for her sake, and it's becoming increasingly hard to hear her over the sound of the wind whistling through the broken passenger window to my right.

"Be happy. You're going..." She coughs, spraying more blood across her car's interior. "You're going to be a bestseller."

"Not without you. Don't start that nonsense. It sounds like you're saying goodbye. Help is coming, I promise."

She shakes her head in a subtle gesture that I nearly miss with my tear-blurred vision.

"I'm tired."

"I know." The amount of blood pooling around her tells me we don't have long. Help needs to get here now, and I don't hear sirens yet. "Do you want me to sing to you? Name the song and I'll sing whatever you want." I'm clutching at straws, willing to do anything to keep Rory awake. My singing voice won't lull anyone to sleep. My dog won't even tolerate my attempts at carrying a tune.

"No. I... I'm scared."

"I am too, but it's going to be fine. One day we'll laugh about this. I promise." My words are lacking any conviction. "Dominic is expecting you. You've been waiting for this day for almost a year. You can't stand him up now." We're not going to make it to our intended location where we were to meet Rory's long-time crush and co-worker Dominic and his friend Mitchell for a double date, but Rory has been talking about this day for weeks. If her excitement is the ticket to keeping her awake, I'll use it. "I'm planning on being your maid of honour one day. Rory McKay. That has a nice ring to it."

The groan emanating from Rory pushes me beyond scared to petrified. She's in pain and aside from shouting information to the crisis-assist responder speaking through the car's Bluetooth, I'm helpless. Hopeless. Afraid.

"Hold on, Rory. This is *not* your last page." Sirens are faint in the background and that sparks a new wave of hope, but optimistic is a far cry from how I feel as I desperately try to keep my best friend from slipping away. "They're almost here."

Vehicles come to a screeching halt at the top of the embankment we've rolled down. I hear blaring sirens and muffled voices. It's hard to hear much beyond the blood pumping through my ears. I never thought I'd find myself in this situation again.

A stranger's face peers in the windshield as the car jolts. The black and yellow helmet on the hulking figure's head reassures me our rescuers have arrived. "We're just securing the car, then we'll get you out of there."

I blubber through my tears. "Please hurry. She's bleeding. She's not talking anymore."

"Stay calm, miss. We'll have you out of there in a moment."

Stay calm? Really? As if that expression has ever brought anyone a measure of calm in the history of time. I'll just "ohm" my Zen right into place and forget about the fact my best friend is dying in front of me.

I take a breath, reminding myself they are here to help and making myself difficult is not going to improve our situation.

So many noises—grinding, cutting, yelling. I can't tell the difference between one rescuer and the next.

A firefighter passes in two blankets through the already broken window and asks me to shield myself and Rory as best I can so they can get through the windshield; using the door isn't an option. I release the handle I was clinging to, which causes my bodyweight to press down on my arm, sending a surge of pain from my fingers to my neck. At least I still *have* feeling. With one arm, I struggle to drape the first blanket over my unconscious friend. I can see her chest rising and falling in shallow breaths, which offers me a glimmer of hope. I pull the second blanket over my face and wait for the sound of breaking glass.

A minute later, the windshield is gone, and the blanket is being pulled off of me, cloaking me with a blast of cold November air.

"Get her first. Please. She needs help," I plead.

Our heroes move methodically, and no decision is made without considering the effects. I want them to move faster. They need to save Rory.

We're both equipped with neck braces and removed from the car; me first, her second. I'm being carried up the hill, strapped to a backboard, my left arm secured against my body.

"Where's Rory? Is she going to be okay?" I choke out, afraid of the answer.

A paramedic with a blonde ponytail sticking out of her black knit toque keeps her eyes focused on the ground. "They're taking good care of her. Let's get you fixed up, then we can see about your friend, okay?"

What do I say in response to that? I'm in no position to fight anybody to get my way, and I wouldn't, even if I was. *Comply. Stay Quiet. Don't make a scene.*

I'm transferred into the back of an ambulance moments later, with no further update on Rory's condition.

"Is there anyone you want me to contact to meet us at the hospital?"

I sniffle, squeezing the pooling tears from my eyes. "Rory's parents, Barbara and Mark Anderson. They're in my phone."

"You don't have family you want me to contact? Someone should be with you."

My eyes shoot wide open as she says those words. "Why? Did something happen? Do you know something about Rory?"

"I just mean, you've been through a lot, and you should have family around. I don't have an update on your friend."

"Um, I guess someone can call my parents. Zara or Zach Haynes. Mom or Dad in my phone."

The paramedic, whose name I see is Charli, uses her own phone to dial a number and has a brief conversation, in which she answers no less than twenty questions. That's a good indication she was speaking to my mom.

"Your parents are on their way. You live in Bracebridge?"

I nod. "Rory and I were going or a double date in Orillia."

"Are you in college?"

"No, I finished a year ago."

"Wow. You're so young." She looks at the health card she retrieved from my handbag and glances at me with raised eyebrows. "You're only twenty-one. That's impressive."

"Homeschool." I don't want to converse at the best of times, but I appreciate Charli's attempts to keep me distracted, even if it's not working.

"What do you do now? For work?"

I swallow the lump in my throat. If I hadn't agreed to go on this date and just stayed home to work on my novel, this never would have happened. We'd be sitting in our apartment, laughing, listening to Taylor Swift, eating our bodyweight in chocolate.

"I'm a writer."

"Like, for the newspaper?"

"No. Books. I haven't published anything yet though, so it's not like you've heard of me."

"That's really cool. I'll definitely keep an eye out for your name."

This is not how I intended to build a fan base. I don't want people to pity-buy my books. I nod before turning my head away. My socializing metre just bottomed out and I don't have the energy to say another word.

I listen to the slushy snow beat against the undercarriage of the ambulance as we speed down highway eleven to the hospital. As if some cosmic joke, the hospital is less than a kilometre from the place we were going.

We arrive at the emergency department, and I see the other ambulance arrived ahead of us. I hope that's good news.

I'm ushered into an examination room as Charli relays some confusing medical speak to the doctor taking over. One nurse and the paramedic who drove flank me, steering me through the wide hallway, which is lined with abandoned medical equipment.

"Where's Rory?"

"Let's get you fixed up, then we can find out about your friend." The doctor repeats Charli's sentiment and I'm not any less frustrated this time around. I just don't have the courage to speak up and defy what the doctor said.

Social anxiety: making every day more difficult since I learned how to speak.

# Eyes Open

2

*Beep. Beep. Beep.*

I don't know why I'm hooked up to this heart monitor; I have a sprained arm. Mom would be a better candidate for a cardiac event, judging by the way she's looking at me. Her medium-brown hair is down in damp loose waves as if she were in the shower when Charli called her. I'm surprised she didn't show up in a robe and slippers.

"Do you need anything, Sweet Girl? I can go get you something to eat or at least a drink  I'll get you a French vanilla cappuccino."

I shake my head. "I want to know where Rory is. She wasn't…"

A warm hand grasps mine. "They'll tell us something soon. I saw Barbara and Mark in the hallway, and they didn't know anything yet, either."

The guilt bubbles over and I sob. Racking, uncontrollable sobs. The heart monitor beeps faster, alerting everyone in a fifteen-metre radius I'm emotionally unstable.

"Shh. Take a breath, Isla. We'll hear something soon."

I'm grateful to my mom for not telling me not to worry or promising everything will be okay. Our anxiety bond makes her a reasonable person in difficult situations. She knows what helps and what doesn't.

"Mr. and Mrs. Haynes, could I speak with you for a moment?" a brown-skinned doctor with greying hair at his temples asks from the doorway.

With a glance in my direction, my parents walk out of my room and fifteen seconds later, the silence is broken by my mom's frantic wailing, saying "no" repeatedly. I don't need them to come in and relay the news to me. I know what that means.

It means my best friend is gone. She's gone, and I wish I could take her place.

When my dad returns, his eyes are glassy, but I can tell from his expression he knows I heard the scene unfold in the hallway. "Hey, Kiddo." He takes a seat at the foot of my bed, placing a hand on my shin, which is one of the few places I don't hurt. "They, uh... they did everything they could, but she—"

"Please don't say it. This can't be real. It can't be."

"I'm sorry. It's not fair." He stands and walks toward the head of my bed. When he leans forward and places a kiss on my forehead, my tears burst from their dams again.

Yesterday, we were sitting in our apartment, dreaming of our successful careers and happy endings. What am I supposed to do if she can't have hers? I can't possibly find my own. I'm left with an injured arm and a massive hole in my heart, ripping open old wounds I tried to forget. How can this be happening again? I wish I could trade places with her.

"Why is life cruel?"

With one hand on my shoulder, my dad replies, "I'm sorry, Kiddo."

What else is there to say?

Hours later, I've cried myself into a state of exhaustion but can't sleep. The last doctor to come visit me said I'll be discharged later today and all I want is to cuddle up with my dog and cry. Once again, my universe has been capsized, leaving me not knowing what to do.

I've already sped through the first four stages of grief, and I'm well established in depression. I think I'll stay here for a while.

"Hey, Troublemaker." My sister Chelsea's ginger hair is pulled back in a tight ponytail, giving me a clear view of the sombre expression on her fair, freckled face. I don't respond, so she walks into the room, taking a position beside the bed opposite our father. She bends over me and starts crying, signalling the start of my tears all over again. She pulls away after several minutes. Her blotchy, tear-soaked face makes me feel even worse. "I'm so sorry, Isla. I told myself to keep it together and be strong for you."

Chelsea and Rory spent a lot of time together over the years. Rory and I were go-to babysitters for my three nephews the odd time Chelsea and her husband Liam wanted a night out, and most times I went to visit, Rory was by my side. My whole family will feel her loss.

"I'll leave you two to chat while I go find your mom. She was with Barbara and Mark, but it's been a while." Dad leaves the room, pulling the curtain closed to give Chelsea and me a modicum of privacy.

Chelsea dries her tears with the sleeve of her black knitted sweater. "What can I do? I know nothing makes this easier, but I need to do something."

I shake my head. "Nothing makes this easier. Nothing."

"It's going to be hard, but we're here for you. You don't have to go through a single thing alone. Me, Liam, the boys, Mom, and Dad, we'll be by your side as much as you need."

I appreciate the sentiment—I really do—but I doubt it's going to help. Nothing can fix this.

Gone are the days of our horrific double dates, making each other laugh until 4am, bouncing ideas off one another, fuelling our creative endeavours. None of those things will ever happen again and right now, there's nothing that will make that okay.

I'll never forgive myself knowing Rory lost out on the opportunity to chase her dream, and the rest of the world missed out on getting to know her. Not to mention how her parents and brother are going to feel.

Once my social battery is at zero, there's no use trying to recharge it with anything other than alone time. I ask my family to leave so I can process the events of today and consider what it all means going forward. They were reluctant, but finally conceded to my request, having plenty of experience dealing with my social limits.

I don't know how to live a life without Rory in it and grasping that reality is more painful than I could have known.

A few hours later, Barbara and Mark enter my room, faces puffy and red from crying. The sight of them is enough to turn me into a blubbering mess, which only makes me feel more guilty. I lost a friend, but they lost their daughter—their flesh and blood.

"Isla, darling? How are you doing?" Barbara asks, her voice cracking with the effort.

I shake my head, trying to rid myself of my tears. "I'm so sorry. I'm so sorry."

Barbara steps forward and sweeps the hair from my forehead before leaning down to wrap her arms around me, avoiding my IV and injured arm. "Sh. You have nothing to be sorry for. Do you hear me?" She pulls her head back to look at me, both of us with tears streaming down our faces. Her Korean-Danish ancestry gives her such unique features—black hair, pale skin, high cheekbones, wide-set eyes—and her daughter was her clone. "I need you to promise me something."

I nod.

"You've become just as much of a daughter to us as Rory. Please, don't let us lose both of you today."

With that, I cry harder than I have to date. Understanding what it means for them to have lost their daughter cuts through me like a knife.

Mark steps up beside his wife, wrapping his arms around her delicate frame. "You'll always be family to us, Isla. Nothing can change that."

The doctor walks in at that moment, drawing our attention to him, and away from the emotional battles we're all fighting. "Oh, I'm sorry. I didn't mean to interrupt. I was coming to tell you once the nurse removes your IV, you can go home." He delivers this information as if it's good news. But how am I supposed to go back home to the place I shared with my best friend, knowing I'm leaving behind her body in the hospital morgue? Like it's that easy?

Barbara and Mark both stare at me and I have to keep it together for their sakes. They shouldn't be the ones comforting me right now. I thank the doctor and with that, he leaves.

"I'll call Zach and ask if he can come pick you up. I'm pretty sure Zara insisted they wait in the cafeteria until you were ready to go, so they won't be long," Mark offers before leaving the room.

Of course she did. Once my mom makes up her mind, there's no convincing her otherwise.

Barbara reaches down to squeeze my bicep. "Promise me, okay? I don't want to lose you too."

"I promise." And it's the hardest promise I've ever made, because carrying on with life like nothing has changed will never be easy.

A new wound forms each time I live through a hard lesson, and this has turned my heart into a pound of scar tissue. I'm not even sure it can beat anymore.

This isn't how I thought I'd say goodbye to Rory. I pictured us, old and grey, streaking around an old age home after we both lost our marbles—and inhibitions. I imagined standing up beside her on her wedding day, crying happy tears because she found her true love. Not shedding tears over her closed casket. It never occurred to me things would turn out this way.

My functioning arm is linked with my mom as we stare at the polished cherry-wood box containing the one human who knew me like the back of her hand. I can barely see through my tears, and I feel sick to my stomach. Music is playing in the background like the end of a heart-breaking movie, and I hate that it's another reminder Rory's life ended in tragedy, not a happily ever after. I knew this day would be hard, but I didn't realize *how* hard.

The volume of the music lowers and the funeral director takes his place at the podium, signalling to the rest of us to take our seats. My family and I are sitting in the second row behind Rory's parents, brother Marcus, aunts, and uncles. If this were a concert, Rory would have been thrilled. Add that to the mental list I've created of moments she wanted and can never experience.

After a few moments of speaking, telling those of us in the audience who Rory was, and how she impacted the world around her, the funeral director calls my name to share a few words. Barbara asked me if I'd like to give a speech, and my instinct was to say no. I don't like crowds, and especially not speaking in front of them, but my mom reminded me this will be my last chance to do something for Rory, and I would regret it if I didn't try. So, here I go.

*Everybody's watching.*

I can do this for Rory.

"Good morning, everyone."

*Good morning? Really? What's good about this morning?*

Push forward. Say what you're supposed to say. Just get through it—for Rory.

"I'm Isla and I am... I was Rory's best friend. Rory and I met at a summer camp when we were thirteen years old. Until then, my only friends were my dog and my big sister." I look at the second row to make eye contact with Chelsea. I continue, pretending I'm addressing her directly. "After three days of sharing the same table for lunch, but not a single word, Rory took it upon herself to speak to me. If you knew her, you'll understand why that was such a notable moment."

I hear Barbara sobbing in the front row, and I force myself not to look at her. If I see her breaking down, I won't be able to stop myself from joining in.

"She was just as shy and anti-social as me—but she was so much braver. Because of her bravery in that moment, we forged a friendship that became more like a sisterhood. We were inseparable. We went on each other's family vacations, and it became an automatic assumption: if one of us was coming, the other was tagging along."

I'm struggling to speak through my tears, prompting my dad to join me, placing an arm around my back. I give him a quick glance to express my appreciation as he rubs my shoulder. His presence won't make this any easier, but it brings me back to the task at hand.

*Everybody's watching.*

I will do this for Rory.

"We shared all of our lofty goals and deepest fears. She was the most talented musician I have ever heard and listening to her strum along to her acoustic guitar in our apartment became my favourite sound. Sometimes my dog would join her, and we'd laugh until our stomachs hurt. She always dreamed of being a song writer for Taylor Swift or Colbie Caillat, and I have no doubt she would have done it. The way she could create the most profound lyrics to match with a melody that you felt in your soul was her greatest gift, and I'm sorry more people didn't have the chance to receive it." Deep breath. "How do I say goodbye"—my blubbering and sniffling are interfering with my ability to speak—"to someone who feels like as much a part of me as my right hand? I don't know who I am without her, but my promise to Rory is that I'll honour her life. I'll cherish everything she taught me about myself. Her impact will never be forgotten, and I'll never take a moment we shared for granted."

I turn to face the photo on top of the casket. "Thank you for choosing me as your best friend. Thank you for reaching inside of me and pulling out a confidence I never would have found without you. Thank you for inspiring me to reach for the stars, but always keep my feet on the ground. I love you."

I step down from the small platform and rush to the nearest exit. My dad is right behind me, but I need a minute out of this room.

*Everybody's watching. They're judging you for leaving. They think you're disrespectful.*

Bursting through the door, I collapse to my knees, sobbing into my hands. "I... can't... breathe."

"We're here with you, Kiddo. Take a breath. You would have made her so proud." I shake my head, unable to catch my breath, but my dad continues, "She knew how scared you were of speaking in front of people. You faced your fear for her, and that would have made her proud."

He's probably right. She was my loudest cheerleader. A wave of grief-induced nausea takes its hold on me, and my head is spinning. This isn't fair. None of it's fair, and I'm not sure how to move on without my cheerleader at my side.

My dad doesn't say anything else. He just holds me, rubs my back, and keeps me from collapsing again.

A few minutes later, I've composed myself enough to return to the funeral. There's not a dry eye in the house as Mark addresses the crowd, talking about how proud he was of his baby girl. As much as I hurt, knowing what he and Barbara have lost rips my useless blob of scar tissue from my chest. He speaks about his favourite moments with her as a child—teaching her to ride a bike, her insistence joining him on fishing trips even though fish and worms freaked her out, standing outside her bedroom door listening to her sing and play her guitar—and it's surprising how much those little things mean when you face the reality of not creating any more memories with someone.

Mark thanks everyone on behalf of him and his family for their love and support in the past few days. I zone out, unable to process this reality. Before I know it, the funeral director is giving closing remarks. Just like that, the chapter on Rory's life is closed. As if we say goodbye and walk out of here to pick up where we left off.

Everyone is invited to meet at the Anderson home to support Rory's family. The thought of being there without her is choking me, but she'd do anything for my parents if the roles were reversed. I've spent the last five days wishing they were.

My parents and sister accompany me to Barbara and Mark's red-brick colonial home north of Bracebridge. The last time I was here was twelve days ago when Rory and I came for a family dinner. Weekly visits were Mark and Barbara's one stipulation when Rory announced she and I were moving into an apartment together. They insisted we come for dinner every Sunday, and since their home is only ten minutes away and Barbara is an incredible cook, it wasn't a hardship. But now, being here without her certainly is.

We walk into the grand foyer, which is littered with discarded shoes and coats, spreading beyond the tile of the entryway, onto the red-oak hardwood flooring. I hear combinations of laughter, crying, and hushed voices throughout the expanse of their main floor. There are people I don't recognize leafing through old photo albums and others inspecting the pictures over the stone mantle.

My mission is to see Barbara and Mark, give Marcus a hug since I wasn't able to at the funeral home, and try to escape without a breakdown. My family was all supportive of my request when I explained my plan to them on the drive over. Talking to strangers on a normal day is hard enough.

Chelsea loops her arm through mine and leads me through the living room. A few strangers stop us to express their condolences and tell me they enjoyed my speech. Enjoyed it? How could you enjoy hearing me sob and talk about my dead best friend? I say nothing rather than question their standard of enjoyment.

*Everybody's watching.*

I accomplish my goal, giving Marcus a hug in which he spends five minutes crying on my shoulder. He's only sixteen, and despite his 5'10" frame being an inch taller than mine, I still see him as a little brother. His heartbreak adds a little more scar tissue.

Barbara abandons her conversation moments later to beeline toward me. We talk for a few brief moments when she reminds me of the promise I made from my hospital bed. She adds in another request: "Don't let your grief stop you from finding your own happiness."

In the two weeks since Rory died, I haven't been able to piece myself back together. I'm Humpty Dumpty, and not even the King's men stand a chance. My German shepherd, Bond, and I moved back in with my parents because I can't handle living in an apartment I used to share with someone who will never return. Not to mention, my arm is still sore, so basic tasks are more difficult than normal—including writing. I may or may not be using that as an excuse.

My editor gave me a one-week grace period after Rory's death to get my next draft back to her, but she's been calling for days, and I haven't answered. I have nothing to send to her. I'm not naïve enough to think that unknown authors regularly get book deals with successful publishers, so it's stupid for me to squander the opportunity, but I am in no condition to meet her deadline. The fact I've been working toward this for a decade makes no difference.

What am I doing instead? Searching grief support groups. Online, of course, because trying to grieve and "people" at the same time wouldn't bode well for me. My comfort zone is the written word, so forums are the extent to which I will speak to other people.

The curse and benefit of living with a counsellor is that she recognizes when someone is stuck. I'm not living in the past, but I'm not moving forward and the guilt I'm holding onto will not allow me to. I feel guilty about wanting to rid myself of the guilt—as if that's discounting Rory's existence in my life.

Rory's death was a freak accident. There's nowhere to place the blame, and I think that's part of my problem. If it was another driver's fault, I could spend my time being angry with them. I can spend the rest of my life hating every road-crossing deer, but it wasn't her fault either. We weren't speeding. She wasn't texting. It just… happened. Her life ended and mine changed forever. The only logical place for me to place the blame is on my own shoulders and leaves me in a permanent state of would've, should've, could've.

I come across a grief group for the Muskoka area on social media. After answering the questions to join—which seemed a little silly, because I can't imagine anyone joining for fun—I sit and wait to see if I'll be approved to grieve alongside other people in the same geographical location.

To kill some time, I open my manuscript, staring at the red lines and notes in the margin, willing myself to apply some of the feedback, but my inspiration is gone. It disappeared the moment the car I was travelling in rolled over four times. Must have flown out the window. It wasn't wearing a seatbelt.

A ping on my laptop notifies me I've been accepted into the Muskoka Grief Support group, so I close my unfinished novel and open my web browser. I scroll through the news feed and see people struggling with loss of loved ones—grandparents, siblings, spouses. My heart hurts for everyone and I question whether this is a good idea. Am I going to ease my grief, or compound it?

I decide to make a post detailing my loss, in hopes someone can relate to what I'm going through and provide me with some magical comfort.

**My name is Isla, and my best friend recently died in a car accident. I'm struggling to process my grief. I don't know how to move on without her. Often, I wish it was me instead.**

I don't know what else to say. For someone who is trying to make a career out of writing, the ability to form words has abandoned me. Maybe my only inspiration was Rory and her music.

It occurs to me to turn on some of her favourite songs, hoping it will bring some inspiration back. Five bars of Taylor Swift's *All You Had To Do Was Stay* and I'm sobbing onto my keyboard.

Another notification forces me to wipe my eyes to see if a well-meaning stranger has the cure to my sorrow. I find a comment on my post from someone named Theo Malinga. Sounds like a porn star name. Not that I'd know.

**Theo: I don't understand why people get so upset over losing a friend. Friends come and go. You can make new friends. It's not like you lost a parent.**

After Reading the message a second, third, and fourth time to make sure I didn't read it wrong, I'm baffled by the response.

I type a response but delete it. Again. I'm not sure how to reply to such ignorance. Finally, I settle on petty with a side of guilt tripping.

**Isla: For your information, Mr. Malinga, I have lost both of my parents. I was orphaned when I was five years old. So are we going to have a grief-measuring contest? If you're not in this group to give helpful advice, perhaps you're in the wrong place.**

**I'm sorry if you've lost a parent because I understand how difficult that is.**

I can't be a complete jerk in response, even if he was. It may be a blob of scar tissue, but my heart still has compassion. Diving into the loss of my biological parents is not something I wanted to do with a complete stranger, but I wasn't about to let him belittle my grief. I mean, face-to-face would have been a different story.

I switch back to staring at my manuscript, unable to accomplish anything, anxious about what kind of response I'll get from Mr. Porn-Star-Jerk-Face. After thirty minutes, he still hasn't responded; I assume he never will. That makes me a bit annoyed because his response was cowardly to begin with, and not replying makes him even more so.

Fifteen more minutes pass, and I notice the icon showing a private message. I open my spam folder and see Theo Malinga's name beside a black-and-white photo of a man whose face does not match his personality, aside from the scowl he's sporting. His hair is cut in a tidy fade, shaped perfectly around his forehead. He's got short facial stubble, probably to make his otherwise-baby face look older. I can't pinpoint his eye colour, but they're definitely dark. They remind me of Rory's near-black eyes. His skin tone is hard to pinpoint in grey, but it looks like the colour of a French vanilla cappuccino—a personal favourite of mine. It's too bad this handsome face is attached to such a wretched personality.

I click his photo bubble, curious about what he has to say.

**Theo: Hey, I'm sorry about earlier. I know it's not an excuse, but my dad died four days ago, and I think I'm stuck at the anger stage in the grief process. My mom and my sister are counting on me, so I don't want to let them down. Please forgive me. I'm sorry about your friend.**

Well. That was unexpected. As much as I want to write him off for being rude, I can't deny that grief makes people do things that are out of character. I respect he was humble enough to apologize, because that's not a quality most keyboard warriors possess.

**Isla: Thank you for your apology. I'm truly sorry about your father.**

I stop the message short of what I really want to say, because I don't want to engage in conversation right now. A moment later, though, I tamp down my social anxiety and say what I intended to.

**Isla: I know we're strangers, but sometimes that makes it easier. If you ever want to talk, I'm here. I may not know exactly how you're feeling, but I will always listen.**

I stare at the screen for a few moments until the dancing dots appear to indicate he is replying. Anxious anticipation increases my heart rate, leaving me with an uncomfortable pounding in my chest.

**Theo: Yeah, thanks.**

That was an anticlimactic reply. No one else replied to my post on the grief group, leaving me wondering if it's worth my time. A group of people all suffering through the same feelings are probably so focused on their own pain, it's hard to reach out to others. That's understandable. I can at least give Theo points for responding, even if it was ignorant. With a sigh, I close the conversation window and force myself to focus on my work.

Navigating through eighty thousand words and three hundred pages is a daunting task. I'm irritated by so many editor notes because she wants to change a bulk of the story. Now, more than ever, the words on these pages mean something to me and I don't want to alter the storyline. Beyond that, as an editor myself, I could never bring myself to change the entire trajectory of someone's work. What's the point of having creative outlets if everyone gets corralled into the same box?

I respect Nancy's expertise and knowledge regarding best-selling books, but she must realize that not every successful book ends with a happily ever after. Sometimes people want pure escapism, reading nonsensical comedy. Some people want a gut-wrenching memoir. I spent so much of my life conforming so I didn't stand out, and my writing was the only outlet that allowed me to be authentically me. It's the one area I'm okay with being different. It's the one place I can share my voice. I'm not okay with that being taken away.

Since Theo first offended… er… replied to me, we've been chatting online. He struggled the day of his father's funeral, but because his mom and sister are counting on him to be strong, he doesn't have many people to talk to. He mentioned he has some friends, but they're all busy with their own lives and he doesn't want to be a bother. I can relate to that—not the friends part, but not bothering people.

So, that leaves me. The stranger who is sympathetic to his pain.

I check my messages first thing in the morning and throughout the day. We know little about each other because our conversations have circled around our individual losses, but I appreciate him as a voice of reason and sympathetic ear.

Checking my messages for the fourteenth time today, a red bubble tells me there's a reply to my earlier check in.

**Theo: I'm doing okay. Just trying to get through the day. How are you?**

I smile at his reply. It's become our daily tradition, messaging back and forth. We ask nothing beyond how the other is feeling. His response is vague, though, and it doesn't sit right with me.

**Isla: That doesn't sound okay. You can be honest.**

As for myself, I'm the same as I've been for the last four weeks since Rory died. Grieving a person and a past I can never have back. Seeing her name still hurts. Hearing her favourite songs buckle my knees. Finding her clothes in my closet feels like a knife through my heart. I'm not okay, but I'm trying to be.

**Theo: Can I get your number? I don't always have internet, so it would be easier. I'll text you.**

How do I reply? I know nothing about him beyond that he lost his dad after a battle with prostate cancer, and he has a little sister named Solana. Is that enough for me to trust him with my phone number? We're not even Facebook friends.

I contemplate my decision for twenty painstaking minutes before I answer.

**Isla: Sure. It's 705-555-4752. Text me anytime.**

Text me anytime? Really, Isla? Like I'm a social butterfly readily available to reply to messages? My editor, Nancy, would disagree. I've answered one of her many emails over the past few weeks, and my response was not what she wanted to hear. I'm well on my way to losing a book deal I never deserved. It was only because of Rory that I took a chance and submitted my work to a publisher. I never imagined it would turn into anything beyond a sent email, but the messages overflowing my inbox say otherwise.

I don't know what I'm going to do with this book because I don't want to ruin my career before it starts, but I'm not in the right head space.

Plus, Rory loved my book the way it was. Implementing the suggested changes feels like a betrayal, and nothing can make me okay with that. Her stamp of approval is one of the last things she gave me. The story was inspired by our friendship, so it's not a matter of deleting and replacing words. Altering the premise for the story feels like I'm deleting her.

My phone buzzes on my desk, interrupting my thoughts. Sure enough, it's Nancy. I should stop avoiding her and face the music.

"Hello?"

"Isla. Wow. So nice of you to *finally* answer." Her tone has me regretting my decision.

I ignore the split infinitive and her sarcasm. "Sorry, Nancy. I'm working through your suggestions."

"Isla, muffin, those suggestions were supposed to be dealt with weeks ago."

I'm itching to respond with an equal dose of sarcasm because if there's one thing Rory encouraged me to do, it was to stand up for myself. However, anxiety says don't rock the boat. Don't burn bridges you need to traverse, and don't make anyone upset with you. "I'm trying, Nancy, I really am, but I'm still dealing with personal issues."

"I'm well aware of your loss, and I'm sorry, but you can't use the death of your friend as an excuse forever. Life moves on. You have fifteen days to turn in your manuscript."

Petty me is irritated by Nancy's abrasive and cold-hearted comments, but I still can't find it in me to stand up to her. "Fifteen days, or what? It's published as is? My contract is cancelled? What are the repercussions for not having it done?"

There's an extended period of silence and I can tell Nancy has been caught by surprise, but this is something I need to know.

"I'd have to look into what your contract states."

"Okay then. Let me know."

*She's going to hate you.*

"Fifteen days, Isla. I want that manuscript back in fifteen days." Click.

I will not apologize, even if I feel guilty for not bending to her every demand. I was raised to respect others, and I always have, but respect has limits.

With Nancy's words replaying in my mind, I buckle down and try to address some of her suggestions. I refuse to change the genre of my book, so I delete any comments pertaining to that. She won't be pleased, but I will not turn my book into a reproduction of a blockbuster movie.

Several hours pass, and my eyes are dry from staring at the computer screen. Bond whimpers to go outside, so I decide some fresh air would be a welcome distraction.

I'm seated in the lone deck chair, bundled in my outdoor gear when my phone buzzes. I assume it's Nancy, so I ignore it, but a quick glance shows a number I don't recognize.

*Don't answer.*

I stare at it, trying to decipher the area code and recognize it as local. Nancy is based in Toronto.

My finger slides the green circle to the right, and I place the phone to my ear. "Hello?"

"Um… Isla? This is Theo."

Wow. His voice doesn't match the boyish features of his photo; he sounds like a man. "Oh, hi. I thought you were going to text." My face feels hot, even though the temperature outside hovers around -10C.

"Yeah, sorry. Is this okay? I thought it would be easier."

"Oh, totally fine. Yep. No problem." *Smooth*. "How was your day?"

He doesn't speak for a few seconds, and I can hear papers shuffling in the background. "Not great, to be honest. It was my first full day back at work, and it was harder than I thought it would be."

That explains why he didn't message me much today. I'm not sure how old he is, but assuming he's finished school, and judging by his photo, I'd estimate around twenty-five. "I'm sorry. What was hard? Was it something you can adjust for tomorrow, or just part of the process?"

He chuckles. "Are you a therapist or something?"

"No, I'd probably be a lot less of a mess if I was. My mom is a counsellor. I guess it's rubbed off."

"Wait. Your mom? I thought you were an orphan."

I wasn't expecting to dive into this today… or ever. "My biological parents died when I was five. I was adopted when I was seven and call my adopted parents mom and dad."

"Huh. Isn't that kind of sad? I mean, just replacing your parents like that?"

Not if he knew my biological parents. This conversation is veering in a direction I'm not prepared to take, so I aim to change the subject. "Are you going to answer my question?"

"I guess it's just harder than I realized to go back to normal, you know? Carry on as if nothing happened. It's barely been three weeks, but I feel like pushing myself back into my old routine is kind of forgetting my old man existed."

"I can understand that. People always say things like, 'oh, he would want you to carry on and live a happy life', or 'she would want what's best for you'. Even though that might be true, there's no time limit on grief, and it's important for you to process your feelings when they come. You can't always be focused on what the person you lost would have wanted. It's normal to miss them."

"How do I process them, Miss Counsellor's daughter?"

"With time. You'll never forget your dad. From what you've told me, he was a great man, and he poured his heart into raising you. That will always stay with you."

"That sounds like a Hallmark card."

I'm not sure what to say in response. This is the most I've conversed with someone on the phone, other than my family or Rory, for… well, maybe ever.

"Listen, Isla. I was wondering if you'd like to meet up sometime. Saturday?"

I'm frozen. Not on account of the temperature. Is he asking me on a date? Does he just want to meet so we can shed tears over our lost loved ones? Is it platonic? I can't ask these things, so I panic and say nothing.

"Sorry. I shouldn't—"

"No, that's fine. I'm sorry. That would be cool." *Could you be more pathetic?*

"Yeah? Okay. We can meet on Saturday at *The Mad Dog Pub*? I promise I'm not a serial killer or anything."

"That's something a serial killer would say." I laugh, knowing he could be a boyishly handsome stalker. I've read *You* by Caroline Kepnes.

"Is it? How would you know unless you're a serial killer?"

"Touché."

"How will I recognize you?"

I don't know how to describe myself. The socially awkward blue-eyed blonde? We're a dime a dozen. I have no idea what I'll wear. I panic again. "Um, I have pink hair?"

"Was that a question? Pink hair?"

"Yes, sorry. Pink hair. That's how you'll recognize me."

"Huh. I didn't expect that." He pauses for a second as I stare at my reflection in the sliding glass door; looking back is a blonde girl who just lied herself into a dye job. "Okay, Isla with the pink hair. I'll talk to you tomorrow. And, uh, thanks for the chat."

"Goodnight, Theo." Bond comes running over after finishing his tour of the yard, ridding it of all other wildlife, and rests his chin on my knee. "I guess I better make a salon appointment."

I spent $193 at the salon to get my hair coloured hot pink. The hairdresser asked me no less than twelve times if I was sure because my natural hair colour was "so beautiful."

I had never dyed my hair before today. I always saw it as a way to stand out when all I wanted was to be invisible. Now with pink hair, everyone is looking at me. Lesson learned; honesty is the best policy.

*Everybody's watching.*

It would be less obvious if I walked around with a bag on my head, but at this moment, waiting for Theo, that's not an option. My pink hair is serving as the only identifying mark I gave him. My generic black fitted sweater and stonewashed skinny jeans, paired with knee-high leather boots, do little to help me stand out in the crowd. This is like a pre-winter uniform for other twenty-somethings in the area.

I'm glad Theo suggested a casual spot to meet. Something formal would feel too much like a date and I'm not sure this is one. This is also one of the few places I never came to with Rory, so I should be able to make it through the evening without too many painful memories popping up. Our dining out experiences were limited to the lame double dates we went on. When it was just the two of us, we preferred to grab our food and eat at home—a home I haven't stepped foot in for nearly five weeks.

"Isla?"

Startling me from my thoughts, I look up to see an insanely tall young man with an oh-so-handsome face I recognize from social media. It's much more striking in person. His eyebrows look like they've been professionally groomed, and his nose is perfectly in proportion and symmetrical. An odd thing to notice, sure, but as a writer, I've learned to study finer details of faces. He has a scar on his left cheek that I want to know the story behind, but aside from that, his face is smooth perfection.

I scoot off of the bar stool and stand to greet him. "Theo. Hi."

He must be 6'4" because even in my heeled boots, he has several inches on me.

*Do you put out your hand? Give him a hug? What's the protocol here? He's going to think you're a loser.*

Before I lose my mind over societal norms, Theo leans in to give me a hug. His confidence is really appealing. He just decides on something and goes for it. Wow.

"Thanks for meeting me. Do you want to sit here, or we can get a table and eat dinner?"

*Let him decide so you don't offend him.* "Sure. Whatever you want."

He nods for me to follow him to one of the open bar-height tables surrounded by four black ladder-back stools.

Like every other Canadian, I struggle to find space for my bulky winter apparel. I stuff my gloves and hat inside my coat sleeve and hang it off an empty stool. Theo has braved the elements and only worn a cognac leather jacket, which he drapes over the other empty stool. Rookie. It looks good with his black long-sleeve tee and medium-wash jeans, though.

"So, uh... can I get you a drink?"

When I make eye contact with Theo for the first time, I notice his eyes are a deep brown, like a 95% cacao chocolate bar. While the deceitful treat is disgusting, his eyes are delicious and hint at a playfulness about him.

With a blink, I break my awkward stare and reply, "I don't drink, actually."

"Oh." He drops his gaze to the floor. "Do you mind if I have a beer?"

"That's fine. Are you not driving?"

"I am, but one drink won't hurt."

If you say so. I'm of the mentality that any alcohol is an impairment, but legally, I know one beer is acceptable. I don't argue. Even if I took issue with it, I wouldn't argue.

When Theo returns to the table with his draught beer, he passes me a menu. "Have you been here before?"

"No, this is my first time."

"Their wings are great. Or their Philly sandwich."

"I'm a vegetarian." *He's going to think you're being difficult.* "But I'll take your word for it."

"Isla the pink haired, non-drinking vegetarian. What else is there to know about you?"

"Not a lot, I'm afraid. I was homeschooled most of my life, so I finished university early. I have an older sister, Chelsea, who has three-year-old triplet boys and is married to her college sweetheart—"

"Oh, those are the kids in your profile picture?" he interrupts.

I nod.

"I wondered if they were yours, but I didn't want to ask."

"Mine? Oh gosh, no. You asked me on a date not knowing if I had three kids?"

His eyebrows rise a few centimetres. "Is this a date?"

*You've stepped in it now.*

"Oh, I... I just... I didn't mean..."

He laughs, but the sound doesn't set me at ease. "You'd have no doubts if I were taking you on a real date."

If we're basing my date experiences off of the random double dates Rory dragged me on, I can't compare to much. I assumed this was just a friendly meet up, but now that the word date has slipped out, I feel hurt by his dismissal of the idea.

*You're annoying, and he's not interested in you.*

"Sorry. I didn't mean to—"

"I wasn't planning on this being a date because we're both going through a lot right now, but I'm not saying no to the idea in the future." He winks at me, and warmth rises up my neck and face.

I fiddle with the paper straw in my water glass, chasing ice cubes around the inside. I am lost for what to say.

*Everybody's watching.*

I'm feeling exposed and under the scrutiny of every other patron in the bar. They can probably sense my awkwardness and smell my stress sweat from clear across the room. I don't know how to move our conversation forward and I'm not good at thinking of questions to ask. Small talk is tantamount to having my eyeballs gauged with a rusty spoon.

After taking a sip of his beer and setting it back on the paper coaster, Theo speaks up. "So, three nephews. What else?"

"Um, I have a Bachelor of Fine Arts in creative writing from UBC—the, um, University of British Columbia. Now I work as a freelance editor, which after working as a copywriter through school, I have a good customer base to keep me busy."

"Wow. How old are you?"

"I'm twenty-one. I started university when I was seventeen and studied online so I could fast track."

"That's cool. So, what do you plan to do with a bachelor of…"

"Fine arts." Now I can really display my nerdiness. "I'm working on a novel right now."

"Hmm. Cool. I'm more of a movie person. Haven't read a book other than for school in… maybe ever." He glances away, flagging down a server walking by. "Do you know what you want?"

Yes, please. The sooner we eat, the sooner we can get this over with. "Definitely."

He nods at me to speak first, so I order a garden salad and potato skins without bacon. The only other vegetarian options are fries or fettuccini Alfredo, and I don't want either. Theo orders the Philly sandwich with a side of fries.

"So, Theo, tell me about yourself." I paste on my best fake-confident smile.

"I work in marketing for a mortgage broker in Bracebridge. It's an all right gig for now, but I don't want to stay there forever. It's only part time now, anyway."

When he says he works for a mortgage broker, it sparks recognition. "So you're the one working for my dad's competition, huh?"

"Competition?"

"My dad's a mortgage broker in Bracebridge too. He's scaled back the past few years because he didn't really need to work. He just kept his business going to help people who wouldn't otherwise get approved for mortgages, but he said his business has been dwindling."

"Oh, I… Um… Shoot."

I chuckle at his expression. He looks terrified. "It's fine. You're obviously doing a good job. My dad is ready to retire now, anyway. It was more something to keep him busy than necessity."

"How old is he?" Theo creases his forehead, leaning back in his seat as the server places down our food. That was fast.

"He's forty-five."

"And he's retiring? How did he manage that?"

I'm not about to tell this virtual stranger that my father won millions of dollars in a lawsuit launched against a company whose neglect killed his parents. As much as I want to assume I can trust everyone's intentions, I know that's not the case. "He was smart with his money. My mom worked and saved her money too, so one day they'd be able to retire and enjoy life while they were still young."

"That sounds like a good goal. My dad… uh, he worked for the electric company as a technician. Spent his whole life slaving away and never got to enjoy it. Now my mom has to pick up the pieces."

"I'm sorry. About your dad and for your mom. Life really isn't fair sometimes."

"It's not. Do you have a cat or something?"

I'm confused by his abrupt change in conversation topic. "A dog. Why?"

"You've got fur on your sweater. I was just wondering. I'm not much of an animal lover. We weren't allowed a pet as kids, so I've never seen the appeal."

Not a book reader; that I could handle. Dad's work competition; no problem. Not an animal lover? I think that's a deal breaker.

I sit in silence after his animal confession, not knowing what else to say. It's clear this isn't going anywhere, and now I'm stuck with pink hair to remind me of another failed social encounter every time I look in the mirror.

After my failed non-date with Theo, I've barely heard from him. I think he sensed it was just as uncomfortable as I did. We have nothing in common beyond our recent losses and our physical locations—though, even then, he lives twenty minutes away, so the chances of ever seeing him again are slim. It's not that I was even looking for a date. I don't want a boyfriend. I really wanted to connect with someone who understands what I am going through. It was just dumb luck that he's insanely attractive.

Pretty to look at. No chemistry.

The only thing I wanted to do when I got home was to cuddle up in a blanket on the sofa and tell Rory all about it. Even though neither of us dated much, I still could use her advice for my attempt at a non-date.

I'm missing Rory more with each passing day, and now that my conversations with Theo have all but stopped, I need to face my battles on my own. Five days remain to get my manuscript in shape, "or else," but the process isn't going well. There are a ton of notes in my apartment, but I can't bring myself to go back there. Barbara and Mark cleaned Rory's stuff out a few weeks ago, and it breaks my heart to imagine how it will look when I return. It won't feel like home without her guitar laying across the end of the sofa, or her tattered sheet music stuffed under books on the coffee table. It won't feel like home without her voice being amplified through the space by nothing other than her raw talent. It won't feel like home without *her*.

I've been staring at my computer screen for a few hours when my phone buzzes, and I fear it's Nancy. I have no update for her, so I don't answer.

A few moments later, it buzzes again. This time, long determined vibrations pleading to be stopped. The screen flashes Theo's name. That offers little relief.

"Hello?"

"Hey. I'm sorry if I'm bothering you." He sniffles.

I sit upright in my chair. "Are you okay? What's wrong?"

A few seconds pass before he responds. "Not really."

"What happened?" Hearing the emotion in his voice pushes every memory of our awkward non-date out of my mind.

"A guy at work was complaining about his dad in the lunchroom and I kind of lost it on him."

"What do you mean, 'lost it'?"

"His dad has Alzheimer's. This guy had the nerve to say his dad is behaving like a petulant child and won't even brush his teeth. Can you believe that? The man who raised him—who gave him life—is suffering from Alzheimer's and this guy is complaining. I understand it's hard, and can sympathize with frustration, but he was insulting his own dad for something he can't control. He went on for about five minutes before I gave him a piece of my mind."

"Did... did you hit him?"

"Are you kidding? You've seen me. I'd be in jail if I punched him. No, I didn't hit him."

That's true. Theo is a big guy, so if he wanted to hurt someone, I'm certain he'd inflict a lot of damage with little effort. "I don't know what to say, Theo. The guy sounds like a grade-A douche, and I'm glad you told him off."

"Yeah? You don't think it was just grief talking? Because that's what my boss told the guy when he complained."

I chuckle at the sound of his voice perking up. "No. I think it was your finely tuned sense of right and wrong, maybe a little amplified by grief. But the guy really sounds like an ungrateful idiot."

"Thanks." Theo huffs out a sigh. "How are you, anyway? Our dinner the other night got a little weird and I didn't want to make you uncomfortable. But I'm glad you didn't block my number."

Wow. He just says exactly what he's thinking. "I wouldn't block your number; don't be silly."

"Could we try it again? I'd like to see you again. I... I could use a friend, and I know you could too."

He's right. Grief is a lonely road you don't want to walk alone, but you don't want anyone else to join you on. Might as well meet up with other people on the same path.

"Okay. What were you thinking?"

"Really? I mean... cool. Yeah. Um. What are you doing now?"

"Now? Right this minute?"

"Sorry if you're busy. I just... I got sent home for the day, so maybe we could meet up."

I glance at my stained t-shirt and holey leggings, asking myself if I possess the energy to make myself presentable and leave the house.

"If you don't want to see me again, that's cool, too."

The resignation in his voice makes my heart clench. "No, don't say that. I'm just a hot mess right now and I was guessing how long it will take me to get ready."

"Where do you live?"

That's a loaded question. I'm not sure where to call home right now. "I'm at my parents'. It's midway between Bracebridge and Gravenhurst. Kind of near the drive-in."

*Why did you say that?*

"We can try that when it's warmer." He laughs. "I have to head home to Gravenhurst anyway, so you tell me a spot and a time."

I settle on one of my mom's favourite spots. "Meet me at *Desirea's Sweets* in an hour?"

"Done. I'll see you soon."

We hang up the phone and I toss my laptop aside, which startles Bond. Once I offer a treat as payment, he forgives me. I rush into the shower, forgo washing my hair, scrub myself clean and contemplate what I'll wear.

Charcoal grey jeans, a burgundy cowl-neck sweater, and black heeled boots make up my outfit. I tussle my hair, making it look decent but not overdone, throw on a knit cap to cover my homing-beacon head, and swipe on tinted lip gloss. The house is empty when I leave because Mom is over at Chelsea's for the day, so I throw on a black leather jacket. It's not painfully cold, but I grab my parka to keep in the passenger seat of my trusty Honda Civic, just in case. It's been drilled into me you can never be too prepared in winter.

Fifty-seven minutes after my conversation ended with Theo, I arrive at the bakery. I stay in my car for a moment, unsure how to proceed. When I said, "meet me at *Desirea's Sweets*," I didn't specify if that was inside or in front of. I don't want to go in and make him wait outside. I don't want to wait outside if he's inside. What do I do?

Text him.

**Isla: I'm here. I'm parked out front, so let me know when you get here.**

A few seconds later, he replies.

**Theo: I see you.**

I find him waiting at the door, and I know he wasn't there when I texted him.

I step out over the one-foot-high snowbank and walk toward Theo. He studies me as I move closer, and it makes me self-conscious under his watchful eye.

*Why is he looking at you like that? Your fly might be down. There's probably something on your face. Pace your steps properly.*

"Hey," I greet with a meek wave.

His smile tells me his ordeal from this morning is long forgotten. He doesn't appear disgruntled or upset. I'm happy he's moved past the confrontation. "Hi. Thanks for meeting me." His navy dress slacks and grey wool coat make him look professional and smart. I learned little about his job, but I appreciate the workwear.

"You'll thank me after you've had some of the fresh-baked goods in here. Have you been before?" I listened to a podcast about small talk topics on the drive here to help me prepare for this.

"Yeah. My mom worked here for a while, actually."

"Really? I wonder if I've met her."

*Now he's going to assume you want to meet his mother. Nice going.*

He chuckles. "Maybe. Let's go inside. This coat isn't well insulated." He opens the door and ushers me inside. "What are you going to get?"

I stare at the display cases full of goodies. Their donuts are heavenly, as are their butter tarts, but once my eyes settle on another option, it's an easy choice. "I'll take one of their dog cupcakes. All proceeds go to the OSPCA."

"You really like dogs?"

"No, I don't *like* dogs. I love dogs. My dog, Bond, is my best friend."

Theo releases a loud, patronizing laugh. "You can't be best friends with a dog."

I glare at him, wishing I had one of those beautiful lemon meringue pies in the display to shove into his face. That would be pie well spent, if you ask me. "I disagree. When I was first adopted, despite everything my parents did, I couldn't sleep. It wasn't until Bond came into my life that I felt any sense of calm. His presence allowed me to enjoy things I otherwise wouldn't have. So, yes, he absolutely can be my best friend."

Theo pays for our order without saying a word. I shouldn't expect today to go any differently from last time. I'm awkward, as is every encounter I'm involved in, so there comes a time when you should just stop trying.

"Listen, I'm sorry. I shouldn't have said that. I guess because I've never had a pet, I don't understand, but I'm glad your dog was there for you. That sounds pretty awesome, actually."

"He is awesome. He's never failed me. Every major transition I've had in my life since he came into it has been made easier because of him." I have never, in my life, felt such a burning need to defend myself, my dog, or my choices. And I've never been more confident doing it.

Theo raises his hands in mock surrender. "Okay, okay. I'm sorry."

I nod in acceptance, relaxing my scowl, but at this moment, I know what my next mission is going to be.

Sure, I should work on completing revisions to my manuscript, but I've been slaving away on it all week, not making any progress. Instead, I'm taking Theo on a special outing. We've chatted every day since our meeting at *Desirea's Sweets* but haven't seen each other since.

When I pull up to his house, I'm sweating profusely, and my knuckles are white from clenching the steering wheel. As I'm staring at the two-storey home with a single attached garage, butter-yellow siding, and a large picture window, my sweat production increases.

*"Hi, Theo. How are you today?"* No, that's lame. *"Hey, Theo. Are you ready for your surprise?"* You are so stupid. *"What's up, buttercup?"* NO.

Mercifully interrupting my practice conversation, Theo walks out the front door and bounds down the porch steps. He's dressed in black, slim-fit jeans, wheat-coloured Timberland boots, and the same cognac leather jacket he wore for our first meeting. I press unlock to make sure he can get in the car, and once the door opens, my face reddens before he says a word.

"Hiya." *That was almost worse than buttercup.*

Theo gives me a sideways glance before turning his head to me, showing off his smirk. "Hiya? You going to karate chop me?"

*You are so stupid.*

"Sorry. I meant to say, 'Hi, how are ya?' and it all came out at once." I'm so mortified, my ears are burning.

"Okay. I'm fine. Curious where you're dragging me at 10am on a Saturday."

I chuckle. "Did I mess up your Friday night plans?"

"I was lying in bed, talking to you."

My already red face heats even more after hearing him mention our phone call. He's given me zero indication he wants anything more than friendship, and I don't think it's something I could handle right now. Regardless, it's nice having someone to talk to who understands loss, and our conversations have become important to me.

I ease in the clutch and set the car in reverse, backing my car out of his driveway, and we're cruising toward Muskoka Road.

"I don't think I've ever known a woman who drove standard." Theo eyes the gear shift as I manoeuvre through the streets of Gravenhurst.

"Why do people seem so surprised? Like driving stick is a skill related to testosterone level?"

"No, I didn't mean anything by it. I'm just surprised."

"It has better control in the winter, so I asked my brother-in-law to teach me when I got my license. I thought it would be safer. That was before they had triplets and he had free time." I laugh.

Theo nods but doesn't comment any further on my driving skills.

As I merge onto highway eleven, the reality of what's up ahead hits me like a brick wall. I drive in silence, with the only sound the hum of the wheels on the pavement and the odd piece of road salt dinging the undercarriage of my car. As the kilometres tick by, the car is filled with the sound of my laboured breathing. We approach the exit for Canning Road, and I have to make a decision.

I can't do it.

A slap of my signal indicates that I'm exiting off the highway, intending to make a detour.

"Are you all right?"

I shake my head, pulling the car over onto a stretch of the gravel shoulder once it's safe to do so. I yank up the emergency brake, open the door and jump out of the car. The cool air helps calm my rapid breathing as I stand next to my trunk, bent over with my hands on my knees.

A few seconds—minutes, I don't know—later, Theo's voice shouts over the sound of nearby highway traffic. "Isla? What's wrong?"

All I can do is shake my head. I stand straight, and as I try to force the words out, I can't. I start sobbing.

*You look like an idiot.*

"Shoot. I don't know what to do."

"Rory..." I start but can't finish my sentence before another sob pours out.

*You're ugly crying. It's not cute. Snot. Tears. Red face. He's judging you.*

"Rory, what?" His voice is tender and low.

"The highway..." I sniffle, wiping my face with my jacket sleeve. "This is the stretch of the highway where..."

Recognition sparks in Theo's eyes, and I don't have to complete my thought. He understands. "I'm so sorry. What can I do?"

I consider his words for a few seconds. "Can you drive? Not past there, but if I navigate, can you drive?"

His expression changes, but I can't understand the meaning behind it. "I… uh… I'd be happy to drive, but I don't know how to drive stick."

I stare at him for a second, but once my brain catches up with his confession, I laugh. Cry-laugh, technically, but it's inching more into laughter territory by the second.

"Wow, way to blow up a guy's ego."

Once I catch my breath that's evaded me for the past several moments on account of panic, crying, and laughing, I feel a little bad. "I'm sorry. I get why you were so surprised now."

"Yeah, yeah. Sue me. Is there something else I *can* do?"

I lean my backside against the salt-covered trunk of my car, knowing it's going to get all over my coat and pants, but I need to relax for a moment. "Just wait here with me? I'll be okay soon."

"That I can do." Theo leans on the car beside me, and although he's several inches taller, I'm not the least bit intimidated by his presence. I'm comfortable, if only for a moment. I'll take what I can get.

"We were headed to Orillia." I turn to glance at Theo, who keeps his eyes facing forward. "That day. Rory had set us up on a double date with her co-workers. We were supposed to meet them at some craft brewery for dinner." I choke up again as a fresh wave of guilt floods my stomach. "I had a bad feeling before we left, but I thought it was just my history of bad dates making me nervous." Tears trickle down my cheeks, which are stinging from the winter air already.

"There was no way for you to know, Isla. One thing I learned from that grief group is that we can't spend the rest of our lives wondering what we could have done differently. Guilt serves no purpose but to rob you of happiness going forward. At least with things we can't change."

I want to argue with him, but every overwhelming thought tells me I should feel guilty. Her parents are left without their daughter, her brother without a sister. There's nothing fair about the whole situation.

With a swipe of my hand, I clear my tears from my face and the salt residue from my back before turning toward my car. I realize I parked with the passenger door against a massive snowbank and send Theo a questioning look.

"I climbed out your door," he says with a shrug.

My car is small, so the image of him dragging his sizeable frame across the front seat has me grinning. "I'll pull up a little so you can get back in."

When we arrive at our destination, Theo looks as apprehensive as he did when I asked if he could drive my car.

"Why did you bring me here?"

"Come on. You'll see why." I open the car door and stride toward the entrance and hear the passenger door close behind me.

"Isla, wait."

I stop, turn around, and face Theo while pulling my jacket closed with my cold, bare hands.

"What am I supposed to do here?" He eyes the building, not with curiosity, but concern.

"Just trust me." I walk in the front door of the animal shelter with Theo in tow.

We greet the staff seated at the reception desk and ask if we can take some time to visit with the dogs they have for adoption. I wasn't planning on adopting another dog, but I wouldn't shut down the idea, either.

"You know I'm not an animal lover. Why did you bring me here?"

I take a breath before facing Theo, wanting to make my intentions known. "You said you never had the opportunity to be around animals, so you didn't understand how anyone could love them so much. I brought you here to show you. Today is your opportunity. You don't have to walk out of here the next Lee Asher, but I want you to relax a little and try to receive what the animals give you." I turn and speed-walk to catch up to the volunteer leading the way.

"What does that even mean?" Theo's footsteps are falling in sync with mine. "Isla. What are they going to give me? Rabies?"

I chuckle. "You'll see."

The dogs are jumping up at the plexiglass barriers, some with excitement and others with aggression. My heart breaks with each one we pass, knowing they're all here because humans have failed them. Theo is walking along the far side of the hallway, distancing himself from the barking dogs.

Céline, the employee showing us around, finishes explaining the basics of how the shelter works. I'm so inspired by the people who volunteer their time to help these animals, and it makes me consider putting in an application to a shelter closer to home—once I figure out where home will be.

When I turn to face Theo, I notice he's not only caught the eye of a dog, but the dog has caught his in return. I look at the information on the dog's enclosure. His name is Charley, and he's a five-year-old German shepherd mix. He's much smaller than Bond and his fur is short, so he must be mixed with a hound or something similar.

"What happened to him?" Theo asks Céline.

"Oh, poor Charley here has been through some tough times. He was hit by a car when he was younger, and his owners had his front leg amputated. They spent so much on vet bills, when Charley later started having medical problems, they surrendered him. He had another surgery to remove bladder stones, and he requires a special diet. He's a sweet boy though."

My heart hurts for Charley. I'm reminded of the Charli who ushered me to the hospital the day Rory died and force myself not to think about her.

"Hi, Charley. I'm Theo."

*Don't cry. Everybody's watching.*

Theo bends down, placing his hand on the glass, and Charley sits at attention, wagging his stumpy, cropped tail. I wonder if that was intentional, or another injury.

"Do you want to take him for a little walk? You're welcome to take him out and get to know him."

Theo's eyes light up as he looks back at Céline. "Really? That would be…" He stands up straight, his face looks stoic and disinterested, but I didn't miss the excitement in his eyes. "That would be fine, I guess. He'd probably like being sprung."

Céline gathers the leash hanging from beside the exit and walks back toward Charley. All the dogs bark and jump, as if they are shouting, "Pick me! Pick me!" It's hard to ignore their pleas for attention, but I want Theo to bond with a dog, not be overwhelmed.

We bundle up for the winter weather again before Céline opens the door to release Charley. Once his leash is clipped on and she opens the door wide, he bobbles his way over to Theo and rubs himself all over Theo's dark pants, covering them in fur. I expect Theo to complain about it, but he's too distracted smiling at the dog.

"It's pretty mild today, but just monitor Charley's paws to make sure he doesn't get too cold. You can come back in whenever you're ready and we'll help you put Charley back in his enclosure."

"Thank you, Céline," Theo replies before bending down to give Charley an ear scratch, which is appreciated. "Okay. Show me what to do because I have no idea."

"You're doing exactly what you're supposed to do. You're accepting what he's giving." I smile at the two of them and I'm reminded of the first time my eight-year-old self met Bond. "Let's take him outside."

We spend our time outside tossing a ball for Charley, who isn't slowed down by his missing limb. Despite what he's been through, he's got an obvious zest for life and a lot of love to give. Theo's face is beaming every time Charley fetches the ball and brings it back to throw again. Watching them connect exceeded my expectations for the day by miles.

When Charley appears tired, Theo sits on a carved tree-stump rubbing the dog's back and telling him how great he is. I chuckle, listening to their conversation, and feel as if I'm observing love in action. I don't believe humans can fall in love at first sight, but I know it can happen between a human and a dog. It happened to me.

Upon returning inside, Céline is cleaning the enclosure of a small fluffy white dog, and tells us she'll be with us in a moment. Theo crouches down, rubbing Charley's chest, speaking to him in a baby voice, and I'm trying not to chuckle. For a guy who never spent time with dogs and didn't see the appeal, I'm convinced he does now.

Céline returns Charley to his space, but he sits at the plexiglass door, staring at Theo. "He likes you."

"I like him too. I… uh, I've never had a dog before, though. Or any pet, actually. Not even one of those fluffy rat things. What are they called?"

"A guinea pig?" I suggest.

"Yeah. Not even one of those. I don't think I'd be the right owner for him."

"Well, if you change your mind, you can fill out an adoption application online. Charley's never responded to anyone the way he did with you, so I don't think he'd be bothered by your inexperience."

Céline is right, but I didn't bring Theo here today to pressure him to adopt a dog. I just wanted him to understand why they're special. Mission accomplished.

"Thanks for hanging out with me, buddy. You're going to find an amazing home because you deserve it." Theo's voice cracks a little, so I glance up at his face. His eyes are glossy, but aside from that, his expression is neutral.

We stroll out of the shelter, thanking the employees for their time and their efforts.

Both of us slide into my car, the doors slamming in unison, and I instinctively place my hand on the gear shift to ensure the car is in neutral before turning the key. I feel a warm hand on top of mine, which startles me and causes me to jolt. Theo pulls his hand away.

"Oh, sorry. That was fine. Totally fine. The hand thing. It just surprised me."

*Smooth.*

"I just wanted to say thank you for today. I'm glad you pushed me to do this." He gives me a one-sided smile before looking back at the shelter.

"You're welcome. I'm glad you enjoyed it. I was a little nervous my efforts would backfire, but dogs are hard not to love."

"Yeah, I get that now." Theo turns back to me as I turn the car on, and a blast of cold air blows out of the vents, chilling the already cold space. His knee bounces, and he's shoved both hands in the pockets of his leather coat. "Are you… uh… are you busy right now? Can I take you somewhere?"

I remove my hands from the steering wheel, rubbing them together, searching my car for a pair of gloves, but really, I'm avoiding eye contact. "What kind of somewhere?"

"My friends are at *The Mad Dog* right now and asked if I'd stop by. You could come with me."

*Meeting friends is a big deal. What if you make a fool of yourself and Theo refuses to talk to you anymore? Never mind IF you make a fool of yourself—it's virtually a guarantee.*

I'm panicking, not wanting to upset him by saying no, but not wanting to risk alienating his friend circle by being my usual self. I have little in common with other people my age and small talk is about as enjoyable as a full physical. Don't even remind me of the painful small talk I subjected my family doctor to last time I had my notorious V.A.G. inspected. She was going on about a speculum and I was telling her I thought she was a really nice person.

*You couldn't shut up and let the woman inspect your cervix in peace, could you?*

"It's okay if you don't want to. I just figured since we're headed in that direction, we could stop in, but if you have other plans, don't sweat it."

"No. It's not that." Might as well be honest. "The thing is…" I heave out a sigh. "I have terrible social anxiety. Sometimes when I'm thrown into unfamiliar situations with new people, my mind goes into overdrive questioning every look or comment. It stresses me out and I unintentionally offend people because I seem rude, but I'm not trying to be."

"Really? I never would have guessed that if you didn't tell me."

"That's the thing. Social anxiety doesn't mean socially awkward. We're good actors, but that comes at a price. It's exhausting. The best way to describe it is I can be around people, keeping up with conversation, but my brain is so hyper-focused on every minute detail, it's like a switch flips and I can't handle any more human interaction."

"Okay. So what do you do when that happens?"

I notch the gearshift into reverse, swing out of the parking space and we pull onto the road leading back to the highway. "Usually, I make up an excuse to leave or separate myself from the situation, and then I go hide for a few hours to recharge."

*He's judging you.*

A minute passes before he responds, and I convince myself in that time he's willing to jump out of the moving car to get away from me.

"How about this, then? We'll go say hi to everyone so I can say I did, and if your switch flips and you want to leave, we can come up with a safe word."

"A safe word?"

"You know. Just something you say that wouldn't normally come up in conversation, so I'll know that's your way of telling me you're ready to leave."

"What do you suggest?"

He thinks for a few seconds. "*Gesundheit.*"

I glance at him with a raised eyebrow. "*Gesundheit?*" I chuckle. "Okay. *Gesundheit.* I'll try, but if you aren't ready to go, I don't want to take you away from your friends, so I can just leave on my own."

"Trust me, I'd much rather hang out with you."

*What does that mean?*

Theo holds the door to enter *The Mad Dog*, allowing me to walk in first. It's not busy, but there is a group of ten people across the room who stare at me as I walk in.

*Smart move with the pink hair. Everybody's watching.*

I wait for Theo to take a few steps before I fall in stride behind him. I'm peering past his shoulder at the group who are smiling and waving. The first two guys to greet us give Theo a handshake and half hug, and I'm praying they don't hug me. I swipe my hands on my jeans to dry my sweaty palms.

"Guys, this is Isla. Isla, this is Shane and Dean."

I give them each a meek wave, still standing behind Theo, using him as a security blanket, but that doesn't stop Shane from stepping around Theo to offer a handshake.

*Yep, he's regretting touching your palm sweat now.*

"It's nice to meet you, Isla—the vegetarian bookworm with pink hair."

*They've been talking about you.*

I'm not sure what to say in response, but before I can reply, Dean chimes in, "You forgot non-drinker."

If someone could harness the energy output from my sweat glands right now, we wouldn't have to rely on nuclear energy. I take a deep breath, focusing on steadying my voice. "It's nice to meet you both."

"Let us go say hi to everyone else, then we'll come back to catch up," Theo says before reaching back to grab my hand. The gesture surprises me once again, but this time I don't pull away. Even if I'm terrified he feels how sweaty my hand is.

We walk toward another pub table with five people crowded around it. Three guys and two girls. The blonde girl loops her arm around the stocky brunette guy sloshing his beer on the table as if she's claiming her territory; she won't get any resistance from me.

The other girl at the table has beautiful auburn hair cascading mid-way down her back, but when she turns to glance at us, it looks like she's trying to use her mental powers to explode my face. I'm not sure I've seen such hatred from another person in my life. It makes me even more nervous.

"Hey guys. This is Isla. Isla, this is Randy and Shawna," Theo says as he points to the couple. "Mitchell, Brent, and Clara."

"Clair," the woman responds, smiling at Theo with doe eyes, pushing her boobs together between her arms. Down, girl. "Clair, not Clara."

"Oh, sorry." He turns to me and clarifies, "She's Brent's girlfriend."

Someone should tell her that because she looks like she wants to climb Theo like a tree. Or a stripper pole.

Not wanting to give anyone the wrong impression, I pull my hand away from Theo's, under the guise of wanting to remove my jacket. Theo offers to hang it for me, but I opt to keep it folded over my arms as an added layer of protection from Clair's glare.

*Everybody's watching.*

After introducing me to three more guys, who all give their condolences on the loss of his father, Theo turns to ask if I want anything to eat or drink. I was too nervous to eat this morning so I'm starving, but I hate eating in front of people I don't know. I decline. He asks me several times if I'm okay, and I appreciate his concern, but I can't help but feel I'm taking his time away from his friends.

Still clutching my coat, I slide into a bar stool around the pub table Shane and Dean are seated at while Theo places his order at the bar. Let the small talk begin.

"So, Isla. Tell us something about yourself we don't already know," Shane suggests.

*What do they know?*

Shane is wearing a toque, but I get the impression it's a style choice, not for warmth. He has dark bronze skin, a black chin-strap beard, and a nose that's been broken at least once. His athletic build leads me to believe it was a sport-related injury. I probably shouldn't ask, though. That's rude. Right?

"There's not much to tell. I'm not very exciting."

"That's not what Theo says," Dean adds. His grey eyes literally twinkle as he looks at me.

*What does* that *mean?*

"Hey now. I told you both to play nice." Theo returns with a pitcher of beer and a plate of fries. He sets the food in front of me. "Not a lot of vegetarian options, so I hope these are okay."

I'm so hungry, I'm grateful he got food, even though I declined. "Thank you. This is perfect."

Theo takes a seat on the remaining bar stool to my left and shoots me a wink. "She's being modest. She's a writer, and she's already got a book deal."

My face flushes.

"No way! That's amazing. Dean here is a reader," Shane says, nodding at Dean as he pours himself a beer.

I've always tried not to judge a book by its cover, but I pegged Dean as the reader of the group the minute we walked in. His ironed khaki pants and tucked in button-up shirt make him an outcast. Even without the thick, plastic-frame glasses set low on his delicate nose, I would have come to the same conclusion. He also looks like he could get a sunburn in a subway tunnel. "What are you writing about?" he asks.

As much as I don't enjoy being the focus of attention, I can talk about my book all day, so I'm glad the conversation ended up here. "Well, it's a spy comedy about two women who don't know each other is a spy for rival companies. When they end up in each other's crosshairs, their loyalty to their employers and each other is tested and they have to decide what's more important."

"Like Mr. and Mrs. Smith?" Theo asks.

I sigh. "No. Yes, but no. The concept is similar, but the two agents are best friends and the way it plays out is nothing like the movie. That's why I refuse to take my editor's suggestion to make one character a man and add a romantic element. 'Sex sells,' she says."

*You just said 'sex' in front of a group of guys. Nice going.*

I shove a few fries into my mouth, avoiding eye contact.

"That sounds pretty cool. What's it called, so I can watch for it?" Dean asks.

"It's called *Double Double Agent*. It's a play on words because both characters are caffeine-addicted Canadians."

The three of them laugh, with Shane spraying beer foam from his nose. I didn't think it was that funny, but I guess that's a good response.

"That's awesome. I'll definitely read it when it comes out. I've never met an author before, so maybe you can sign it for me."

"I… I guess I can, but really, I'm a nobody. Who knows if my editor will push it forward because I refused so many of her suggestions. I don't want to change my vision for the book, you know?"

*Nobody cares about your editor woes.*

"Isn't there another option? A different publisher or something?" Theo asks, elbows on the table, leaning in toward me.

"No, it's not that easy. Honestly, I was lucky I even got picked up by them in the first place. I never would have submitted my manuscript without..." A tear springs to my eye. "Without Rory insisting on it."

Theo places a hand on my knee under the table and gives it a gentle squeeze.

"Who's Rory? An ex-boyfriend or something?" Shane asks, but I can't find the words to respond before he yelps and gives Theo a glare.

"Rory was her friend who passed away," Theo clarifies.

Everyone around the table is quiet and the level of awkward is so far beyond what I can handle when I'm feeling emotional. I fake a sneeze so I can say, "*Gesundheit.*"

Without a second's hesitation, Theo pushes his half-full beer glass forward, stands and says, "Sorry, guys. I gotta get home. Mom asked me to help with some stuff around the house. You know how intense she can be." He takes my coat from my hand, pulls my chair out so I can stand, and holds it up for me to slide my arms in. "Give me a call sometime soon, eh?"

"It was nice meeting you guys," I choke out, trying to pull up my zipper.

"Likewise, Isla. Hopefully, we'll see you around. Good luck with the book thing," Shane concludes.

Once again, taking me by the hand, Theo leads me out the door, all the way to the driver's side of my car. "I'm so sorry about that. Are you okay?"

I nod. "It's fine. They didn't know. I brought her up, so I kind of walked into it. You don't have to leave because of me, though. You can stay if someone else can drive you home. I'm really sorry."

"Isla, look at me."

Tears are burning my eyes, but I force myself to meet his gaze.

"I'm only here because you came with me. I wanted to spend time with you, and even after seeing my friends, that's still what I want."

"Why did they say they were sorry about your dad?" I address that nugget of information but ignore the confession he wants to spend time with me. That's ridiculous.

"Those guys in there, I've known since Little League. We don't get together a lot, but we still support each other when we can. Still, Shane and Dean were the only ones to come to my Dad's funeral, and to be honest, that stings. I'm happy to see them, but I'm just as happy to leave. Leaving you though, that, I'm struggling with."

*What is happening? What do you do? Tell him you like spending time with him too? No, that's desperate. Are you breathing too fast? You probably smell like body odour. You're blinking too much.*

I feel paralyzed. My back is against my car. I can't move; I can't speak.

If I'm being honest with myself, I want to kiss him, but that adds a complicated dynamic into our blossoming friendship. This was never an issue with Rory. We were always just friends.

Like a tsunami, a fresh wave of grief and sadness washes over me, and I sob into my hands. Theo wraps his arms around me.

"I'm sorry, Isla. I didn't mean to freak you out."

Oh no. He thinks I'm crying because of what *he* said, and that couldn't be more wrong. That makes me cry harder. I pull away from his embrace and climb into my car. I'm freezing, I'm embarrassed, and I'm confused.

This is a cruel existence.

Yesterday, I dropped Theo off at home without speaking another word. I didn't know how to say what I was feeling and needed time to wrap my head around everything. Once I was back at my parents', I took a few hours to recover from the social interactions of the day by snuggling up with Bond and a book. Then I spent two hours crafting the perfectly worded text message for Theo so I could apologize for the way the day turned out.

This is what I came up with:

**Isla: I'm so sorry. I can be a lunatic sometimes.**

Pulitzer Prize stuff.

It took three hours for him to reply, and his response didn't resolve much either.

**Theo: I'm sorry too. I didn't mean to make you cry.**

Dagnabit. He didn't make me cry, but I don't know how to explain to him what did without sounding like a stage-three clinger. I can't exactly say, "I really wanted to kiss you, but I don't want to lose you as a friend, then when I realized I considered you a friend I felt guilty for replacing my dead best friend and that made me cry."

So, when my phone buzzes around noon on Sunday, I'm surprised to see Theo's name lighting up my screen. I'm terrified to answer.

"Hello?"

"Hey."

*What is proper phone etiquette? Is it his turn to speak because he called? Or yours, because he spoke last?*

I wait silently, not knowing how to proceed.

"Isla, I'm so sorry about yesterday."

What do I say? "There's nothing to be sorry about. I was just being stupid, trust me."

"No, obviously I upset you and that was never my intention. I was... Well, I was hoping I could run something by you to make it up to you. I have a proposal."

A what now?

"A business proposal, I mean. For your book," he rattles out. "I did some research last night and called some of my old classmates. Can we meet somewhere?"

The cursor on my computer screen is blinking, taunting me. I'm supposed to have this back to Nancy tomorrow, "or else," but I can't implement any more of her changes without changing the premise of the book.

"Isla?"

"Sorry. I was just contemplating how much work I have to do, but I think I've done as much as I can for now. We can meet at *Carly's Coffee* in an hour?"

The excitement that was missing in his voice so far in our conversation appears. "That's perfect. I'll see you there at one."

Forty minutes later, I'm hopping across the floor on one foot, trying to pull my skinny jeans on over my insulated socks. It's a challenge to put the socks on afterward, but I'm not convinced this order makes things any easier. When my heel finally pops through the narrow opening, I pull them up, grab my jacket and my purse, and run downstairs to find my boots. I'm going to be late. I hate being late.

A voice sounds from behind me while I rustle through the closet. "Where are you going in such a hurry?" I spin my head, acknowledging my dad.

"Going to meet a friend for a coffee. Have you seen my other boot?" I hold up the brown, salt-stained boot, more concerned with warmth than fashion.

"You mean the one right there?"

I look where he's pointing, and the boot is laying right at my feet. It was literally under my nose. "Thanks." I pull both boots on and throw a knit cap on to hide my pink hair I've tamed into two Dutch braids.

"What's got your feathers ruffled?"

I look at my father, who's movie-star handsome with his dark blonde hair and chiseled features, but his kind heart and gentle nature are far and away his most beautiful qualities.

"Running late. I'll be back soon. Love you, Daddy."

"Love you too, Kiddo. Drive safe, okay?"

I nod in response. To be frank, the thought of driving anywhere since the accident with Rory has sent me into a minor panic. I don't know how many car accidents it takes in a person's life to relegate them to public transportation, but I'm guessing any more than two would do the trick.

I pull up to *Carly's* seventeen minutes later with seconds to spare. Theo is waiting at the door. I was stressing so much about getting here on time, I didn't play out potential conversation scenarios in my head and now I'm feeling caught off guard.

*What does he want to talk about? What is he going to propose? Whatever you do, don't say 'hiya' again.*

"Hey, thanks for meeting me," Theo greets me first. It's cold enough today he's wearing a toque and a dark-teal bomber jacket. He opens the door to the café, allowing me to step in.

"Sorry I'm late. I couldn't get my pants on."

*Why would you say that?*

Theo chuckles. "That's an important step before leaving the house. You weren't late, though. I only got here a minute before you."

*You couldn't get your pants on? Seriously?*

The rush of heat from inside the coffee shop doesn't help my anxiety-induced body-temperature woes. I unzip my coat, draping it over my arm, and stare at the menu board.

"Are you ready to order?" a woman asks from behind the counter.

I glance at Theo, who gives me a nod to go first. "A French vanilla cappuccino, please."

"Are you sure you don't want something to eat?"

"No, it's okay." I pull out my wallet so I can pay.

"No, I got it. Let me pay. I invited you."

"Theo."

His lips curl up into a smile, exposing a hint of his teeth. "I insist. You go find us a table."

I place my hand on my hip and tilt my head. There are four tables and we're the only two people in here. "Are you trying to get rid of me?"

He looks down at his feet as they shuffle in place. "No. That's the last thing I want to do."

A rush of anxiety floods my nervous system, fearing we're treading into dangerous territory again. I don't want to risk our wires getting crossed. "Fine, I'll go get a table."

I choose one table meant for two people, saving the four person tables for any potential larger groups, but it doesn't appear we'll have to battle anyone.

Moments later, Theo is sliding onto the chair across from me. "Perfect choice. Stellar table choosing." He slides me my drink and places a box of baked goods on the table between us. "Take whatever you want, but I promised I'd bring something home for my mom." He laughs.

"I'll save her something. Thank you." I look at the sweets on offer, selecting a maple donut. Maybe it's the Canadian coffee shop inspiration I need to finish my book edits. "Tell me about your mom. I'm assuming she's pretty amazing."

"Why would you assume that?" He levels me with another devastating grin, and I choke on my donut, causing me to cough and tears to form in my eyes. "Are you okay?"

I swallow hard, washing down the sweet, sticky dough with a sip of coffee. "Why do I always end up with tears in my eyes around you?"

*Why can you never think of anything normal to say? You always make people uncomfortable. Now you've hurt his feelings and he'll think he makes you cry.*

"I'm sorry. I didn't mean it like that. You don't make me cry. But I assume your mom is amazing because she raised you."

His wide grin is little more than a smirk now. "My mom is a tough lady. She and my dad moved here from Cuba when she was eighteen. They married young. She only has a public-school education, so she worked odd jobs here and there to make ends meet. My dad's job was our bread and butter, but it was just enough to get by, so my mom worked hard so we could have little extras. You know, like winter jackets and shoes without holes. Both of my parents came here, never having seen snow, and settled in an area that was predominantly white—not from the snow. No offence. I'm not projecting onto you because you're white."

"None taken."

He nods, taking a sip of his coffee. "Life wasn't easy for them. It wasn't easy for me when I started school either, because me and Shane were the only black kids, but my parents had it so much worse. My mom is tough because of it. Not much rattles her, but she doesn't put up with nonsense either." He chuckles. "When Solana and I were younger, we wouldn't dare speak back to our parents or step out of line. To be honest, it started out as fear, but it grew into respect. Once I understood their intentions as I got older, I realized they were doing their best to raise us to be decent peop e."

"Do you have any family here at all?"

He shakes his head. "Mom's family is in Cuba, but most of my dac's family is in South Africa. My parents wanted to come here for a better life, but I'm not sure they got it." He stares down at his cup, his lips in a terse line, as he fiddles with the edge of the donut box.

My stomach lurches. I assume he's thinking about his father. "Does your mom want to move back to Cuba now?"

Theo stares into my eyes, lips slanting into a grin again. "No. I don't think so. This is home. We might deal with three seasons on any given day, but it has its appeal."

Before this conversation goes back into scary-for-me territory, I ask, "So, what did you want to talk about?"

Theo scans the area, as if he's looking for eavesdroppers. We're still alone. It's a delay tactic, and that sets my nerves on edge again. Why is he so nervous?

"Right. So, like I said on the phone, I did a lot of research, and I had an idea."

He pauses, so I prompt him to continue, "I'm listening."

"Have you heard of self-publishing?"

I nod. "I considered it, but it's a lot of work. You're no longer just a writer. You need to outsource editors, proofreaders, cover designers, formatters, and marketing is probably the hardest part. I wouldn't even know where to start, so I gave up."

"That's my idea. I'll be your marketer."

I quirk a brow at him. "You want me to hire you to market my book?"

"Yes! No. Yes, I want to market your book, but no, you don't have to hire me. I'll do it for free."

"Theo, I can't ask that from you. It's a lot of work. Never ending work. It's not just a matter of launching the book and forgetting about it. It's a constant game of playing your intended audience. I could never expect you to do that for free. Plus, I'm a nobody."

He stares back at me with a straight face. "You are not a nobody; you're an unpublished author." After a quick nod, he relaxes his features. "I want to do it for you. It's just as much for me, too. I'm bored out of my mind marketing mortgages. Do you know how demoralizing it is spending every day coming up with ideas to encourage people to take on a mountain of debt they'll spend half of their life repaying?"

I never considered that.

"Besides, I hate the idea of you having to change your book. Sure, I've yet to read it, but I already know it's amazing, and if we do everything ourselves, you can keep it how you want."

I see the appeal in that, but I also fear that Nancy wants me to change it because it's not marketable how it is. What if I agree to this and Theo spends hours on a marketing plan, but the book just isn't good? I stare at my half-eaten donut for a moment, weighing my options. Do I continue down the road with the demanding editor who wants a cookie-cutter story, or do I take the risk and release the book I want to share with the world?

"What did your research tell you?" I ask, curious if he's found some magic formula I missed.

Theo spends the next fifteen minutes relaying all the pros and cons of each publishing method, and aside from the marketing clout my publisher brings, there's not a lot of appeal with them anymore.

At the top of the list of pros for self-publishing is the one thing that I keep coming back to: creative control.

Had Nancy accepted my manuscript and only made some tweaks to it, I wouldn't hesitate to comply. But I can't get past the reality that changing the story feels like a betrayal of Rory.

The characters were inspired by our friendship, and if I change that now, she'd really disappear. I'm not letting her go without a fight.

"Like any big business, they're out to serve themselves. They aren't going to change their ways for you. We need to change it ourselves. We can do this, Isla."

I think for a few minutes before I reach my conclusion. "I'll look into a few things first, so I'm not saying yes. But I am saying, maybe; if it's possible."

Theo jolts up, bumping the table, and I reach up just in time to steady my drink. It's only lukewarm and nearly empty, so it's not going to do any damage, but I'd be sad if it spilled.

"Sorry. Sorry. I'm excited. I'll research some other books like yours and study their marketing plans. See what worked and what didn't. Are you on social media as an author? Because that's a good place to start. Generate a buzz and get people excited about the book."

"Wow. Slow down. I still have to look through my contract and see if I can get out. I had a termination clause written in because I didn't want to be in a position where they could sue me if I didn't finish it, but I have to read the fine print."

"Right. Sorry."

Thanks to my anxious brain, I always have a backup plan in place. My book contract was no different. I thought of every scenario before I signed on the dotted line, but it never occurred to me I'd finish the book and decide to escape their clutches so I can present the story how I want it. How Rory wanted it.

I chuckle at Theo's face. He's smiling ear to ear, and he's more excited than I've been about this book since I wrote THE END. "Just one stipulation if we do this."

"Okay, hit me with it."

"Actually, a few stipulations."

He nods.

"One, this business arrangement will not interfere with our friendship. I enjoy talking to you, and you're literally the only reason I've left the house for weeks, so I don't want to ruin this." I wave my hand between the two of us.

He pretends to pull a pen from behind his ear, and leaf through imaginary paper on his palm. "Okay. Friendship first. What's next?"

"We'll create a contract outlining a royalty payment schedule to make sure you get paid for your work. You will not be doing this for free."

"Isl—"

"No. It's non-negotiable. I have a lawyer who I'll need to contact regarding the other contract anyway, so he'll draft something for you to sign. You will be paid for your time."

"I thought business wouldn't come in between friends."

"It won't. Because we'll have a contract to make sure your business end is taken care of. You're excited now, and I appreciate that, but I don't want you resenting me down the road, and it doesn't feel good to be taken advantage of. I don't want you to feel that way."

"I wouldn't."

"We're not taking that chance." I take the last overly sweet sip of my drink, scrunching my face up after the sugary assault on my taste buds. "My final term is that, *if* you decide you want out, please just tell me. I know you're busy with your job and your family. I don't want it to become too much for you."

"Not going to happen. I'm all in."

"Those are my terms." I reach my straightened hand out across the table. "Do we have a deal, Mr. Malinga?"

Reaching his hand over to mine, he says, "Deal, Miss Haynes." Taking a sip of his coffee, he turns up his nose. "This is ice cold now. Do you want another one?"

I shake my head.

"I'm going to grab a refill. While I order, think of some books I can research." He slides his chair back and walks over to the counter to replace his coffee.

Am I really going to do this? Is my book ready to be seen by the world? What if people read it and they hate it? Without a publishing house to hide behind, I'm thrust into the forefront to receive any criticism. Will people even buy it? I'm a nobody, and there are tens of thousands of talented authors struggling to have their work seen. What would possess anyone to pick up mine? To be a successful author, you need to stand out, but I've spent my entire life trying to blend in.

The self-doubt—the plague of most creative types—can be crippling. It prevents you from moving forward, but once there's a story in you begging to get out, it's impossible to shove it back in. I don't know what else to do with what I've created now. Surely the fact a publishing house was willing to take a chance on it means it has some promise, but without the requested changes, is it still worth publishing?

Until now, I've been Isla, the writer. But once my book is out there, I become Isla, the author. If no one buys my work, does that still make it true? Who am I if I'm not a writer?

I'm not sure.

"I was just thinking, I should read your book too, so I know what it's about. Or maybe you can give me the CliffsNotes version." Theo laughs as he sits back down across from me.
My switch has flipped, and I've become so overwhelmed figuring out every future scenario, I need space. I need to catch my breath and calm my heart. I do the only thing I can think of.
*"Gesundheit."*

I rushed out of *Carly's Coffee* ignoring Theo's shouted pleas behind me. Once I got home, I collapsed on my bed, wrapping my head around what I agreed to. It was fine when it was theoretical, but knowing I'll upset big-wigs in the publishing industry—which is massive, but small at the same time—is stressing me out, and confrontation is not something I'm comfortable with.

I've avoided Theo's phone calls for the past thirty-six hours, but I responded with text messages to explain why I freaked out. I didn't dive into the convoluted reasoning, but I wanted to make sure he understood he did nothing to upset me. His excitement and encouragement in this endeavour mean a lot to me.

Monday morning, the moment of truth has arrived. I stare at my phone for several minutes before I work up the nerve to call one of the five people left in the world who call me. I'm about to knock that down to four.

"Hello, Isla. I trust you have good news for me."

*She's going to hate you.*

"Um. I guess that depends on your perspective." I cuddle in beside Bond on my bed, seeking the comfort he readily gives.

Nancy releases a frustrated sigh. "Are you done the revisions or not?"

"Not."

"Isla, we had an agreement. Fifteen days, you'd be done. You can't use your friend's death as an excuse anymore. Life goes on."

Now I feel less guilty about disappointing her. "I can't apply your suggestions, Nancy. I never set out to write a romance, and I refuse to turn this story into one. It's not what I want. I was calling to tell you my lawyer will send over documentation for me to be released from my contract."

"Are you kidding me?" Her voice is shrill despite the gruffness evident from years of smoking. "After everything I've done? My team and I put more than 100 hours into your manuscript and you're what? Just going to scrap it?"

"I'm not scrapping it."

"Your contract states you can't take it to another publisher. Did you neglect to read that part?"

"I'm not doing that either. I'm going to self publish."

Her laugh is alarming. "Are you trying to make yourself a laughingstock? Do you not realize how rare it is for reputable publishers to take a chance on a nobody?"

I remember Theo's words from the coffee shop. "I'm not a nobody; I'm an unpublished author. There's a difference." I take a breath to calm myself so I don't say something and burn every link to a future in traditional publishing. "Your time and effort are appreciated, and I realize I'll need to pay for services rendered, but this story is too important to me to sacrifice my vision for it. I can't turn it into a mass-market paperback just to make a profit."

She laughs again. "You're going to get eaten alive. There are hundreds of thousands of books published each year. Good luck making a career out of it when you don't bend to fit the box people want."

"Thanks for your input, but my mind is made up."

"You're making a mistake. You get one chance at a first impression."

The reality of that statement terrifies me. "Thanks, Nancy. All the best."

I hang up the phone, throwing my arm over Bond, rubbing my face in the short fur on his head. My pounding heart slows with each stroke along his side. He shifts onto his back, giving me access to his belly, which makes me laugh. Hard moments are bearable with him.

I get sucked into tummy rubs for thirty minutes before I conclude I should report in with Theo. He deserves an actual conversation.

My phone says it's just after 11am, but I dial anyway, knowing he's at work.

*Please let voicemail pick up. Please don't answer.*

"Isla?"

"Hi… uh… hi."

"Why do you sound surprised? You called me?" He chuckles.

Because I wasn't expecting you to answer. "Sorry. I just got off the phone with Nancy… my editor… well, my former editor."

"Really?" His voice is animated. "That's fantastic. What did she say?"

"Well, short version, she told me I was making a mistake because I'm a nobody and I won't have any success if I don't bend to fit in the box people want to buy."

He laughs. "So, it went well."

"Could have been worse, but she's not wrong."

"She is wrong. People are going to love your book."

Huffing out a laugh, I reply, "I wish I had your confidence."

"I didn't suggest this to make you doubt yourself. But for now, I'll have enough confidence for us both, okay? Until you can find your own."

That comment leaves me sputtering. "I'm not sure I'll ever find any, so that could be a long-term commitment."

"I'm good with that." A few seconds of silence pass between us again. "So, do you want to meet up one night this week to work on a plan? I have a lot of questions before I can make a marketing strategy."

"Whatever works for you. Technically, I'm unemployed, and it's not like I have a social life. As long as my dog doesn't make plans for us, I'm wide open." The fact he's still willing to help me when my reputation in the writing community has taken a major hit makes me envy his determination.

"Okay. I'll call you later tonight and we'll make it a date. I mean... not a date, date. You know. Business meeting."

We end the call with the understanding we'll talk later, but he's at work, so I feel guilty about keeping him any longer.

I turn to Bond, who is snuggled into my underarm. "You wanna see the kids?"

He pops up, raring to go with the energy of a puppy. I call my sister to ask if she's busy and invite myself over for the afternoon. I could use some sister time.

When I walk into Chelsea's house, not stopping to knock, my three favourite munchkins come running to greet Bond and me.

"Auntie I-wa!" Lenox cheers the loudest and wins the race to be picked up. It's getting hard to hold them now, as they approach kindergarten age, but I won't stop until they're as tall as me.

"Hi, little penguin. You're getting big!"

"I know," he says with a glimmer in his eye. He's always been the smallest of the three, and looks like the little brother of twins, but it doesn't deter him when they decide to start a good old-fashioned wrestling match.

Lincoln and Hudson both greet Bond first, then latch themselves onto me. I trudge across the room holding one forty-pound child in my arms with two more attached to my legs.

"Thanks for coming. They're full of beans today. I'm exhausted." Chelsea walks around her kitchen counter after setting down her coffee and gives me a hug.

"How is that different from any other day?" I set Lenox down and tickle the other boys' armpits until they release their death-grips on my legs.

"It's not. I'm happy to see you." She observes me for a moment, focusing on my face. "You look stressed. What's up?"

Wow. She's good. I glance down at the boys, not wanting to sacrifice my time with them, but I could use some life advice from my big sister. "Let me play with the boys for a bit, then I could use your input."

"Sounds stressful. You're going to leave me questioning every worse-case scenario?"

I chuckle because I am well aware she doesn't need cause to panic. "It's nothing. Book stuff... mostly." Before she can reply, I throw up my monster claws, let out a roar and chase after the screaming hooligans who light up my world.

An hour later, the boys are sprawled out on the family room floor watching *Paw Patrol* and Chelsea gestures for me to take a seat in her living room. I oblige.

"Tell me what's happening with your book." She's probably been running through every scenario since I arrived, so she doesn't waste time digging for the facts.

"Well, things weren't going great with my editor."

"Not great how?"

I take a breath and brace myself to explain the long list of issues, which ramble on for a full minute.

Chelsea stares at me with her wide blue eyes. "Okay. So what now?"

"I met this guy." The eyes observing me widen further. "His name is Theo, and we met online in a grief support group because his dad died, so it's not what you're thinking. He's just a friend"—who I want to kiss sometimes—"and we understand each other's grief. Anyway, he's in marketing and when I told him about my issues with my editor, he suggested I self publish so I can tell the story my way, and he'll market it for me."

Chelsea sits silently for a moment. "Just…" She looks away, taking a sip of her coffee, which I'm certain is empty.

"Just what? I need some guidance, here."

"You know I think you're amazing. Your writing is amazing, and you're going to end up on the New York Times bestseller list someday."

"Boosting my ego doesn't sound like what you really wanted to say, Chels."

"I think the idea of self publishing the story you want is great." She gives me a meek smile. "But, you know the saying, 'don't put all your eggs in one basket'?"

I nod.

"Don't allow your entire career, or your life, to get tied up in this Theo guy. I know he says he's going to market your book, and that's great, but don't become dependent on him to launch yourself as an author. Do you get what I'm saying?"

Chelsea learned the hard way not to rely on a guy you barely know for your livelihood. In her case, it was cocaine, but the premise is the same. She's right. I'll accept Theo's help, but he is not going to chart the course of my career. That's up to me.

A snowy Saturday in February would normally be a perfect day for me to cuddle up with my dog and my laptop and get some editing work done, but Theo asked me to tag along with him somewhere. He didn't tell me where and despite my anxiety gnawing away at my nerves, I'm trying to trust him. I did the same thing to him when we went to the dog rescue, and he followed along.

In order to have a semblance of control, I offered to pick him up at his place. The last thing I want is to go somewhere unfamiliar and be trapped.

As I pull up to Theo's house, I don't even honk or go ring the doorbell before he walks out the door, but it appears as if he's sneaking out. He comes skipping down the stairs with his lips in a wild smile. That smile could melt every bit of the snow falling.

Instead of walking around to the passenger side, he opens my door and bends down to face me. "Hey. Can you come in for a sec? I want you to meet someone."

*Meeting family? What will you say? How do you explain who you are? Is it helpful or upsetting to give your condolences?*

The only vehicle in the driveway is Theo's SUV. I don't think his sister is old enough to have a car, so it must be her he wants me to meet. Okay. I can do this.

I unbuckle my seatbelt and swing my legs out of the car. Theo reaches his hand toward me to help me out, earning him a smile. The anxiety I was feeling lessens. Hopefully, his sister is as easy going as him.

He gestures for me to walk ahead, but with each step, my anxious thoughts are raging back again.

*What do you say when she greets you? Don't say 'hiya,' whatever you do.*

At the top of the stairs, I step to the side to allow Theo to open the door. His smile is so wide, I can't help but stare at him with a smile of my own. Even from behind, I can see his rounded cheeks and squinting eyes. He must really love his sister.

When he opens the door, I'm greeted by the last thing I would have guessed.

"Charley?" A sweet, bouncy tri-pod shepherd waits on the other side. "What is he doing here?" I ask as I bend down to give Charley a proper hello.

"I adopted him a few days ago. I've been dying to tell you, but I wanted it to be a surprise."

Standing to face Theo, with a glance down at Charley's waggle bum, I'm elated to see how happy Charley is, and Theo clearly feels the same. "This... this is amazing. What made you decide to adopt him?"

He bends down, ruffling the short hair on Charley's head. "I thought about him for days after we went to the shelter. I kept telling myself that I didn't know the first thing about dogs and couldn't justify having one. But as weeks went by, I became more convinced that he belonged here. I had such a strong feeling that no other home would be a better fit for him. When

I called the shelter, they said he'd had no interest, and he was depressed despite everything they tried to do for him. I couldn't leave him like that."

"Wow. I'm so happy for you—for you both. Charley isn't depressed anymore!" I kneel beside him and he licks my face. "Are ya, boy? You love your new home, dontcha?" He reduces me to a fit of giggles in no time flat, and the more I laugh, the more eager he is to lick my face and wag his tail. Several moments of my life pass with dog slobber and laughing, and I haven't been so happy in a long time.

When I stand, I can't help but think Theo's face must hurt from smiling. It warms my heart seeing how happy he is and knowing that I helped him to see how the love of a dog is so special.

"You were right, you know," he says as he looks into my eyes.

"About…"

"A dog can be a person's best friend. I swear, this guy has been here for four days and everyone in the house has been smiling again. I wasn't sure that would ever happen." He steps closer to me. "Thank you."

*You're breathing too loud. He can smell your breath from this distance. He can probably hear your heart beating, too.*

I take a step back, breaking eye contact with Theo.

He clears his throat and asks, "Are you ready to go then?"

"This isn't what you wanted to show me?"

"Partly. But we still have one more stop to make."

We pull into *Carter's Forever Rescue and Sanctuary,* and I'm transported back to the many years ago we came here to get Bond. Every few seconds I glance at Theo, hoping he'll give me some sort of clue why we're here, but his face doesn't budge from the wide smile he's sported all day.

"This is where I adopted Bond from. I never told you that."

"Really? That's so cool. I'm sure they'd be happy to hear that he's been loved all this time."

"Why are we here? Are you adopting another dog?"

Laughter reverberates through my car. "No. One dog is enough to start. Come on. I'll show you."

Once I'm parked, Theo and I walk toward the entrance of the shelter, which doubles as a residence. He's walking with such confidence, it's a stark contrast to the day I took him to the animal shelter he adopted Charley from. He walks right in the door and a petite, brunette woman with olive skin greets him with an enthusiastic, "Hi, Theo!"

How does she know him?

"Hey, Lucia. How are you?"

And he knows her? I recognize her from when we adopted Bond, but I doubt she'd remember me.

"I'm good, thanks. We weren't expecting you today. I didn't see you on the schedule."

"Oh, I'm not on the schedule. I just wanted to bring my friend, Isla, to show her around. Do you mind?"

Schedule? What's happening?

"Go on ahead. You know your way around."

After a quick thank you, and a nod of acknowledgement from Lucia to me, Theo marches down a hallway that brings back memories from when I was a child. Everything looks so different but feels exactly the same.

"Theo, what's going on?"

He stops walking and spins around to look at me. "When you took me to the other shelter, I realized something."

"Okay… which was?"

"Dogs are amazing."

I laugh at his epiphany. "Indeed, they are. And I don't hate to say I told you so."

He smiles so big, his dimples are more pronounced than ever. "I've only been here for a week, so I didn't want to say anything. I don't want you to think I brought you here to showboat... Really, I just wanted to thank you. If you hadn't taken me to meet Charley, I would have missed out on something amazing."

"You're welcome?" My words come out as a whisper. I don't think I did anything noteworthy. Honestly, my decision to take him to the shelter was selfish because I wanted to justify the love I have for my dog. "Actually, I don't deserve any credit. Your decision to adopt a dog and volunteer your time is squarely on your shoulders. I bet ten thousand people have walked in and out of Ontario shelters this month and only a handful will do either, let alone both. So, what you're doing, it's because of who you are and your heart. It's got nothing to do with me."

His face is unreadable as he stares at me. "We'll have to agree to disagree, because I know I wouldn't have made this decision without you."

The next few hours pass in a blur. We visit with each dog on site, spoiling them with attention. I'm amazed by how natural Theo is with the dogs—even ones that clearly came from bad situations. His ability to read a dog's body language and switch from playful to tender is baffling. He has so much confidence around each animal, I'd never know that he only got his first dog a few days ago.

When it's time to leave, I can barely see my car on account of the fallen snow. Getting out of the parking lot will be difficult enough but driving home could prove even harder.

"I'll brush the snow off the car. You get in and warm it up." Theo winks at me, still wearing a beaming smile. I'm about to argue as he pulls on a pair of gloves, and I realize I don't have any.

Once the car is clean and warm, I throw it in reverse and the tires skip on the slick snow. This is going to be a nightmare.

The snow is falling rapidly, coating the road in a familiar slick sludge. I've never enjoyed winter driving, but after my experiences with deadly winter car crashes, I'm finding it hard to breathe and drive at the same time.

"Maybe we should find somewhere to wait out the storm. Once the roads are plowed, we can get back home," Theo suggests.

Just then, my phone rings through my car's Bluetooth speaker. It's my mom.

"Hi, Mom."

"Oh, Sweet Girl, where are you?"

I glance at Theo as he mouths "sweet girl" and smirks at me.

"I'm in Bracebridge, but it's snowing really bad."

"I know. The road just north of us is closed because of an accident, so I wanted to make sure you were okay."

My breathing speeds up, as does my heart rate. "Is Dad home?"

"Yes. He got home a while ago. Just stay put wherever you are. Why don't you go wait at your condo for a few hours? You should check in, anyway."

Theo spins to glare at me with wide eyes.

"I'm not sure I'm ready for that."

"It will be strange, but you'll need to do it sometime. Better to stay somewhere warm and safe for a while."

I stare into space for I don't know how long before Mom interrupts my silence. "It will be fine. Just call me back if you need someone to talk to when you get there."

"I'm not alone." My eyes dart open, realizing what I just said. "Uh… I have a friend with me right now. We were visiting the animal shelter."

"That sounds nice. I'm glad you won't be alone. We'll give Bond his dinner and make sure he's looked after. Don't rush to get here until it's safe."

Resigning myself to the fact there is little choice with the road closed, I agree. My parents live in the middle of nowhere, so it would take an extra twenty minutes on a clear day to detour around the closed road, but I'd guess a full hour in these conditions. That's too risky right now.

I say goodbye to my mom and turn to face Theo. "Are you okay with coming to my place?"

"You have a condo here?"

I nod. It's never come up before.

"Why don't you live there?"

I don't reply. Explaining why I don't hurts too much. He doesn't press me and sits silently as I drive the two kilometres to my abandoned home.

Before we walk into my ground-floor condo from the patio entrance, carrying the food we picked up on the way, I turn to Theo. "Rory and I lived here together. I… uh… I haven't been back since…" A tear rolls down my cheek and I can't bring myself to look at his face.

He doesn't say a word. He holds my shaking hand for a moment before taking the key and sliding it in the lock. "This might be hard, but you're strong, and I'll be right here."

I nod before I step forward, turn the key, and open the door. The blast of warmth and stale air greets me. It doesn't smell like home anymore. I stomp my boots off on the colourful woven bohemian mat as I step inside. I stare at it for a moment, reminded of the day Rory and I chose it.

Barbara and Mark came to remove Rory's stuff quite a while ago. Knowing that makes me afraid to look up. How is it supposed to feel like home without the sound of her strumming serving as a constant soundtrack?

I can't do this. I stand in place and cry into my hands.

It takes only a second before Theo has his arms wrapped around me. He's removed his coat, but I haven't, and it makes me feel guilty he's getting wet from the melted snow stuck to my clothing. I shake my head so he'll let go and I can at least take my coat off. He releases me and stumbles backwards.

*Nice going.*

"I'm sorry. I thought… I'm sorry." His expression compounds my guilt.

I want to explain to him, but I'm crying and can't speak, so we stand there in silence, allowing the miscommunication to go unaddressed.

I excuse myself to the powder room. There's an ensuite off of my bedroom, but to get to it, I'd have to pass Rory's former bedroom and I'm not ready for that. Who knows if I ever will be. The water runs for a moment since it hasn't been turned on for months, then I splash my face to help stem my tears. Looking at myself in the mirror, my hair is styled by static electricity from removing my toque; my face is splotchy from a combination of cold, crying, and smudged makeup; my eyes are red. I remove a washcloth from the vanity so I can try to salvage my face. Theo shouldn't have to see me like this. I don't even want to see myself like this.

A knock at the door causes me to jump. I've stopped crying, but I'm afraid to leave this safe space. Rory and I rarely used this bathroom because we each had our own, so this feels like neutral territory. The rest of the place—well, there are memories in every corner. Artwork. Furniture. Dishes. Nothing is safe.

"Isla. Are you all right?"

I open the door. Theo is leaning against the wall opposite the powder room.

"I'm so sorry. You probably think I'm an idiot," I mumble.

He steps forward before stopping himself. "You're not an idiot. I don't think that at all."

"I wouldn't blame you. Gosh. How many times am I going to come completely unhinged in front of you?"

"You're allowed to take the time you need to grieve. Don't feel bad about it. I get that this is hard. My mom is still sleeping in our living room."

How could I be so stupid? So self-absorbed? It didn't even occur to me that Theo and his family are left living in a house with all of his father's things. No one came to remove the reminders of him.

I'm not sure how to explain my thought process to him, so I change the subject. "Wanna eat?" I squeeze past him, avoiding any contact between us and walk to the kitchen.

Theo placed the bags of food on the light grey marble before coming to knock on the bathroom door, so I busy myself taking the items out of the bags one by one.

"What can I do to make this easier for you?"

"Can you grab plates, please?" I nod my head toward a cabinet behind me.

Theo walks to the cupboard at a snail's pace. "I mean being here. How can I help?"

"Yeah, I know." I stare down at the spoon I'm twirling in my right hand. "Trust me. Grabbing plates is helping. Rory's parents came to clean out her things a few weeks after she…" I swallow the golf-ball-sized lump in my throat. "After she died. I'm not sure what they did or didn't take, and I'm not sure I'm ready."

He responds with a kind smile before removing two plates from the cabinet. "Pink plates?"

I shrug at his discovery, not turning around to look. My condo had a very modern aesthetic when I moved in, and I wanted to make it more creative and fun. Rory and I decorated the entire place with boho elements, hoping it would inspire us both in our different pursuits. The blush pink dishes are the outlier in the otherwise cohesive decor. "I like pink."

He chuckles. "Me too." He stares at my fading pink hair with blonde roots.

*What does that mean?*

With an increased heart rate, I lead Theo the few feet to the dining area, which, once we've cleaned the layer of dust off, is more comfortable to sit at than the bar stools at the counter. That's too close. Too intimate.

"You guys don't have a TV?" Theo asks, disturbing the growing silence.

"There's one in the family room. That's where we spent most of our time." We. Us. That's past tense. There is no Rory and me anymore. "I use the living room for writing mostly, so there was no need for a TV in there." I stare at the glass doors overlooking the patio, remembering the late nights I spent there crafting my novel, hearing Rory strum her masterpieces from the other room.

The snow has accumulated at least two feet up the door. We're not going anywhere soon.

After chewing a bite of pulled pork, Theo struggles to carry the conversation forward. "This is a really nice place. Have you been paying rent all this time?"

How do I answer that without sounding pretentious? With honesty, I guess. "No. I… um… When I was working on my degree, Rory was taking her Bachelor of Arts in Music production online, too. We knew we wouldn't get the traditional college experience, so we decided we'd at least get our own place. You know… trying to adult." I shovel a mouthful of parmesan mashed potatoes in my mouth, debating how much else to explain. "My parents agreed but insisted on helping us find a place. Because of Bond, they knew renting would be hard, especially since my work is all freelance, so they bought this condo." I shrug, acting like this is a normal gift for nineteen-year-old students to receive.

Theo looks surprised but blinks his expression back to neutral. "That makes sense. I guess with your dad being a mortgage broker, that made financing easier, too."

I'll just skip over the fact there was no financing required. Delving into my dad's tragic past is not going to make this already-emotionally draining day any easier.

"It's a good thing you still have this place, though. It looks like we're going to be stuck overnight."

Theo fluffs the pillow I grabbed from the linen closet, punching it into submission on the sofa before he lies back, draping his legs over the armrest. The couch is about five feet long and uncomfortable for me, so I feel bad, but the alternative is him sleeping in Rory's room. He's made it clear he won't do that until I'm comfortable having someone else in her space. Whether that will ever be possible, I don't know.

"Are you sure about this? You can't be very comfortable."

"I'll be fine. It's just one night."

I stare at Theo for a moment, unable to move my feet. My condo is a long, narrow layout, which allows for the living space to cover about sixty percent of the square footage, and both bedrooms are at the opposite end. That means I have to walk past Rory's bedroom door to get to my own. Part of me wants to ask Theo to walk me to my room, but I know that's pathetic. He has to live in the house his father spent the last two decades in. He's functioning like a normal human. Open doors aren't causing him panic. I don't know why this is so hard.

"Isla?"

I'm staring. "Sorry. Sorry. I'll let you sleep." Heat creeps up my cheeks and down my neck, which is not remedied by Theo's chuckle.

"Are you gonna be okay getting to your room?"

I can't move or blink. My chest is heaving as I labour with each breath. This can't happen. If Theo can live in his family home after losing his father, I can find the guts to walk to my bedroom. I called this home for two years. Part of the issue is it doesn't feel like home anymore, but that's not Theo's problem.

*He's watching you. You're making a fool of yourself.*

I blink several times to bring myself back to the task at hand and nod before turning to leave the room. One unsteady foot in front of the other, I toddle down the hallway. As I near Rory's bedroom door, it's closed, and I want to peek inside, but right before sleeping is not the time for that. I walk through my open bedroom door, scanning the Scandinavian décor and my dead houseplants, and collapse onto my teak queen-sized bed face first.

My heart breaks again, recalling the nights Rory and I had slumber parties because living together wasn't enough. We'd stay up until the early hours of the morning, talking about our goals and dreams. Rarely we'd talk about boys—Rory, more so than me—and that guilt rips through me with another sob. It's not fair that I'm here with Theo—though 100% platonic—and Rory never got to tell Dominic how she was crushing on him for over a year.

I hear tiptoeing down the hallway, but the sound stops a few feet away. I force myself to get it together before Theo comes in like a wannabe knight in shining armour again. He's sweet to want to comfort me, but he's dealing with his own grief. Mine is not his responsibility. The footsteps move in the opposite direction, heading back where they came from.

Once I complete my nighttime routine, I climb into bed, flipping over my tear-soaked pillow, exposing the solid orange colour on the back side of the colourful geometric patterned sham. I lie down on top of the matching duvet, blocking out thoughts of how much dust has accumulated on my bedding in my absence. Instead, my mind drifts to Bond. I haven't slept a single night without him by my side in thirteen years. He's either cuddled in between my parents right now, or Mom has relegated Dad to the sofa across the room so Bond can sleep beside her. I miss him, but like Theo said, it's only one night.

After a lengthy battle with my pervasive and unrelenting grief, I drift off to sleep.

"Isla? Isla. Wake up."

My heart is racing, I'm drenched in sweat, and I'm disoriented. I clamber to the head of my bed, where I sit for a moment and take in the who, where, and how. Theo. The voice is Theo. My condo bedroom. Snowstorm. I come back to reality, taking deep breaths to slow my pounding heart.

"You were screaming and thrashing around. Sorry if I scared you."

I shake my head. A night terror. It's been years since I had one. Even after Rory died, I had a few nightmares, but not the full-fledged horror of a night terror. The only good thing is that I never remember what they were about upon waking. They seem real, and how I physically respond to them is evidence of that—my hands are clammy, and sweat is dripping down the back of my neck. I'm so embarrassed—sitting here looking like I tussled with an alligator, no bra, twisted shirt, and feeling really exposed.

"Sor… Sorry. I didn't mean to wake you."

Theo sits at the edge of my bed. The gesture has me squeezing myself as tightly as possible against the headboard. That doesn't go unnoticed, and Theo stands in response.

He stares at the dead aloe vera plant on my nightstand. It's a remarkable feat to kill a resilient cactus, but they don't thrive with little sunlight, in a room with the heat turned down, and no water. A moment later he speaks again, his voice quiet, eyes downcast. "Are you okay?"

"I will be. I'm really sorry for waking you. This hasn't happened in a long time." My cheeks are burning, which isn't helping my body temperature to drop.

"Night terrors?"

I'm embarrassed he recognizes what happened, but it makes me curious. "How did you know?"

"Remember Shane?"

I nod.

"He used to get them when we were kids. He outgrew them though; at least, as far as I know."

"I thought I had, too. They're common in kids, but in most cases, kids outgrow them by their teen years... I... Hopefully this was just a one-off because my dog isn't here. Normally he sleeps in the bed with me and having him there helps me sleep." I wave my hands around the room. "This is all just too much for my idiotic brain, I guess."

"You're not idiotic, Isla. Today was a lot, and I get it. Don't feel bad about how you respond to it."

I swallow down my emotions, but my mouth rivals the Sahara. Pretty sure I cried out every drop of hydration my body had. "Thanks. I'm really sorry for waking you."

Theo sighs. "You don't have to be sorry. I'm just glad you're all right. Do you want to go back to sleep? Or we can hang out and watch a movie or something?" He looks shy. It's adorable.

"To be honest, I'm afraid to go back to sleep because I don't want it to happen again, but I need a shower. I'm… sweaty." And I can't even imagine how I look right now.

His eyes shoot wide open and I'm even more embarrassed than I was thirty seconds ago.

*Did you really need to tell him you were sweaty?*

"Oh, right. Yeah. Sure. Okay. Um… I'll just go out to the couch and find a movie, and you can come… um… you can join me when you're done."

By the time I enter the family room, Theo appears to have fallen asleep. I turn to tiptoe back to my room when he speaks. "I'm just resting my eyes."

"My dad says that all the time, but it's code for 'I can't keep myself awake.'"

His eyes dart open and he sits up straight, patting the sofa beside him. "No, I'm fine. I was just waiting for you. Did the shower help?"

Heat creeps up my face as I recall the embarrassment over my night terror. "I'm fine. And sorry… again."

"Stop apologizing. It's fine. Nothing was your fault."

I sit on the sofa, kicking my feet up on the coffee table, and attempt to change the subject. "What are we watching?"

"No idea. Whatever the lady chooses."

"What if I pick *The Notebook*?"

"Sure, but I have my doubts you'd choose that."

I face him, trying to analyze his reasoning. "Why?"

"Because I might not be a reader, but I know that book lovers always think the book is better."

He's right. "The book *is* always better."

He laughs, pressing the right arrow on the remote, scanning our options. We settle on *A Dog's Journey* and watch the entire movie in virtual silence, with only a few comments made throughout. By the end, I'm a blubbering idiot because dog movies always make me cry regardless of a happy or sad ending. I can't even watch *Dogs with Jobs* anymore because I bawl my eyes out.

We sit on the sofa talking for a while as the sun finally rises, casting light on the amount of snow that accumulated overnight. The building manager has already plowed the parking lot and shovelled the pathways, but the snowbanks are at least three feet taller than they were yesterday.

Life in Canada.

I move to get up from the couch when Theo places a hand over mine and freezes me in place. "Isla?"

I nod.

"Will you go on a date with me? A real date."

As I stare into the front hall mirror, I barely recognize myself. Every other date I've been on in my life, I went because I thought it was my friendly duty to accompany Rory. I've never been on a one-on-one date, and beyond that, I've never *wanted* to go on a date, so I've never put effort into it. But today, I was like a NASCAR as Mom and Chelsea whipped around me, helping me choose an outfit, doing my hair and makeup, spritzing me with *Chanel No. 5*, leaving me looking back at a stranger. Dare I say a pretty stranger? I've never felt pretty before.

My charcoal sheath dress hugs every curve of my tall frame, ending with a scalloped hem just below my knees. The medium-width straps allow for a push-up bra, and I'm alarmed by the cleavage on display. I'll probably end up dropping pasta down there at dinner. Still, it's a better option than the off-white dress Mom had recommended. That, for sure, would have looked like one of my nephew's finger paintings by the end of dinner, even with a cardigan.

Chelsea has to rush home because Liam is handling dinner time with the kids and she wants to get back to help him, so she gives me a kiss on the cheek, wishes me luck and rushes out the door with instructions to call her tomorrow.

Theo will arrive in about five minutes, assuming he's on time, so I put on my black three-inch heels which make me an even six-feet tall. It's a good thing Theo is tall because I lost count of how many times I ended up on a date with guys whom I towered over. Like I need more reason for people to stare at me—I don't want to look like I'm dragging some poor bloke around by force.

My coat is black with a faux fur shawl collar, so I don't need a scarf or other winter accessories. No way am I putting on a hat after the time mom and Chels spent on my hair. Despite my legs being bare from the knees down, I'm warm. When Mom's phone pings, indicating someone is at the driveway gate, she presses a button and shoots me a look. Leaving no room for misinterpretation, she says, "Do you want me to stay down here to meet this Theo, or should I make myself scarce? I can call Dad down too."

Oh please, no. My dad is a teddy bear, but I don't want to scare Theo.

"Well, your facial expression just cleared that up. I'll go upstairs and keep your dad busy."

"Ew. Please don't say that."

She gives me a hug, giggles, and rushes upstairs. Part way up, she turns back to add, "Just focus on staying in the moment, okay? Enjoy the night and try not to think about the past or the future."

I nod. If logic controlled my thoughts, I'd say that was good advice. "I promise I'll try."

"Love you, Sweet Girl."

The doorbell rings. "Love you too." I blow out a breath and step to my left to open the door. On the other side is a startled face holding a colourful bouquet, instantly deflating every ounce of confidence I had built up with each layer of foundation or hairspray. "Hi."

"Wow." His eyes scan me from top to bottom. "Are you going to be warm enough?"

Oh. My. Gosh. Seriously, man? Each second that passes between us has my heart rate accelerating because I'm just waiting for him to tell me he doesn't want to be seen in public with a pink-haired, pale-skinned Amazonian woman. I knew this was a mistake.

"You look amazing. I mean, you always do, but wow… You are stunning."

I hear his words, but given his initial reaction, I'm certain he's only saying that because he knows it's proper date etiquette. "You look nice too."

"I brought these for your mom, actually. I hope that's okay."

Melt. He's redeemed himself. It might be hovering around freezing, but I am remarkably warm. "She'll love that. Thank you." He has no idea that him bringing my mom flowers means so much more to me than if he brought them for me. "Let me put them in water and I'll be right back. Come in for a second."

He steps through the door, closing it behind him. "This is a nice place."

I shout from our kitchen in the open-concept space. "Thanks. My dad bought it when he was a bachelor. Just him and his sister lived here for a few years before he and mom got married. Then he quickly went from bachelor to full-fledged family man." I giggle, recalling how fast the entire process happened for him, but he never hesitated and never made us feel like he had to work up to loving us. He just did. If I settle down someday, my future husband has big shoes to fill. When I glance at Theo, that thought makes me blush. I can't be thinking about marriage on our first date. Lunatic.

When I walk back to the front hall, Theo reaches his hand out to me. "Are you ready for this?"

Am I? I don't know. I halt my steps forward. "Theo."

His face flashes concern as he looks at me to reply, "Yeah?"

"If you changed your mind, it's okay. I mean, I don't want to lose you as a friend, so it's okay if you don't want to do this." I wave my pointed finger back and forth between us.

He furrows his brows and tilts his head. "I've been looking forward to this for weeks."

"You only asked me five days ago."

"I know." He winks and my guard drops. My walls are crumbling down around him, and he doesn't even have to try.

We walk hand-in-hand in silence toward his navy-blue GMC Terrain. He opens the door, allowing me to slide in. I've spent quite a bit of time with Theo so far and we've had awkward moments, but things have started getting easier with him. He slides into his seat a few seconds later, and since he kept his car running, we're driving away as soon as his seatbelt clicks.

"Where are we going? I never asked."

"I noticed." He smirks. "It actually means a lot that you trusted me to decide."

That confuses me. He's never given me a reason not to trust him. "Why wouldn't I?"

"I've never dated anyone who didn't want to have complete control." He shrugs as he continues, "I don't mind handing over the reins; I'm not a misogynist, but it's nice to plan an evening out." When he reaches his hand over to mine, I turn into a puddle. "I'm grateful you're letting me show you how special you are."

There are no words in my brain right now. Words are my area of expertise and I've got nothing.

He clears his throat. "Anyway, we're going to *Mountainside at Muskoka Inn Resort*. I wanted to stay close to home so we don't get stuck anywhere again. Not that I'm complaining about that."

I blush when he reminds me of our night snowed in at my condo. Nothing romantic happened, but things shifted between us. I was vulnerable, but it didn't scare me. "That was smart thinking. I've never been there before."

"I called ahead to make sure they had vegetarian options on the menu, so I hope you can find something you like."

My jaw drops. That is… wow. That's so above and beyond. "Thank you." I squeeze his hand in return and recognize how clammy my hand feels, but I don't dwell on it. For once, I just enjoy his touch.

We pull into the parking lot at *Muskoka Inn Resort,* a whopping ten minutes after leaving my driveway. He really kept close to home.

"I'll drop you at the door and go park. I don't want you to get cold."

Chivalry is not dead. My stomach clenches at the thought of Theo's dad and imagining him teaching Theo about being a gentleman. I want to thank him. I want to tell him he did an amazing job. Tears spring at the corner of my eyes, so I stare out the passenger window, hoping Theo won't notice. But he does.

"What's wrong?" Panic is obvious in his voice.

*You ruin everything.*

I shake my head. The last thing I want is for him to think I'm upset with him. "Nothing. I'm sorry. I was… um… just thinking about your dad." A small smile tugs at my lips, trying to lighten the emotional turn in the conversation. "He did a good job raising a gentleman, and how I wish I could thank him." As those words spill out, so do a pair of tears.

Theo reaches over, wiping a rogue tear with his thumb. "He taught me how to cherish what's important."

For a split second I wonder if he's going to kiss me and note how badly I want him to. But he doesn't.

"I'll go park and meet you inside."

A wave of embarrassment rushes through me. Why would he want to kiss me? I'm me.

With a nod, I avoid meeting his gaze, open the door and hop out. I walk down the brick path to the timber-framed building. It's stunning, but as I catch my reflection in the windows, I don't feel pretty anymore.

I pull the door to wait inside, where a gentleman in a server's uniform asks to take my coat. I reluctantly hand it over, assuming this is not a place where you hang your bulky coat on the back of your chair.

Moments later, I see Theo striding down the path. He walks with such confidence; I'm jealous, because aside from the fleeting moment I had earlier tonight, confidence is not something I recognize in myself.

When he opens the door and steps inside, he catches sight of me and trips on something invisible. He takes a stutter step to right himself before standing next to me. "If I was going to die just now, I'd go a happy man."

*What does that mean?*

was already feeling awkward standing here alone but having Theo's gaze on me isn't helping. I swivel around, taking in the rest of the faces in the room and meet at least ten more pairs of eyes.

*Everybody's watching.*

My body temperature is skyrocketing, enough I may need to go sit in a snowbank, and that's preferable to being the recipient of the gaping-mouth stares of multiple strangers.

The hostess catches my attention when he addresses Theo. "Table for two?"

"Yes, please. I made a reservation for Malinga."

"Oh, lovely. Mr. Malinga, if you and the missus could follow me this way, I'll get you seated."

Theo doesn't correct him, and I don't have the nerve to. Instead, he takes my arm, and we follow the auburn-haired gentleman, weaving through the other occupied tables.

"Theo," I whisper. "Is it just me, or is everyone staring at us?"

He leans his head toward me and whispers back, "No, they're staring at you."

That was the last thing I wanted to hear, having my suspicions confirmed.

Before I can turn around and run out the door, the hostess pulls out a chair belonging to a beautifully set table for two near the windows. Because of the time of year, the sun has already set, but it's still a stunning view of the snow-covered golf course. The downside is that I can clearly see my reflection again in the darkened windows and several faces staring at my back.

*Everybody's watching.*

I've never been so self-conscious about sitting in a chair in all my life—and that's saying something.

"I'm so sorry," I mutter to Theo the moment our hostess is out of earshot.

The man is going to end up with pre-mature wrinkles if he spends much more time with me because he looks back at me with his eyebrows stitched together. "What are you sorry for?"

"Everyone is staring at me. I'm sorry for embarrassing you." I focus on the folded black napkin set on top of a hardcover black menu in front of me. "We can go."

"Why would I be embarrassed?"

I take a breath, calming my frantic breathing. "Because I look like a pink-haired freak-show parading around in this dress." I place my elbows on the table and drop my face into my hands. My cheeks feel warm enough, they're probably the same colour as my stupid hair.

Theo chuckles—actually chuckles. "You really don't know why they're looking at you?"

"Of course I do. Look at me," I whisper-shout. "They probably think a unicorn just walked through the restaurant. Six feet of pale skin and pink hair. Oh my gosh. Can we go?"

I can't bring myself to pull my face from my hands, but Theo does. He gently tugs my left hand down until I lift my eyes to meet his. "Isla, they're staring at you because I guarantee you're the most stunning woman they've ever seen in real life. They're staring at me thinking, 'damn, that guy's lucky. Why is someone like her with a schmuck like him?'" He pauses for a second, his smirk growing wider. "Plus, unicorns are majestic."

A laugh escapes me that is a mortifying mixture of a bray and a snort like I can't decide which farm animal I want to imitate to make this situation worse. I could throw in a moo for good measure, but I don't. "You're ridiculous. No one is thinking that; trust me."

"Want me to ask?" He smirks again, and the longer I stare at him, the less I care about the other eyes on me, whatever their reasoning is.

"Please don't. You'll just have to take my word for it. People always stare at me. I've spent my life avoiding eye contact because I don't want to get lost in a cycle of trying to determine everyone's intentions."

"How 'bout I just glare at them all until I make them uncomfortable and they stop looking?"

I laugh again, but Theo hardens his face the best he can with his boyishly handsome features and scans the room, pausing at those whose stares are lingering.

"There. They got the message."

He's got me in a fit of giggles, which would normally make me cower in the corner, but right now, I can't help it. "Thank you. My knight in shining armour."

"At your service." He pulls his menu out from underneath his napkin and begins examining its contents. He drags his gaze from the menu to me. "Seriously, Isla. You look like a goddess. I was struck dumb when you opened the door at your house, but when I walked in here and saw your dress... wow. That dress.

You. I tripped over my own two feet because I forgot how to walk."

I take several seconds to formulate a reply. "It was my mom and sister. They were an amazing pit crew. This"—I circle my face with my hand—"is all because of them."

Theo blows out a breath and reaches for my hand again. "You're forgetting I've seen you with wet hair in your pyjamas. I've seen you with puffy eyes from crying. I can confirm it's not the hair, makeup, or dress that makes you beautiful."

Mercifully, we're interrupted by a smiling server who introduces himself as Todd. Theo sits up in his chair a little taller, clears his throat, and declares we're ready to order. I ask for a Mediterranean salad, and Theo orders the mushroom ravioli.

When we regain our privacy, I give him a questioning look. "You ordered a vegetarian meal?"

"I figured that way we can share... I mean, if you want any."

Rory is going to die when she hears about this.

My face drops.

"We don't have to share. I just thought the option would be nice. You know, a little of this, a little of that?"

I choke back my emotions because I don't want to ruin Theo's night again by being emotionally unstable. "Thank you. That's really sweet of you." I huff a quiet laugh as I stare at the condensation dripping down my glass of ice water. "I was just thinking how I'd love to talk to Rory about you."

He surprises me with his response. "Really? What would you tell her?"

How can I answer that? I'd love to tell her that he sets my skin on fire with a single touch. Our interests are vastly different, but I've never felt so understood. That he's compassionate, intelligent, and thoughtful. How it means the world to me that he's opened up his horizons to include things that are important to me. I can't tell Theo any of that. "I'd tell her this is the best first date I've ever been on."

"Me too. Maybe it will be our last first date ever." His eyes shoot open as those words pour out of him. I think they caught him as much off guard as they did me. "I... sorry. My mouth worked faster than my brain."

Though what he said did shock me, I don't hate the idea. On the surface, we have little in common—if anything—but when I'm with him, the world fades away. I care more for what he thinks about me than anyone else, but I don't feel anxious about it. "I'd like that."

The smile that appears on his face is the most beautiful thing I've ever seen.

Our meal passes with comfortable conversation and Theo's declaration that vegetarian food "isn't all that bad." As we're finishing, he throws a curveball at me. "Tell me about your parents... your biological parents."

I stare at him for a moment, unsure if that's a wound I want to open. Instead of diving into the dark past I try to keep hidden, I pacify him with the simple truth. "They died in a car accident when I was five. I don't remember much about them."

"I'm sorry. That must have been hard."

He has no idea how hard, but I'd like to keep it that way. Maybe someday I'll explain the whole story, but today has been nice, so it won't be now.

"I remember the day it happened; we had a good day... the best day, actually. They took me to a farm, and I got to ride a tractor and pick apples. It was such a simple outing, but it's the only good day I remember."

Theo's eyes question me without him saying a word. I shouldn't have said that, and I refuse to ruin our night with my tragic history. There's no reason for me to be bothered by it now, all these years later.

"Anyway, I was too young, so I remember little about them. I can't tell you which parent I look like or who I have more in common with." It's preferable I have nothing in common with either of them.

"I'm sorry. I shouldn't have asked."

With a shrug of my shoulders, I try to brush off the topic. I don't want him thinking he's upset me by bringing up my birth parents. "It's fine. It's been a long time. I was lucky Zach and Zara took me in when they did. Foster care was worse than you could imagine, so without them, I'm not sure I'd be here."

*Now you've made it worse.*

I stutter, "Now, I'm sorry. Oh gosh. Just ignore me, please."

He pushes his chair out and stands beside me, holding out his hand. "Are you ready to get out of here?"

Of course he wants to leave now. I've ruined our evening. I swallow the lump in my throat and give a silent nod. After I remove the napkin from my lap, placing it beside my empty plate, Theo takes my hand and leads me to the area where our coats are. This time, walking through the crowd, all eyes are on me, but I'm so disappointed in the abrupt end to our date, I can't be bothered to question everyone's motives for staring.

While he helps me into my coat, he whispers in my ear, "It's a shame to cover this dress."

"I'll let you borrow it. I doubt I'll ever need it again." My words come out with more tension than intended, but I can't fight back how much it hurts to be ushered away like this. He asked a question, and I answered. It's not my fault I had a less-than-ideal childhood, but that doesn't define me.

"I was hoping you'd wear it again on our next date."

I crane my neck back to look at him, which leaves our faces only an inch apart. His breath is warm on my cheek and his eyes are intense. "Next date? Right. You can't seem to get out of here fast enough, Theo. I'm not expecting another date." I step forward out of his reach because I hate myself for wanting to kiss him. One minute he's talking about us being on our last first date and then he's rushing me out the door. I'm getting whiplash.

Before he can stop me, I walk out the door, but realize I have no idea where he parked.

"Isla, wait. Why are you running off?"

I can't stop the emotion from choking out as I step into the cool, late-winter air. "It's fine, Theo. Please, just take me home."

"Not until you tell me what just happened, because I'm confused. I thought we were having a good time, and now you're running away."

"I get that I didn't have the ideal childhood, but it didn't occur to me that you'd think less of me because of it. Please. I just want to go home."

"Hey… wait for a second, please." His voice is tender, with every trace of annoyance gone. He places a hand on my arm, stopping me from going any further. "The only reason I asked if you were ready to go was because I could tell you were getting upset and I felt like a jerk. I thought if we had a change of scenery you could forget about me asking stupid questions I shouldn't have asked. I'm not trying to get rid of you." He steps forward, close enough his body heat permeates my coat. "In fact, I can't imagine ever wanting to get rid of you."

I hate myself for doubting him and reading too much into situations that are easy to misinterpret. Such is the plight of social anxiety and why I'm a disaster at conversing with other humans. The tension I was feeling melts away and my shoulders finally relax. Before I can respond with words, I lean in and plant my lips against his. I'm not a kissing expert, so my anxious thoughts are running rampant, but Theo quickly takes the lead. His hand moves from my arm to the back of my neck, pulling us closer. His soft lips brush against mine, and I feel like we're inside a snow globe, with nothing outside of our bubble existing.

When Theo pulls away, he's left holding me up because my legs are weak. He leans his head down to rest his forehead against mine, not releasing his hand from behind my neck, his other hand secured around my lower back.

"Does this mean I'm forgiven for my terrible date etiquette?" He smiles at me, but his eyes are closed.

"I'm the one who needs to be forgiven. I misread situations and jump to conclusions, but I'm sorry. You've been…"

"Shh. It's fine." His eyes open, and he leans down to kiss me again. "I've found my new favourite hobby."

I giggle. "Charley will be disappointed if belly rubs are pushed down the list."

"He'll understand." With a step back, he says, "You're probably freezing. Do you want me to go get my car, or do you want to walk with me?"

I'm not cold at all because heated blood is coursing through my veins. "I'll walk."

Hand-in-hand, Theo leads me to his SUV, which is parked 150 metres away. Halfway there, under the lights of the parking lot, he spins me to face him and kisses me again. The effect has my body re-heating and missing his absence as soon as his lips are no longer touching mine.

Like a gentleman, he opens my door. Thankfully, no fresh snow has fallen since yesterday, so he is able to jump in and turn the heat on. The immediate blast of cold air makes me shiver.

"Where to now?" he asks, then laughs at my reaction, which is complete surprise.

"I assumed you were taking me home."

"I can if you want me to, but I was hoping we didn't have to say goodnight yet." The smirk that he sends my way could have me agreeing to just about anything

I look down at my outfit and out the window at the weather. "I'm not really dressed for the outdoors."

"No, you're not. You're dressed to kill." We both laugh at Theo's stupid joke as he pulls out of the parking lot.

"We can go somewhere and talk for a while."

Oh yay. My favourite pastime: talking. Though, with Theo, it doesn't seem like work. He makes me feel safe, and that's something I'd like to hold on to for as long as possible.

A few minutes later, Theo pulls into *Riverview Park*, and parks under a streetlamp. There are no other vehicles around, which I'd expect on a Saturday evening in February. Neither of us speaks a word for a few minutes, allowing the final bars of John Legend's *All of Me* to play through the radio. I don't know if Theo was listening as intently as I was, but the lyrics hit me differently after tonight.

"I guess you probably don't want to walk to the lookout in those." He points to my shoes.

"Probably not. That's an accident waiting to happen."

"I had a really great time tonight." He changes the topic of conversation abruptly.

"I did too. Aside from my unnecessary tantrum, which again, I'm really sorry for."

"No, I'm sorry for bringing up your parents. That's not really first date material."

"It's fine. To be fair, our friendship hasn't been conventional from the start, so I think we're beyond typical first date conversations."

"Friendship? Is that all this is? Because I don't know about you, but I don't kiss my friends like that."

Lordy... those dimples will be the death of me.

"I... I'm not sure what to say to that. The past few months, you've become one of the most important people in my life, both personally and professionally. But I'm not kissing anyone else at all."

With a gentle tug on my upper back, Theo pulls me in for another kiss and his touch sends my whole body alight.

"Good. Because I don't want to kiss anyone else." He releases me and leans back so he's centred in the driver's seat, a serious expression taking over his face. "You know, the first time I asked you to meet up, I had no idea who I was meeting."

I think back to that night, which seems like a lifetime ago, but it's only been three months.

"Your profile picture online was your nephews, and I couldn't find a photo of you anywhere. Your Facebook is sealed up tight because I searched." He laughs at himself, and I can't help but chuckle. "I didn't know how old you were, what you looked like, or anything aside from my assumption you were female, which I'm happy I was right about."

"I guess I had a head start because I saw your profile picture, but I didn't search beyond that."

"Ouch. I wasn't even worth a little internet stalking? That cuts deep." His hand is placed over his chest like he's nursing a physical wound, but the mischief on his face makes me snicker again. "Anyway, before we met up, I was assuming you were a middle-aged mom of three having some sort of identity crisis with pink hair."

"Theo!" I can't stop the full belly laugh from escaping. "I have to tell you something."

"Do you have three kids? Are you having an identity crisis?"

I shake my head, catching my breath between giggles. "When you asked what I looked like, I panicked. I didn't know how to describe myself beyond blue-eyed blonde."

"Blonde?"

My laughter is undeterred as I try to speak because the reality of the situation is so ridiculous. "I was blonde. But I blurted out that I had pink hair, so I thought I should follow through."

"Wow, wow, wow. Wait a minute. You're saying that you dyed your hair pink because of me?"

I nod, still laughing. "I guess so. This is a nearly $200 dye job, thank you very much."

He's silent for a moment, studying my face, which squashes every bit of laughter bubbling out. "Do you want to know how I'd describe you?"

Not really... but curiosity killed the cat. "How?"

He reaches for my hand, pulling it to his mouth, placing a kiss on my knuckle. "Gorgeous." Kiss. "Kind." Kiss. "Smart." Kiss. "Beautiful eyes." Kiss. "Sunshine."

I'm staring at my hand in his, visualizing each kiss across my knuckles, speechless. That's not really a good way for me to describe myself to someone else, but I'm not going to argue with him.

"I was blown away when I walked into the pub and saw the most gorgeous woman I've ever laid eyes on. I didn't ask you to meet me that day because I expected to end up here, but there's nowhere else I'd rather be."

When Theo dropped me off the other night, I had to force myself to come into the house. I could have stood on the porch with him until I froze on one leg, like a flamingo. He didn't pull the macho move, waiting three days to text or call after our date; he messaged me the minute he got home. We stayed awake another few hours, messaging each other back and forth.

Today we're meeting up to discuss marketing ideas for my book launch, which we've scheduled for May 14th, giving us less than three months to advertise and generate a buzz. Given that this is Theo's first attempt at marketing a book and my first time publishing one, I'm not setting my expectations high. I'm under no illusions that this route will be easy, or profitable, but I believe in this story and being able to release the version that I want is worth more than topping any bestseller charts.

I surprised myself when Theo asked where I wanted to meet. He's working all day at his office job, so I offered to meet him at my condo when he's done. That gives me time to go early, grab something for us to eat, and get myself organized before he arrives.

After gathering my things—laptop, clothes, Bond's paraphernalia—I walk downstairs to tell Mom I'm leaving. Her lips turn up into the biggest smile I've seen on her face for months when I inform her I'm going to my condo to meet Theo and I'm going to spend the night. Despite my last effort, this time will be easier with Bond by my side. Logic keeps gnawing away at me, reminding me I can't leave the place empty forever.

With a peck on the cheek and a grizzly grip mom hug, she sends me off with instructions to call if I need anything. I love her for that, but I also know she's gone above and beyond to accommodate me the past fifteen years—never more so than the past three months.

Bond follows me out to the car, where I open the back door and help him climb inside. He's getting old and his hips don't always cooperate, but he never lets that stop him.

Forty minutes later, I'm parked in front of my condo with a steaming hot bag of takeout. I arrived five minutes ago but haven't worked up the nerve to go inside. Bond knows where we are, and his tail is thumping in a steady rhythm against the backseat. This is home.

"Well, buddy. Let's do this."

I hoist my backpack from the passenger seat, walk to the back door and open it for Bond, and before I can issue a command, he's bolted to the patio with pep in his step. His excitement to be home makes walking inside less daunting.

When I open the door, he strolls around, sniffing every surface and comes to settle at Rory's bedroom door, pawing at it and whining.

"She's not there, buddy." That's all it takes to send me into a downward spiral. Racking sobs pour out of me with an intensity like never before. I sink into a puddle on the floor, collapsing onto my knees, face in my hands. Bond nudges me and I fall back onto my bum, wrapping my arms around his neck and crying into his fur. He doesn't budge. He just lets me cry and offers silent comfort.

A knock at the patio door startles me some time later, but I don't have the strength to get up to answer. Bond serves as a doorman, pawing at the glass, pleading with the person on the other side.

The door opens a crack, and I hear Theo call my name. I can't offer more than a sniffle and a quiet, "I'm here" from my spot behind the couch on the floor.

As soon as I utter those words, I hear the door open wide and close quickly and frantic removal of shoes, in addition to the obligatory dog scratches.

Bond seems quite proud of himself as he struts over, leading Theo to my position on the floor.

"Isla, what's wrong?" Instead of pulling me up to stand, he drops to the floor beside me, leans against the back of the couch, and pulls me into his arms. "Take your time. Let it out."

I do. I let the snot and tears fall until I'm exhausted. How many times is this man going to watch me collapse into an emotional heap and keep trying to comfort me? He's grieving too. Is it selfish of me to put him in this position? Probably.

"I'm so sorry," I mutter as my breakdown eases.

"Stop apologizing." He uses his thumb and forefinger to turn me to face him. "I'm proud of you for coming here. You don't need to apologize because it's hard."

I nod, wiping the remaining tears from my eyes. "Still. I'm sorry you keep seeing me like this."

He doesn't respond with words first; he leans in to give me a sweet kiss. It's as if he stitches me back together piece by piece each time. "Do you want to talk about it?"

"No, I'm fine. I'm just being dramatic." I place my hands on the floor in front of me to get up and force myself to move on with the evening. Theo came for a reason, and I can't monopolize his time.

Before I can push myself to stand, he grabs my hips and pulls me into his lap. "Come here for a second."

I yelp as I crash into his lap, which has Bond sending Theo a "look" that lets him know his antics are not appreciated.

Theo placates Bond with a pat on the head and a heartfelt apology. Then he turns to me. "I didn't get a proper hello." With a gentle hand on my cheek, he kisses me hello, properly, and I never want to say hello another way again.

"Hi," I reply once I'm able. "I bought food."

He laughs. "I'm starving... but there's something I want to do first."

I assume he means kiss me again, but he lifts me to stand and pulls himself up beside me. He clasps his fingers between mine and leads me down the hall toward my bedroom.

"Theo... I'm not..."

"Just trust me, okay. You might be hesitant, but I promise you'll feel better."

What in the hell? If this guy thinks he can just sweet talk me into...

We stop at Rory's bedroom door. He stares at me, concern etched on his face. "I'm going to open the door, okay? And before you protest, just listen.  know this seems like an impossible step and you think you're not ready, but there will never be a right time. Moving on is never an easy choice, but it is a conscious one. So, I'm going to open the door, and I'll be right here with you."

He's right. Keeping this door closed and hiding out at my parents' house is not allowing me to move forward. If Bond and I had moved back in months ago, I would have already addressed these feelings. So as much as I want to protest, I nod, and Theo slowly opens the door.

Her bedroom is unrecognizable. The bed is made, but aside from that and a dresser, everything else is gone. Her artwork, her clothes. The very essence of Rory is no longer here. It doesn't feel like her room—it feels like a void.

I'm already exhausted from crying, so I don't have many tears left, but what I do have fall quietly down my cheeks. I step inside, spinning in a circle, taking in everything remaining, but mostly everything that's missing. Most notably, Rory.

"Her… her guitar." I point to the empty corner beside her bed. "Her music." I stare at the top of the dresser that only holds a thick layer of dust. "Everything is gone." I sit on the end of her bed and cover my face with my hands. I don't want Theo to see me cry again. "She's really gone."

The bed dips beside me from Theo's weight as he sits next to me and pulls me into a one-armed hug. "I know."

It takes several minutes to compose myself while Theo keeps one arm wrapped around me, probably not knowing what to say. I needed to take this step, and I'm grateful to him for pushing me, but that doesn't make the hurt more bearable.

When I finally work up the nerve to open the top drawer of her dresser, I find one lone sheet of paper covered in Rory's elaborate cursive.

### ***More Like You***
*We were both shy when I first met you,*
*A couple of kids with big ol' dreams.*
*No faith in ourselves,*
*But so strong as a team.*

*Change the world like a tornado,*
*Deal anxiety a deathblow.*
*Dream 'bout the day when you wake up and see,*
*Your name at the top of the NYT.*

*This is me confessing,*
*Saying, "You changed my life,"*
*You need a boost, and this is my cue,*
*Our future ain't nothing but dreams,*
*And in my dreams,*
*I realize I wanna be more like you.*

I try to read further, but I can't. "She... she wrote a song about me." My eyes meet Theo's while I'm still processing the paper in my hands. "She never showed this to me."

"Maybe she wasn't done yet."

"She always started with a melody. She'd constantly quote Roger from *101 Dalmatians*, 'melody first, my darling, then the lyrics.'" I laugh, remembering her impression of him. "But this is just lyrics."

I set the paper down and start opening the other drawers. When I find nothing, I lift the corner of the mattress, as if that's the next logical place to look. I scour her bathroom, her closet, but find nothing.

"I'll never know how the song goes. How am I supposed to have her song in my head if I don't know how it goes?" I crash my body into Theo, unable to cry another tear.

"It'll come to you," he replies with such certainty, I almost believe it.

We spend the rest of the evening eating our reheated takeout, discussing launch ideas, and setting a schedule to release my debut novel. I vetoed nearly every suggestion Theo made because they all involve interacting with people, and that's a recipe for disaster. Isla-plus-people, no go.

Apparently, most book launch strategies require me to "put myself out there," and that's so far out of my comfort zone, I'm questioning whether it's worth it to publish anything at all. Perhaps I'm better suited to continue life as an editor, or someday as a ghost writer. That thought sparks an idea.

"Maybe we can just list you as the author and I'll be your silent ghost writer. What do you think?"

Theo looks at me with a raised eyebrow. "Not happening. The entire world is going to know that it's you with the talent, and eventually, Jane Austen will come to you for advice."

I burst out laughing. "Theo, Jane Austen died in the 1800s. But I wish I could pick her brain about her marketing strategy, because she became one of the best-selling authors in history without selling herself on social media." I grumble, dreading this task Theo has given me to set up social media accounts. Until now, I've been happy to survive in the stone age.

A gentle hand grazes my cheek and with one brief touch, this "business meeting" could turn personal very quickly.

"You're going to be great. With social media, it's like you're putting yourself out there without having to be 'out there,' you know? You can interact with people—readers, other authors, bloggers—but you don't have to think on your feet. With every response, you can take your time to reply, and share only what you want. Think of it as the best of both worlds, okay?"

I consider his words and he's right, but still the whole "social" part of social media terrifies me. I guess it's like opening Rory's bedroom door, though; it's terrifying until I take the plunge and do it.

"I promise I'll try my best."

Theo takes a deep breath, releasing a long exhale as he squeezes my hand. "I hate to say this, but I really have to get going."

My heart clenches at the thought of being here alone, but it's time for me to act like an adult. I already faced one major milestone today, so what's one more?

"Do you want me to follow you home to make sure you get back okay?"

I'm touched by his chivalry, but realize I forgot to tell him my intentions for the night. "Actually, I'm staying here. I... I figured it was time."

Theo's smile splits his face, it's so wide. "I'm so proud of you right now."

I chuckle at his reply. "For staying in my apartment I've avoided for three months? You're setting your standards for pride a little low."

He stands from the couch, reaching his hand down for mine, which I take, and he pulls me into a hug before kissing my forehead. The second his lips leave my skin, I miss the contact.

"Not at all. This is a big step for you." His words warm my entire body, because to most people, such a simple thing would seem trivial, but he doesn't judge me for struggling.

Thirty minutes later, after a long, drawn-out goodbye, Theo is walking from my patio into the darkness of the parking lot.

"Text me when you get home," I shout after him.

He turns back and, with the dim lights of the parking lot, he's little more than a shadow. "I will. Goodnight, Isla."

Bond and I return inside, flicking the door lock and turning off the exterior light once Theo's brake lights disappear. I want to shower before I go to bed, so although it's 11pm, I head into my bathroom and rush to shower so I don't miss Theo's call.

I blow dry my hair and note how terrible it looks with the faded pink and grown out roots. It's probably time to return to normal, blending into the background as another unremarkable human—just how I like it.

Forty minutes later, Theo still hasn't replied, and I'm getting worried. I send him a quick text to see if he's arrived home and forgot to tell me, but my message stays unread. His house is only twenty minutes away, but he might have had to stop somewhere on his way home. Options are limited this time of night, so I'll give him another twenty minutes before I really panic.

Lies. I'll panic now.

My fear is growing like E. Coli, doubling every few minutes, threatening to have the same effect on my digestive system. Before I allow myself to spiral out of control, I pick up the phone and dial.

After three rings, a groggy voce picks up, "Sweet Girl, is everything okay?"

I blow out a breath, overwhelmed by guilt for waking her. "Yeah, Mom. I'm sorry. Go back to sleep."

"It's not nothing if you called. Out with it."

"It's silly… really. Um… well, Theo was here working on our marketing plan, and he was supposed to tell me when he got home, but he hasn't."

"That's not silly. I can understand why you're worried. Chances are it's just late, and he fell asleep before he remembered to call."

"I know. I just… after everything… you know… I just worry, I guess." *So poetic, Isla.*

Silence.

"Do you want me to take a drve to his house to see if his car is there?"

I laugh at her response, grateful she'd implement stalker-mode to ease my mind. "No, that's okay. I'll try calling again, and if I don't hear from him… I don't know. But I'll let you go back to sleep. I'm sorry for waking you."

"Never be sorry for needing me. I love you."

"Love you too."

I hang up the phone, not feeling any better about the anxiety pooling in my stomach. Bond has spread out on my bed, so I snuggle my face into his soft fur. I focus on his steady breathing, trying to calm my own to match his pace.

*"Hiya." Such an idiot, making the man think you were going to Karate chop his throat. "I couldn't get my pants on." Moron. "Sex sells." Could you be more pathetic?*

Unable to sleep, I pull out my phone again, checking to see if Theo has read my text message, but he still hasn't. I try to push my nerves aside, so I spend the next few hours opening social media accounts and learning how to navigate them. Three, four, five o'clock passes, and still no word. I use my new social media accounts to check local law enforcement's news feed, hoping to not find anything about fatal accidents in the area. Nothing.

Just before 7am, I'm exhausted from lack of sleep and the emotional toll worrying has taken when my phone rings. Theo's name lights up the screen, but for the first time in a long time, I'm afraid to answer his call. What if it's someone else reaching out to his contacts to say he's died in a horrific accident?

Reluctantly, I answer. "Hello?" Sniffle. I hadn't noticed tears started falling down my cheeks.

"Oh, *Mi Alma*, I'm so sorry." Theo's voice sounds panicked.

"Are you okay?"

"I'm fine. I got home last night, and my mom was having a rough time, so I spent a few hours with her. By the time she fell asleep, it was after two and I passed out. I'm so sorry. You weren't worried, were you?"

I'm not about to make him feel guilty for being a good son. "No, it's fine." However, *I* feel guilty for consuming his time and taking him away from his family, who obviously need him.

"Can I come over after work?"

"Theo—"

"I'll bring food this time."

"You should spend some time with your family. They need you right now, and the last thing you need is to be dealing with me."

He heaves out an exaggerated exhale. "Isla, I'm not 'dealing' with you. I enjoy spending time with you."

I love having him around—so much so, it terrifies me. "Your family needs you, Theo. I can't take you away from them."

After a few seconds of silence, he replies, "I have a proposal."

Him and his proposals.

"Either you let me come over and bring you dinner, or I go home, pick up my mom and sister, and we'll all come over to hang out. That way, we both get what we want."

I roll my eyes at his "proposal," not convinced he'd follow through. "Nice try."

"I'm serious. I want to see you. If you don't want to see me, or you're busy with something else, that's cool. I shouldn't assume you have nothing better to do…"

Of course I have nothing better to do. He's quickly become the best part of my days and seeing him eases the sadness that consumes me. But that also comes with a healthy dose of guilt. Not to mention how terrified I am to let someone else become my entire world, just to have them ripped away.

"I'm not doing anything else. I was trying to get all of this social media stuff in order."

"It just so happens that's my area of expertise. So, am I coming over with or without my family?" He chuckles.

"Theo…"

"Isla…"

"Fine. Come over." There's no way I'm ready to meet his family. That's a step in signifying commitment and I don't think we're there yet, but it gets me thinking.

"I'll see you tonight."

With that, my worries he had been hurt are put to rest, but new fears surface and I'm not sure how to combat those.

The night after Theo's failed check-in, he came over after work, and it was as if the entire evening passed in a blur. We've become so accustomed to each other's presence, I flip-flop from being so elated I can barely breathe to choking on guilt, feeling like I've replaced Rory. Either way, it's suffocating. Still, that didn't stop me from inviting Theo to my parents' house for Chelsea and Liam's sixth wedding anniversary celebration today.

I'm not sure how typical family meetings go, but Theo and I met nearly four months ago, and I realized I can't get more invested in him without my family's approval. To my surprise, he didn't hesitate to say yes when I asked.

Bond and I have been living at my condo since Monday and despite a few meltdowns, I've been handling it okay. Today is my first time back at my parents' house in five days, but gauging the strength of my mom's hug, you'd think I'd returned from eighteen months abroad. I arrive early so I can help set up and deal with food.

Our family members arrive an hour later, and Mom and I had little time to talk because she was so busy—I didn't mention that Theo was coming. Most of our conversation was about what goes where, and how she is glad I went back to my natural hair colour. Me too. Theo hasn't seen my hair change, nor did I tell him, so I'm curious what he'll think.

Before I blink, the open-concept living space is filled with people. Fred and Alanna Levy, my grandparents, were first to arrive, followed closely by my aunt Jasmine and her husband Rafael with their infant daughter, Isabella. Mom's sisters, Lexi and Noa, arrive with their husbands, Lorenzo and Henry, respectively. Their adult children, Oscar, Ethan, Hollis, Caleb, and Sophie, show up minutes apart, everyone except Hollis bringing a significant other. It's weird seeing Oscar with a girlfriend, because I'll always picture him as the little monster who chased us around with his boogers. Hopefully he's outgrown that.

Liam's parents, Dola and Ian, walk in just before Chelsea and Liam arrive with their boys, who immediately run through the house, increasing the volume level tenfold, but everyone can't help but smile at their excitement. It's cute when you don't have to deal with their non-stop energy fifteen hours a day. It's hard to believe they'll be starting school in a few months.

"Hey Troublemaker. Thanks for helping mom with all of this. I've been missing you lately. We never see you anymore."

I know that's her way of asking how I'm doing because I usually visit them a few times a week. Since switching to self-publishing and spending my free time with Theo, I've been a terrible sister and aunt. More guilt.

"I'm sorry, Chels. I've been swamped getting my book prepared to send out to readers and navigating marketing, which, turns out, is 100 times harder than writing a book."

"It's fine. I just wanted to make sure you're okay. I've missed my sister time."

More guilt. Not intentional, I know, but my visits are sometimes Chelsea's only adult interaction in a day, so I feel like I'm failing her.

A knock at the door sends goosebumps across my body. I don't even need to look to know who it is. When my dad opens the door, I spot Theo on the other side wearing a black bomber jacket and a knitted beanie. I can't get across the room fast enough. I abandon my conversation with Chelsea—more guilt— so I can intercept the curveballs my dad, a former college pitcher, is bound to lob at Theo.

"Thanks for having me, Mr. Haynes."

I see my dad's facial expression morph to confused because no one was aware Theo was coming. I probably should have given them a heads up, but I wasn't willing to face the third-degree that would accompany a warning.

"And you are?"

Oh gosh. Please no.

"Dad, this is Theo," I chime in as I step into the entryway, noticing Theo is carrying a large, wrapped gift and another bouquet—I'm assuming neither is for me, and that makes me swoon. "Theo is… my friend. I invited him."

Dad looks at me, then back at Theo, his confusion disappearing, making way for a stern facial expression. Oh, fun. He's going to play this tough dad game. It might be more effective if Theo wasn't a good three inches taller.

"Well, come on in. We're happy to have you," Dad finally adds, changing up his tactic. You catch more flies with honey, or something like that.

"Hi," I say as the door closes behind him, but I don't step forward to give him a hug under my dad's watchful eye.

Theo's eyes stare at my hair and I worry it's a mess from the frazzled party-prep session. I never freshened myself up afterward. "Hi," he returns.

"Um, let me take that so you can get your stuff off, then I'll introduce you to everyone."

"I'll take it, Kiddo. You help Theo get acquainted." When my dad takes the items from Theo's hands, then winks at me as he turns away, I can't stop my jaw from dropping. What is happening? How did he go from alpha-male to wingman in the blink of an eye?

"So that's my dad," I say once he's out of ear shot. "I swear he's not bi-polar or anything. He's just... protective."

Theo steps in close as he removes his coat and exposes his dark-wash jeans that hang perfectly on his long legs, and his light grey dress shirt with the top button undone. His baby face is covered in the first signs of facial hair I've ever seen on him in person and, well... I'm a fan. His sharp jawline is accentuated by the neatly trimmed goatee. "I've missed you," he whispers.

My breath hitches. I want to kiss him, but I'm not ready for that show in front of my entire family. "I missed—"

"You must be Theo," my mom's voice rings behind me.

I mouth, "I'm sorry," trying to pre-emptively apologize for whatever embarrassing things are about to happen. Theo laughs and his wide smile just about drops me to my knees.

"I am. Thank you for having me, Mrs. Haynes. I've heard nothing but good things about you."

She slaps his arm playfully. "Oh stop." When she looks at me, she starts the embarrassing moments right out of the gate. "You didn't tell me he was so good looking. I might be ready to trade my ball and chain in for a newer model." She winks... actually winks at me.

Why? Why must everything be so awkward?

Theo laughs, but not in an offended way, like he's ready to run the other direction—which I wouldn't blame him for. "I'm afraid your husband would really have a reason to dislike me then."

"Oh, don't worry about him. He's just protecting his baby girl. As long as you don't give him reason to dislike you, he'll be fine."

"I don't plan to, ma'am."

"Well, come in and meet everyone. I think they've all stared long enough; they're owed introductions."

"Is you a giant?" Lenox interrupts our conversation, inspecting Theo.

Before I can reply, Theo is down on his knees, meeting Lenox at his level. "What's your name?"

"Wenox. Who's you?"

"I'm Theo. Can I tell you a secret?"

Lenox nods.

"I am a giant, but I'll tell you my secret so you can be a giant one day, too."

My little ginger nephew's eyes widen as he awaits Theo's confidential information, hanging onto his every word.

"You have to eat all of your dinner every night, even the vegetables. And, you have to go to bed on time."

Lenox nods, and without another word to Theo, spins around to run toward his brothers, yelling to "Winkin' and Hudson" that he has a special secret of how to grow bigger than them. I don't think Theo realizes how happy that made Lenox, who has always been the "runt." After watching their exchange, I might as well serve Theo my heart on a platter.

"You're good with kids," I state, no question in my voice.

"No idea. I've never been around little kids before."

The next thirty minutes pass as I introduce Theo to everyone in the room, and he meets them all with a smile, never faltering or hesitating. His confidence is one of the most attractive things about him, and I wish for one day I could channel some of it for myself.

When we finally get to Chelsea and Liam, Theo gives Liam a bro-hug, and it seems they form an instant connection.

Chelsea introduces herself and adds, "So, you're the reason my baby sister has ditched me."

Theo could take offence, but he laughs it off again, and I'm grateful because I know Chelsea meant it in a joking manner. "I guess I'm guilty."

"Well, just know, if she's spending her time on you, you better be worth it."

"Chelsea!" I shout, drawing looks from everyone else in the room. I drop my voice to a whisper, "Please be nice."

Theo wraps an arm around my back and it's the first physical contact we've had since he arrived. "No, it's okay." He leans in and kisses my temple, making my face burn hot. "I'm trying to be worthy of her."

*What does that mean? Everybody's watching.*

Theo and I spend the next few hours socializing. Everyone in this room—minus him—have been a huge part of my life. I'm more comfortable than I normally would be in a crowd; even so, the constant dialogue running in my head exhausts me. I need a few minutes to recharge.

He doesn't follow me when I give him a pleading look and walk up the stairs to escape socializing for a few moments. I'm grateful for that because him following me would be a whole other awkward situation.

A short time later, I'm sitting in my childhood bedroom, Bond at my feet, when I hear a knock at the door. It swings open and in steps my mom. "Hey Sweet Girl, we're about to have dinner. Are you coming back down?"

I nod, but before I can get up, she shuts the door behind her and sits on the bed next to me.

"That Theo is really something."

"Yeah." I exhale. "I keep waiting for the other shoe to drop. For something to come up and rip him away, and it scares me to death."

"It sounds like you've got it bad."

"So bad. I've tried to keep myself from falling, but my heart just jumped without permission."

"And what's wrong with that?"

I let out a sigh, refusing to let tears fall. "I feel guilty. About a lot of things, but mostly about Rory. Knowing she'll never get her happily ever after weighs on me every time I'm around Theo and it keeps me from really letting him in."

"And this guilt? Is there anything you can do to change the situation?"

"No, obviously not, but that doesn't mean I can toss it aside."

"Isla, one thing I know is that guilt only serves a purpose to better us if there's a course of action to correct whatever we feel guilty about. If someone steals from another person, they should feel guilty and return what they took. If we say something that hurts another person's feelings, we feel guilty and apologize. But this guilt you're carrying, all it will do is prevent you from healing."

I consider her words, but I'm not sure how to apply what she's saying. The past few months I've been living under a perma-raincloud and while there are moments of sunshine, sadness still looms overhead, threatening to pour down on me at any moment.

As if she reads my mind, she asks, "What's the remedy to sadness?"

"There isn't one. That's the problem."

"Oh, but there is. And you know what it is?" She places her hand on my knee and doesn't continue until I'm looking at her face. "Happiness. The only thing that can cure sadness is happiness."

That sounds like something you'd see on a t-shirt. *Positive vibes only. Love yourself. Happiness cures sadness.*

I'm not sure what to say, so I nod. "Let's go back downstairs before everyone thinks we're taking a nap. We can talk about this later."

No emotional dragons are being slayed today.

When I descend the stairs into the living room, Theo is on the floor being attacked by three little monsters. He's putting in a valiant effort, but he's no match for their triplet powers. He lets out a roar like he's a mythical swamp creature, and instead of scattering, the boys double down, hanging off his limbs; their giggles are the happiest sound in the world.

Theo makes it to his feet, Lincoln clinging to his left leg, Hudson on the right, and Lenox dragging across the floor with each step, grasping Theo's ankle. The sight is comical, and I can't help but laugh.

"What are you guys doing to my friend?" I ask, and the four of them smirk.

"I'm pretty sure your dad paid them with cupcakes to wrestle me." Theo laughs, and when I glance over at my dad who is snickering alongside Liam, I have a feeling Theo's on the right track.

Mom tells everyone dinner is ready and the boys release their hold, scrambling to their feet. Theo bends down to whisper in Lenox's ear and gives him a wink. Lenox races off to be first in line for dinner.

"What did you say to him?"

"I reminded him about my secret to becoming a giant." Theo sits beside me. He's worked up a sweat in battle, but he looks happier and more content than I've ever seen him. It's not lost on me how seamlessly he fits in with our entire family, and that makes my resistance drop a little more. "Are you all right? I was getting worried about you."

"I'm fine. Just needed a break from socializing for a few minutes. I was afraid if I didn't take a break, my switch would flip, and I'd be done for the night."

"It was hard for me not to fo low you. I wanted to make sure you were okay, but I wanted to respect your need for time alone. Plus, your dad sent the kids after me and I got caught fighting for my life."

I laugh again, and it feels good

We stand together to join the buffet line formed around the long dining room table. When Theo dishes up some fried chicken, I see Liam come barrelling over with his hand above his head. He looks like a deranged psychopath, about to finish what his children started. I mean, really, it's Liam, who's as nice as they come, but I am like a little sister to him, so I can't be too sure how far that protective nature goes. Before I can step between him and Theo, Liam shouts, "Heyyyyy! Team Carnivore! Up top, man!"

Without skipping a beat, Theo lifts his free hand to high-five my brother-in-law and they laugh together, bonding over their love of edible animal flesh in a family of vegetarians. Chelsea and I make eye contact, laughing between ourselves. Amongst our immediate family—Mom, Dad. me, Chelsea, Liam, and the boys—Liam is the only meat eater. It appears he's excited to have company.

Liam places an arm around Theo's shoulders and faces me. "I knew I liked this guy, Isla."

Seeing how my entire family has embraced him so naturally, I can't help but reply, "I do too."

After dinner, Chelsea and Liam start opening their gifts. I'm curious to know what Theo got them, so I can't stop myself from asking.

His unhelpful reply is, "You'll see." He looks nervous, which seems foreign for him.

Each gift unwrapped makes my curiosity worse. I bought them a camera Chelsea had been eyeing for a while, and her glassy eyes tell me she's happy with my choice. I'm glad she likes it, but I'm dying to know what Theo got them. The fact he even brought anything impresses me.

"Please tell me," I beg.

"You'll see." He nods toward Chelsea as Liam hands her the package Theo arrived with.

I'm practically bouncing in my seat with anticipation. My guess is it's some sort of photo, based on the dimensions.

Chelsea rips away the white and gold wrapping paper, and to my dismay, the item is in a plain cardboard box. I shoot a glare at Theo, who smirks, but he still looks anxious. I place a hand on his bouncing knee and soften my expression into a smile.

When Chelsea pulls the item out, with Liam's help to hold the box, she gasps. For a split second, I wonder if Theo gifted them a nude photo or something based on the shock registered on her face, but tears glide down her freckled cheeks, assuring me that's not the case.

She looks directly at me when she spins the item around to show the rest of us. The image in the frame is a watercolour silhouette of a couple with Liam & Chelsea written at the top, and lyrics from *"Me"* by Taylor Swift and Brendon Urie superimposed over the couple. I recall mentioning one time Liam and Chelsea's love for *Panic! At the Disco*. The fact he remembered that and gifted them something so perfect has me lost for words and my mom sending me a knowing look, smiling ear to ear.

"Isla told me you guys love Panic! and… uh… I know you were close with Rory, and she loved Taylor Swift, so I thought I could make something that honoured her too, which is why I picked that song," Theo adds, justifying his gift.

"You made this?" Liam asks, his jaw slack.

"Yeah," Theo replies, looking at the floor.

"Isla, I'm going to marry your boyfriend." Liam laughs, walking across the room to pull Theo in for another bro hug. "This is amazing. Thank you."

Theo's shoulders finally drop back to neutral, and he appears to relax. I'm surprised, and a little perplexed that he doesn't correct Liam's use of the term "boyfriend." He beams as Chelsea walks over to hug him. Seeing my sister embrace this man who has become so important to me is all I need for the last bit of resolve to weaken.

I examine Chelsea's new prized possession, reading the lyrics, and I couldn't imagine a better gift. Knowing that Theo made it makes it so much more special.

Rory and Chelsea used to play that song every time we were together. The memory makes me feel as if a ratchet strap is being tightened around my chest, out not from sadness.

I'm so in love with this man.

That's scary.

Theo doesn't race to leave after the party dies down. He sticks around, assisting with cleaning up so Chelsea and Liam can get the boys home to bed. While we're carrying bags of recycling out to the garage, it's hardly romantic, but it's the first time all day we've been alone. The second the garbage bags are dropped, Theo cages me against the wall with his tall frame and kisses me.

I moan into his mouth, which seems to urge him on. When he takes a step back, I'm left craving his body heat. He makes me feel so safe, desired, and, dare I say, confident. That might be a stretch.

"So, Liam wants to marry your boyfriend." He smirks at me, and my face instantly heats enough to cook an egg.

"Ignore him. I never told him that… he just assumed. But you won him over with your meat-eating."

"Is his assumption wrong?"

I look at Theo's playful smile, trying to gauge whether he's being serious or pulling my leg. My skills at reading people always end up leaving more questions than answers though, so I stay silent.

"I know going on a garbage run in your parents' garage isn't the most romantic setting, but ever since he said that, I've been waiting to ask. Maybe not so much to ask, but let you know where I stand and let you decide what you want."

I tilt my head, still studying his expression, my heart hammering my ribcage. "Where do you stand?"

"Physically, I'm standing in front of the most beautiful woman I've ever seen in my entire life, wondering why she'd give someone like me the time of day."

I laugh and slap at his chest. "Oh, stop. You're crazy."

"You're right. Because emotionally, I'm crazy about you, Isla. So what do you say we make what's happening between us official?"

"Another proposal?" *Why would you say that?* "I... Sorry. That was supposed to be a joke, but it was terrible timing."

He stares into my eyes for a moment before he replies, "This may not be a marriage proposal, but make no mistake, I wouldn't be asking you this if I wasn't serious about you. We're good together. Let's see where this goes."

I can't stop the tears from forming in my eyes. The last time I remember my heart feeling this full was the day I adopted Bond. "Okay. Let's see where this goes."

Theo bends down to kiss me again just as the garage door opens, and I stare up at my mom's wide-eyed expression. Without a word, she smiles and closes the door, but she's going to make this awkward later. That's her thing.

I giggle at Theo, who has the same expression as my nephews when they're caught sneaking candy from the pantry. "Don't worry. She'll just have something totally embarrassing to say when we go inside."

"I just hope she doesn't tell your dad I was feeling you up in the garage. I don't think he likes me much, and that's not the impression I want to give him."

"Are you kidding? If he didn't like you, he wouldn't bother with you. Consider it his way of testing you."

"Testing me?" His crooked smile reappears, and he leans in toward me, his face hovering inches above mine. "And how am I doing so far?"

"I'd say you're an 'A' student." I duck down and slide my way out of Theo's reach. "Let's go back inside so my mom can embarrass me while we finish cleaning." In any other scenario, I'd be fending off complete panic, but right now, it doesn't seem so scary.

With a few long strides, Theo catches me before I open the door. "Wait. Next weekend… Saturday, will you meet my mom and sister?"

Now that, *that* seems scary.

Despite my reluctance, I agreed to meet Theo's family, so here I am pulling into his driveway after listening to a podcast about small talk conversations on the drive here. I may or may not have listened to a few last night as well. Okay, I did. And two on beginner's Spanish, because Theo has informed me his mom mostly speaks Spanish at home, which he only mentioned to apologize in advance.

Nothing like a good pre-emptive apology to set your nerves at ease, right?

As soon as my e-brake is up, Theo opens the door and stands on the porch, both hands in the front pockets of his black jeans. He's more casual today than I've ever seen him, with a plain black hoodie and what appear to be slippers. Doesn't make any difference in how my heart races at the sight of him.

"Hey." He greets me with his signature smile as I ascend the steps, and no Muskoka winter can compete with the warmth that sends right down to my toes.

"Hey. I… uh… I wasn't sure what to bring, so I made vegetarian *paella*."

He reaches down to take the dish from my hands as I reach the porch and leans in to plant a chaste kiss on my cheek. "You made a Spanish dish?"

It never occurred to me I was making a Spanish dish to bring to a Spanish woman's house. My food could never compare, and I panic over her perception of my offering.

"I… uh… oh no." I place my face in my hands and I can feel the heat in my cheeks. "Theo, let me put it back in my car. Please. I can't take that inside."

He chuckles at my reaction, but I'm not sure he understands how embarrassed I am. "Not going to happen. I can't wait to eat this."

"Theo, I'm serious—"

The door flies open and on the other side is a striking middle-aged woman with warm brown skin, the same dark eyes as Theo, and a full head of thick, dark hair. She locks eyes with me but doesn't acknowledge me. Instead, she smiles and addresses Theo. "*¡Qué mujer tan guapa!*"

I have no idea what that means, except *mujer* means woman—I think. The only thing keeping me from diving off the porch, headfirst into the adjacent snowbank, is the fact she is smiling.

"*Si, Mami*. This is Isla. Isla, this is my mom, Carlota."

I reach my hand out to shake hers, but she pulls me in for a hug, muttering something else in Spanish that doesn't seem to be directed toward anyone in particular.

I'm happy she's so friendly, but there's also a part of me that wants to melt into a puddle and slink away right now.

Theo must sense my unease because he chimes in, *"Aye, Mami. Let her come inside before you attack her."*

Is it going to be okay to attack me inside?

His mom pulls away and I see a flash of annoyance at her son, but she holds my hand and pulls me inside where Charley and another stunning young woman await. Carlota wastes no time introducing me, and I understand what it's like to be a show-and-tell item.

"This is my daughter, Solana," she says with a beautiful Spanish accent.

Solana is not a hand-shaker either, pulling me in for a hug. When she steps back, I study her features, which are more like her mother's than Theo, leading me to think he looks like his father. The only differences between mother and daughter are Solana's incredible hazel eyes and her dark hair falls in tight coils. "Thank you for convincing my brother to get a dog." She laughs.

I chuckle and it's the first time since I reached the top step that my heart rate decreased. "I didn't convince him of anything. He decided that all on his own." Looking back at Theo, he's smiling while bent down scratching Charley's ears. It's hard to believe, seeing how natural he is, that he'd never had a dog before.

"That's not the way he tells it." Solana smirks at her brother, and I notice she has the same dimples, but hers only ramp up my anxiety, wondering what Theo told them about me before I arrived.

"Play nice, you two. You promised you wouldn't scare her away." Theo snickers and places an arm around me. "I'd be heartbroken."

His mother is beaming at us both and with the combination of nausea and my pounding heart, I'm dizzy. She carries on saying something in Spanish and I get the impression it's not because she forgot to speak in English, rather, she is saying something she doesn't want me to hear.

"*¿Qué estás esperando, Theodore?*" She slaps him with a dish towel that was hanging over her shoulder. "*¡Qué rápido pasa la vida!*"

He looks down at me and smiles. "*Tienes un punto, Mami.*"

I thought seeing Theo play with my nephews was the peak of how attractive he could be, but I was so wrong. Theo speaking Spanish is so next level, even though I have not the slightest clue what he said.

I question him with my eyes, and he leans down to kiss my temple. The display of affection in front of his family makes my already-fragile social state crumble further.

His mom approves of whatever he said, because her eyes are literally sparkling, but I'm so uneasy not understanding what's being said about me.

Solana offers the first bit of reassurance since the conversation turned cryptic for me, the sole unilingual person in the room. "Don't worry. It's all good things."

I offer her a small smile to thank her for saying that, but I'm going to ask Theo later what was said. Socializing is exhausting enough in one language; dealing with a language I can't guess is doing my head in.

"I'm going to give Isla a tour. We'll be back in a minute." Before I can protest, Theo is pulling me by my hand down a short hallway to the left. He yanks me through the second door on the right, closing it behind us.

The second the door closes, Theo asks, "Are you okay?"

I heard what he asked, but I'm too busy scanning my surroundings. This must be his bedroom, but it's immaculate and minimalistic. There's a shaggy grey carpet on the floor, a black metal bedframe holding a queen bed, white bedding, and a large black bolster pillow across the top. He has only one end table to the right, holding a lamp and a few books—that I will definitely inspect at my first opportunity—abstract art over the bed, and a dresser with nothing but a watch and cologne on top. I figured Theo was a simple guy, but this confirms it; no bells or whistles for him. The thing that catches my eye is a beautiful Gibson acoustic guitar sitting in the corner.

"You play?"

He follows my eyes but doesn't answer my question before repeating his. "Are you okay? You were shaking, and I was worried your switch was ready to flip. I'm sorry if that was a lot."

I hadn't realized I was shaking, but now that I've had a moment to breathe, I can feel the tension in my body. The fact he was so in tune with my physical reaction is mind-blowing. "I didn't know what anyone was saying. I struggle to read people when they're speaking English. None of the podcasts I listened to covered any of what you said."

He chuckles. "You listened to Spanish podcasts?"

My face flushes once again. *You're such a loser.* "What did you and your mom say?"

Theo raises a hand to the back of his neck and turns away. He spins back toward me and plants a kiss on my lips, but I swat at his chest.

"Oh, no you don't. You're not going to distract me with kisses. Please, just tell me what you guys said, otherwise I'll spend the rest of the afternoon obsessing over it until I'm exhausted and have to leave before I shut down. I don't want to make a fool of myself, and maybe it's stupid, or rude of me to want to know, but please tell me."

"It's not rude. We were rude for having a conversation you couldn't understand, and I'm sorry."

"Theo…"

"Okay. Basically, my mom said you're a beautiful woman."

Well, that's embarrassing. I'm not sure how to process that because his mom and sister are beyond stunning.

"And?"

He blows out a breath. "I agreed. Then she told me life passes too quickly and asked what I was waiting for."

"Waiting for what?" Oh… Oh! I understand what he's implying a second too late. My cheeks are burning with renewed intensity.

"Don't mind her. My parents were married three months after they met, and I think my mom assumes it happens the same way for everyone. But I don't want to rush anything, Isla."

He steps closer to me, drawing his lips into a smile. "I want to do this right."

I know Theo said he doesn't date unless he's serious, but I may have underestimated how serious he is. A subject change is much needed, so I draw his attention back to the guitar. "Do you play?"

His expression looks uncomfortable, and I can't help thinking I've said something wrong.

"I did. I mean, I do. I can. Just… my dad taught me when I was younger and since he… It just doesn't feel right playing without him anymore."

His response surprises me because for the past few months, I'd barely seen a hint of grief from him. I assumed he was coping fine, but maybe what I see on the surface is not the whole story.

"What's wrong?" he asks, cradling my face in his warm hands.

I'm not sure what to say because I don't want to upset him, but I want to acknowledge the hurt in his eyes. "I guess I'm just surprised that losing your dad affected you enough to stop playing music. All this time, I thought you were so well-adjusted and coping with losing him."

He steps back from me, creating a distance between us I didn't want, but can't protest. "Trust me. I'm not well-adjusted or coping. I have to pretend to be for my mom and my sister. There are days when I want to fall apart, but I have to keep it together."

Those words create a cavernous crack in my chest. "Theo… that's not fair to you, and I'm sure it's not what your mom wants. She wouldn't want you suffering in silence. I know that's not what I want."

I couldn't possibly feel worse than I do right now. What kind of useless girlfriend am I, ignoring the pain he's dealing with because I'm too consumed by my own?

"It's fine. Most times I can deal. Let's get back out there before they send a search party—which would be Charley."

He's shutting me down, and I don't want to push, but his admission leaves me with a lead brick in my stomach. I hate myself for being so self-absorbed and failing to be the support he needs. That's why we met—he was looking for grief *support*, and I've been nothing but a grief tax. He's so in tune with me and my needs, he picks up on things before I do. Yet, I haven't noticed all this time that he's still struggling? But I don't want to push him to open up if he isn't comfortable with that.

He moves away to exit his bedroom, clasping my hand in his. As we walk out, I notice the three books on his bedside table are ones I recommended for him to look into that are similar to mine. I'm grateful he's taking book marketing so seriously, but I'm left feeling nauseous, wondering if he's distracting himself to avoid dealing with reality without his father.

We step out his bedroom door, and he glances back at me, so I try my best to neutralize my expression. He continues down the hallway without another word. I'm not sure how to proceed from here, but I have to trust him to take the lead and tell me what he needs.

The evening passes in a blur of accelerated heart-thumping, a Spanish inquisition, and insanely spicy food. I'm mortified by my attempt at *Paella*, despite the compliments everyone gave. Compared to Carlota's food, it probably tasted like toilet paper. Now I will have plenty of material to obsess over when trying to fall asleep tonight, replaying every comment and change in body language from this entire evening.

All in all, it was a nice evening and Theo's mom and sister were very welcoming. Theo uttered a few things to his mother in Spanish which made his sister chuckle, but the smile never wavered from Carlota's face, so I'm trying to convince myself they were good things. I definitely need to listen to more podcasts in the future.

As I stand in Theo's living room, I scan the space and find a photo of a man wearing a white fedora sitting poolside in swim trunks, an open button-down t-shirt, and a killer smile. I'd recognize that smile anywhere.

"That's my husband." Carlota startles me.

"I can see the resemblance. Theo looks just like him." I give her a tight-lipped smile, not sure what to say or not say. I add, "I'm sorry for your loss." Then I continue to drone on in a panic because I don't want to make her sad. "I know that doesn't help anything—me saying I'm sorry—but I am. From everything Theo has told me, you two loved each other very much."

She places a delicate hand on my arm. "Thank you, *hija*. I love him with everything I am. His death can not take that away from me, even though it causes me much pain."

My stomach sinks. I feel terrible for encouraging this conversation with my nosiness.

*Isla: Always here to ruin the day.*

"*Mami*," Theo interrupts, walking to my side. "Are you scaring my girlfriend again? A guy can't even turn his back to wash dishes?"

Now I'm causing contention between Theo and his mom and panic rises in my throat.

*Don't vomit. Do not vomit.*

"She was admiring the photo of your father," Carlota says as Theo places a peck on my temple. "I was telling her how much I love him."

"I... I'm sorry for upsetting you both. I didn't mean to. It was just—"

"Hey. No one is upset with you." Spinning me to face him, Theo continues, "I can't blame you for looking at him. He was a handsome guy. Like father, like son." He waggles his eyebrows and, as much as I want to laugh at his goofiness, after our conversation earlier, I can't help but think he's sidestepping an emotional conversation again.

Carlota silently vacates the room, leaving Theo and me standing next to the photo of his father.

Regardless, my tolerance for socializing is heading speedily toward capacity, and I want to make my escape before I make a fool of myself. Theo and I can sort through his feelings when he's ready to talk, and now is not that time.

I whisper to Theo, "I think I need to go."

He stares at me, his eyebrows stitched together and his lips in a grimace. "*Gesundheit*?"

"Yeah. *Gesundheit*." I try to smile back, but I'm too busy swallowing down my rising panic. My skin is crawling, and I feel as if a colony of ants is storming around my entire body.

"*Mami*, Isla is leaving. I'm going to walk her out."

Carlota and Solana peek out of the kitchen and tell me they were happy to meet me, and I'm welcome back. I return the sentiment as I slide on my boots.

Theo and Charley walk me to my car, but Charley darts off to find some snow-covered landscaping to mark while Theo cages me against my car door. I want to feel comfort in this moment with him, but all I can focus on is the impending social shut-down I'm headed for.

"I need to go." Tears prick my eyes, but I refuse to let them fall. Not yet. I can't let him see me cry again.

"I love you."

'm not sure I heard him correctly on account of my heart pounding against my ribcage and blood pumping through my ears.

"What?"

He chuckles. "I thought it was obvious by now, but that doesn't mean I don't need… don't want to say it."

As much as I want to tell him I love him too—because I do—I can't help the flood of negative emotions coursing through my veins. This isn't fair. It's not fair to Theo because I can only love him in between bouts of sadness, and he deserves so much more than that. And no matter what my mom tells me about happiness curing sadness, none of this is fair to Rory, because she never got the chance to fall in love.

I need some space. My mental, emotional, and physical limits have been reached, and I'm shutting down.

"*Gesundheit.*"

I ignore the shock that registers on Theo's face as I escape into my car. This is too much right now.

I expect him to offer some resistance, but he lets me leave without a fight.

He shouldn't love me.

To say I've had a difficult time sleeping the past two days would be an understatement. Theo came over after his day job yesterday so we could work on my book marketing, but we completely ignored the bombshell he dropped on me the night before. Neither of us acknowledged what he said, but I'm not an idiot; I know my response hurt him, and that tears me up inside. He's done nothing to deserve my avoidance, but that scares me. What if I keep hurting him because I'm not in the right space to love him how he deserves?

Logic tells me there's no reason *not* to tell him I love him. I have been made painfully aware of how short life can be, and that should motivate me to take life by the horns and live every moment. But the truth is, I'm terrified.

Not terrified of loving him. Not in the least. That came naturally without giving logic a say in the matter.

Me, the girl who is scared of drive-thrus, phone calls, and eye contact. Afraid of breathing too loud in the presence of others, saying the wrong thing, and unwanted attention. Petrified of small talk, lulls in conversation, or what strangers think of my walk.

There are plenty of things I'm scared of, but loving him isn't one of them. I might not be good at speaking to people, but his heart has been so in tune with mine, they communicate directly. There's a connection between us that doesn't need words, but that doesn't mean words aren't needed to express my love for him.

What scares me most, then?

Losing him.

Having his love ripped away like Rory. Like Theo's father. And I guess in my own twisted way, like my parents.

Failing him.

Not being able to give back to him all he gives to me.

Do I love him enough to put my heart at risk again? Am I selfish enough to make us work when I know we're both navigating through things we need to address on our own? Can I really open myself up to him despite how scared I am? It's stupid, really, because I already love him. I love my family, and while it scares me to lose them or fail them, I don't dwell on it; I just love them. Why it's so different with Theo, I don't know.

Why is this so hard?

Our conversation last night didn't end well, and I assume that's because things were emotionally charged, and necessary words were left unspoken—by me.

Theo, trying to stay business-focused, insisted I do a "book tour" in the area and get into as many bookstores or libraries as possible. I resisted the idea because the thought of interacting with people doesn't appeal to me. It's not that it just doesn't appeal to me—it terrifies me. He doesn't see the big deal, even though I've been honest with him about my social anxiety. He seems to think it's something I can ignore to get a job done but doesn't realize that it never shuts off. Sure, there are times I'm more comfortable than others. Occasionally I can relax and not question every word that escapes my lips or every louder-than-normal exhale, but those moments are rare.

Intentionally going into a crowd where I don't know who will be there, what will be expected of me, what will be said, or having attention on me? Well, that's recipe for a living nightmare and I've had enough of those.

Anyway, we had an argument and haven't spoken since he left. I've been up all night, even after not sleeping the night before, and I'm exhausted in every sense of the word. Even

Bond's affection hasn't eased the tsunami of emotions ravaging my shores.

I send Theo a text because I owe him more insight into why I am the way I am. He deserves an explanation why I struggle with things that seem like basic tasks for a majority of the population.

**Isla: Can we talk?**

Message delivered. Now we wait… and wait… and wait.

Thirty minutes later, he hasn't even read my text, and I can't help but feel like he's avoiding me. I hurt him, frustrated him, and ran away from him like a coward. There's only so much a person can forgive.

I dial his number and pray he answers.

On the fourth ring, he answers. "Hello?" His voice sounds groggy, with none of his normal enthusiasm.

"Theo. I'm sorry."

I hear rustling in the background and his phone shifting to a different position. "Hey. You don't need to be sorry. It is what it is."

*What does that mean?*

"I… Theo… can we talk after work?"

He blows out a breath into the phone. "I didn't go to work today."

"It's Tuesday."

"No kidding. I barely slept and couldn't focus on anything, so I didn't go. You woke me up when you called."

I feel terrible about that last sentence for three reasons: one, I woke him up; two, my emotional immaturity or whatever it is, is causing him distress; and three, now he's missed a day of work at a job he needs to provide for his family.

"I'm so sorry. I know it might not matter anymore, but I'd really like to explain myself." Considering that reality—that he might be over making an effort with me—stings like rubbing alcohol in the gaping chest wound where my heart once was.

"Might not matter? Seriously? Isla, you're basically all that matters to me. You, my family. Everything else is just noise and distractions."

Gulp.

"If you want to talk, I'll come over so we can talk."

"Thank you." My words are barely more than a whisper. What will I say when he arrives? Beats me, but it's time I say something.

I busy myself by showering, getting dressed in black leggings and a knitted sweater, throw my hair into a messy bun, and tidy my condo before Theo arrives. I've been really proud of myself lately, leaving Rory's bedroom door open, and even though sometimes walking past knocks the air from my lungs, it is getting easier. There's not an ounce of doubt in my mind that I'll never stop missing her, but I know my mom was right. The cure for sadness is happiness, and that's going to take intentional effort.

It's time for me to put in that effort with Theo.

Two hours later, Theo is walking into my condo looking like he's just gone five rounds in a boxing match… more like a tennis match. No blood, but he looks exhausted and dishevelled. His grey trackpants and loose-fitting sweatshirt are a new level of casual I've never seen on him. He doesn't lean in to greet me with his usual hello kiss, but Bond receives his mandatory ear rub upon entry. The price of admission into this place is non-negotiable.

"Hi." Guilt drips off the lone syllable I'm able to utter.

"Well, I came." His words are clipped, and I tense at his response.

"You did. Thank you." This doesn't feel like Theo—my Theo—in front of me. He's a distant stranger and the palpability of this chasm growing between us only makes my pulse race. I have to fix this. "Do you want to ccme sit?"

He doesn't reply; he just toes off his shoes and walks into the living room, sinking down into the sofa.

It's now or never.

I f it weren't Theo sitting beside me, I'd probably high tail it out of here, but I owe him this. There's nothing I want more right now than to bridge the gap that's opened between us.

"I want to explain to you why I have a hard time with some things that might not make sense to you."

He nods, but there's no warmth in his eyes. Just hurt. "You don't have to tell me anything."

"I want to tell you. You know my parents died in a car accident, but I didn't explain the whole situation." I take a deep breath and make eye contact with Theo, seeing a nearly imperceptible nod to continue. "My mother was an alcoholic."

Theo's dark eyes widen as he stares at me, but he remains silent.

"She was better off out of the two of my parents. My mom just liked hard liquor, but my dad, he did whatever he could get his hands on—whisky, marijuana, or heroin. Anything in between."

"Isla… I'm so sorry."

"It's not your fault." I shrug, trying to lessen the severity of their addictions. "As I've gotten older, I realized a lot of it wasn't even *their* fault. They were probably medicating themselves because of something, but I'll never know what that was. I never really knew anything about them aside from they were drunk, high, or angry all the time."

He reaches a hand out, holding mine on my lap, and I don't move. I allow the warmth of his hand to comfort me so I can explain the reality of my childhood.

"Anyway, life at home wasn't great, but I didn't know any different. I spent as much time as possible in my room staring at the pictures in the worn out books I'd looked at hundreds of times. I couldn't read yet, so I'd spend hours imagining myself inside those pages, coming up with my own stories, escaping my reality. I was young, but if I stayed quiet and didn't ask for anything, I was more likely to escape a beating for that day."

"They… they beat you?"

I let out a crass, one-note laugh. "Oh gosh. That's a nice way of putting it. I basically looked like I was from *Avatar* because my skin was blue. I had several broken bones that didn't heal correctly, and I was in pain most of the time, but I didn't dare cry about it." I hold out my hand and stare at the slightly bent fingers of my left hand, recalling having them slammed in the trunk of our family car for something I can't even remember.

"Nobody helped you?"

I pause for a moment and choke on my words. "I was the big sister. It was *my* job to help."

"Big sister? You have a sibling?" Judging by Theo's narrowed eyes, he's got an idea where this conversation is headed.

"Had." My tears choose this moment to trickle down my cheeks. "I had a little sister. Her name was Misty, which, believe it or not, my parents named after *Canadian Mist Whisky*."

Theo's eyes are moist, and he sniffles while rubbing the back of his free hand across each eye. "I don't know what to say. I'm so sorry, Isla."

There's nothing he could have done about it, and there's certainly nothing he can do about it now. He shouldn't be feeling guilty about my miserable childhood. "It's fine. I'm not telling you this to make you feel bad. I'm explaining this so you understand why some things are hard for me."

"How can I not feel bad? What you're describing, it sounds like Hell. I hate that you had to live through that."

"No. I lived through it, but that's the point. I was born fine and now, I have a good life. My dreams are out there for me to chase, and my family at home for me to love. Misty never got that chance. She was born with Fetal Alcohol Syndrome, and she had more health problems than I could count. She was underdeveloped from birth and nearly deaf. My mom drank straight through her pregnancy with no regard for my sister's life." I pause for a moment because saying these things out loud is emotionally taxing. Tears are streaming down my face with no sign of letting up. "She was a needy baby, but it wasn't her fault."

"Of course not. But I'm assuming your parents didn't handle it well?"

"They barely handled her at all. They carted her off to neighbours or friend's houses because my parents played the victim, complaining about how hard it was to have a disabled child—which, it no doubt was, but they always failed to mention it was their fault. The poor-me card was their favourite schtick, and they disregarded that it was Misty who suffered most."

"Why didn't they send you to neighbours or friends, too?"

"Because I could talk."

Theo nods again, understanding what I mean by that. Snitches get stitches—or in my case, they wouldn't. They'd get neglected, gaping wounds and broken bones.

"Anyway, point being, I learned to keep quiet. If I didn't talk, I didn't attract attention to myself, and it was safer. That became my defence. To just sit down, shut up, and not make myself a target. My only protection was not being noticed—not existing."

"That makes sense to five-year-old you, but you're not that girl anymore."

"I'll *always* be that girl. I spent a long time attempting to 'get over it,' but those fears are embedded in me." Theo's eyes are on me, but I can't look at him anymore. "That day I told you we went to the farm, we stopped at one of my dad's 'friend's' houses on the way home. We were there for hours. My mom was drinking who knows what, and my dad injecting anything and everything into his veins. We got in the car to drive home, and on Highway Eleven, near the airport, my dad crossed the median and slammed head on into another car."

"You were in the car?"

"I was. I was..." This is still painful to say, even after all this time. "I was the only one to survive, but I spent six weeks in the hospital recovering."

"Did you have any family to take care of you?"

"Nobody wanted me. I was too 'troubled' for either of my parents' siblings to bother with me. Even when I moved into foster care, no one wanted to deal with me because I didn't talk, and my night terrors kept me up at night. Every time I closed my eyes, I replayed the accident over again—seeing my family dead in front of me. I'd wake up screaming, which disturbed Miss Deborah too much, so she gave me a thread-bare sleeping bag and put me in the basement. My life there was just as bad, maybe worse than with my parents. I had to 'earn' necessities like food, clothes, or even going to the bathroom. If it weren't for Zara, I wouldn't have survived it; she was the first person I could talk to. She made me feel like a person and not a problem. I didn't fear her and developed a trust with her I'd never experienced before." I stare down at my hands wringing together, overcome with guilt for piling this on Theo. This should have been something I confessed months ago, but I didn't want to address it again. I didn't think any good would come from opening old wounds or making excuses for myself. "All that to say, the way I handle things, my irrational fears and my struggles that might seem like nonsense to everyone else, well, I am this way because everything I spent years recovering from came hurdling back when Rory died the same way."

Despite looking like he's going to be sick, Theo squeezes my hand and says, "You say you lost your family in the accident, but you never mentioned your sister before. Did she…"

A sob escapes my lips when I think back to that day. Theo moves closer and wraps an arm around my back.

"She… she wasn't strapped into her car seat. I should have buckled her, but I was five; I only knew how to buckle myself. When we crashed, she was ejected out of the car and died on the road. Like an animal, Theo. My two-year-old baby sister died right there on the road."

"*Mi Alma*, I'm so sorry."

I cry into Theo's sweatshirt, trying to absorb the comfort he's offering, but it's no use.

"This is the last thing you needed. I'm sorry for dumping this on you. Really, I was doing so well, honest. My anxiety was under control and my night terrors had gone away. I swore I wouldn't live my life being a victim of my crappy childhood because my life is good now, but this all… everything with Rory, it was too much. I'm sorry."

He kisses my shoulder and rests his forehead above my ear. "You're amazing, Isla. I know talking about this must be hard. I never questioned your anxiety or your night terrors before because they're just parts that make up the whole, and everyone has some broken bits. But that doesn't make me love you any less."

"Theo—"

"No, it's fine Isla. You don't need to love me back. Just don't run away from me *because* I love you."

"But I do. I love you and I didn't run away because you told me."

Theo's wide, unblinking eyes meet mine. "Say it again."

"I... I love you?"

"Are you asking me?"

"N... no. I love you, Theo. It wasn't in my plans, and initially I thought you were irritating and obnoxious..." I clap my hand over my mouth, horrified I just said that. I speak through my hand, "I'm so sorry."

He laughs, removing my hand from my mouth. "And what do you think of me now?"

I formulate my words in my head before I allow myself to blurt out anything else, carefully calculating what to say. "I think you're everything."

Theo asked me to tag along with him for a weekend volunteer shift at the dog rescue. How could I say no to a day with dogs? I'd love to volunteer here, but I don't want Theo to think I'm only doing it because he is. My goals and ambitions are my own, and even though I know my intentions, social anxiety makes me far too concerned about how others perceive things.

When we arrive at Carter's, we're asked to help with cleaning up the yard and walking a few dogs, giving them some individual attention. The first dog I tend to is a hound mix named Nick. He's a hyper guy, but having been disappointed by humans in the past, he takes a few minutes to warm up. I sit on the ground and wait quietly until he's curious enough to come investigate me. After a thorough sniffing, he allows me to pet him and shortly after, we're best of friends.

"You're a natural. Have you always had dogs?" Theo asks, beaming at Nick and me.

"I've always loved dogs, but Bond was the first dog I had. Well… the first dog I got to keep, anyway."

"What do you mean?"

Now that Theo knows the reality of my life with my biological parents, it feels like a whole new world of conversations has opened up and I can share things from my past that I've never shared with anyone but my family or Rory.

"Uh… when I was young—maybe four—my dad brought home this chocolate lab from somewhere and told me he got me a dog. I was thrilled. I had so many books with dogs and puppies, even though I'd never been around them, I always loved them, from the pictures alone."

"That was nice of him." Theo's face relaxes and for a flickering moment, my dad redeemed himself, but that's not the end of the story. "What did you name him?"

That's the only funny part in the story. "Don't laugh."

Theo's lips quirk before he bites his smile and nods.

"His name was Teddy. But he was brown, and to my four-year-old self, he looked like a teddy bear."

A booming laugh fills the space, making Nick flinch, but Theo quiets himself. "I'm flattered you named your first dog after me. Now I can be your Teddy." He winks.

My face is far too warm now. "Don't flatter yourself. Anyway, Teddy was not trained, and I had no idea what to do other than feed him and cuddle h m. He had a terrible habit of stealing food that was left unattended. One night my dad ordered pizza, and when he got up to get a drink—or heroin, who knows—Teddy ate the entire thing."

"Oh no. You can't mess with a man's pizza."

"Especially not an angry drunk." Tears spring to my eyes, but I choke them back. "He kicked Teddy; he was so angry. I remember screaming and crying, trying to get in between my dad and the dog, which earned me a few bruises for my trouble, but Teddy was protecting me, too."

"Oh, Isla. I'm so sorry. I shouldn't have brought it up."

"No, it's fine. I mean, it's not fine. I woke up the next day and Teddy was gone."

Theo pulls me to stand and wraps me in his strong arms. His comfort makes me more emotional, but I refuse to cry here. Nick is just starting to get comfortable, so I need to focus on him.

"I don't know what to say, but I can promise you, this Teddy isn't going anywhere. And I'd do anything to protect you too."

That's all I need for the floodgates to open and my body shakes along with my sobs. It's been seventeen years since that day with Teddy, but it still hurts just as much. Not physically, but that wasn't the worst pain. "I love you," I choke out, attempting to calm myself.

"I love you too, *Mi Alma.*"

"You still haven't told me what that means."

He winks again. "Someday. Now let's get these dogs some exercise. I've got a couple of eager chihuahuas ready to rock 'n' roll."

I laugh, which is all I need to stop my tears. Both on account of Theo's comment, and the sight of him standing with two chihuahuas. He's a very tall guy, so the dogs are barely higher than his ankles, but he's taken such a liking to canines in general, he doesn't care about their size. That makes me love him more.

On our walk, we talk about happier times. For Theo, that includes his entire childhood, and I love that his happiest memories are simple things like playing ball with his dad, or watching his parents, who both grew up in a tropical climate, learn to snowshoe. For me, my happiest moments came after I was adopted, which, until then, I had never felt like a person. I reminisce about our first and only camping trip when Bond went missing for three days. After losing Teddy how I did, those days were devastating, but Bond came back safe and sound.

Twenty minutes into our walk, both of the dogs Theo is walking start lifting one paw at a time, refusing to walk for more than a few seconds. "I think their paws are cold." Without a second's hesitation, he unzips his coat a few inches, and places both dogs inside his coat. He talks to them in a soothing, gentle voice, and both dogs look at him like he is their hero.

Watching this giant of a man baby-talk a couple of chihuahuas in his coat, I'm a goner. It wouldn't be possible for me to love anyone else as much as I love Theodore Malinga. He's continued to surprise me, day after day, and brought light to my life in a time I was suffocating in darkness.

"What?" he asks, one brow raised.

I give my head a shake, realizing I was staring at him with a goofy smile on my face. "Nothing."

"Why were you looking at me like that?"

"I... uh... I was just thinking about how much I love you. Every time I think my heart is at capacity, you fill it up more." I scrub my hands over my face and exhale an intentional breath. "Sorry. That was so cheesy. Double-cheese pizza."

*Double-cheese pizza? You thought* that *was going to make the situation better?*

He chuckles and I feel my face flush against the cool late-winter air.

"There's nothing I want more than to fill your heart up more." He takes a step toward me and places a hand on the back of my neck to pull me in for a searing kiss. I could get lost in the moment, but we're interrupted by a pair of chihuahuas licking our chins and a hound dog jumping up against Theo's leg.

We burst out laughing.

"These two want in on the action, and this guy is pushing me away." He leans down to scratch Nick on the top of his head. "Don't worry, buddy. I'll let you have her today, but she's mine every day after." He looks in my eyes as he says that, and there's nothing about that statement I want to argue.

Theo drives us back to my condo after we finish our tasks at the rescue. The roads are coated in slush as the temperatures rise and everything begins to melt. I stare at the window, watching the dirty snowbanks pass by in a blur, listening to the radio.

"We don't have a song yet." Theo reaches forward to press the scan button for the radio. "What do you think it should be?"

"Loser."

Theo's eyes shoot open. "Did you just call me a loser?"

"No. The song… Loser?" I wave my hand around in front of my face, trying to summon the song to his mind or something. I don't even know what I'm doing. Surprise.

"I'm a loser baby, so why don't you kill me?" he sings to the tune of the song by Beck, and I'm taken aback by how effortless that was for him.

"No, not that one. It's a song by Julian Moon. Basically, it says doing simple things together like getting takeout to eat at home or shopping at a used bookstore doesn't feel so lame when we do it together."

"Hm. I like it. I don't think I know it, but that sounds like us." He reaches over to grab my hand. "Speaking of bookstores, are you going to give me a copy of your manuscript so I can read it? I need to know what to market to bookstores."

"Do you have to read it?"

He chuckles again. "I want to read it. Which is saying something because I've never *wanted* to read anything."

I heave out a sigh. "Fine. When you drop me off, I'll print you a copy. Or I can email it. Whatever works."

"I can't wait to read the world's next bestseller."

When Theo called on his way to work to tell me he finished reading my book last night, I was concerned by his tone. He didn't seem the tiniest bit excited or impressed with it, and despite the approval I've gotten from everyone else who has read it, including Rory, I can't help but feel crushed. His vote of confidence is important to me, and beyond that, he's worked so hard on this, I don't want to fail him.

So, he's on his way here after a full day at work so we can discuss his take on what he read. To say I'm nervous is a massive understatement.

His knock on the patio door startles me from my self-deprecating, internal monologue. Time to face the music, I guess.

"Hey." He smiles his devastating dimpled grin at me and for a fleeting moment, I forget about the potential derailing of my career I've dreamed about since I was a child.

"Come in. I ordered food."

He sets his laptop bag on the floor, greets Bond, and removes his shoes. Before he speaks again, he sweeps me in for a kiss and it's nice being back to normal. No, not normal—better than ever. "You have no idea how much I miss you when I don't see you for a few days."

I'm pretty sure I do. Living alone, not including Bond, is lonely, even for someone as socially inept as I am. "I missed you too."

With Theo's work, family, and volunteer schedule at Carter's, sometimes we go days without seeing each other, but the last thing I want is to come across as clingy. That makes admitting to missing him, even after he's said the same thing to me, far more difficult than it should be. When we went through our rough patch a few weeks ago, part of it was because I was afraid to be honest about my feelings. That should scare me straight and encourage me to be open with him, but all it's done is make me question everything I say and do in his presence because I don't want to upset him again. I can't deal with hurting him.

"Do you want to get some work done first, or do you want to eat?" He interrupts my thoughts again, and I doubt he has any clue how much I needed him to.

"I can't eat until you give me your feedback on my book. You... you didn't sound like you liked it and I've been stressing about it all day. I probably smell like a samosa from the stress sweat."

*Why would you say that?*

My shoulders slump, but he pulls me in again, wrapping his arms around me as I deflate against him.

"I really loved it. And you smell amazing."

"Don't lie to me to spare my feelings, Theo. Reviewers won't hold back, so if it's totally awful, I want to know so I can fix it before scathing reviews come in."

"I'm not lying. I really loved it," he confirms with a chuckle.

A modicum of tension releases from my shoulders, but I'm not convinced. "Then why did you sound so... I don't know... blasé about it this morning?"

Taking my hand, he walks me to the couch and sits, patting the cushion beside him. "I don't want you to take this the wrong way, and I don't want you to be upset about it either."

That's all I need for my heart to thunder in my chest. He hates it.

"It's nothing to do with the story itself. I'm not a reader, and you know that, but I thought the book was amazing. I kind of assumed I'd have to 'get it over w th' and force myself to finish it, but I loved every minute."

Deep breath. "What is it then?"

"I'm probably being over-sensitive—"

"Oh my gosh. Just tell me, please!" I screech.

"So... uh... when you describe your characters, I noticed that you have some with bronze or brown skin."

I nod, anticipating his words with wide eyes. "I wanted to show a diverse cast of characters."

"And that's amazing. It's just... uh... you described skin tones for people of colour, but never for white characters. Like being white is the default, and anything else needs to be mentioned."

I stare at Theo, my mouth stretched open, because I replay my book in my mind and realize he's right. I flip through the pages of the manuscript on the coffee table, and I'm horrified. How did I not notice that? How dic it slip by everyone else who's read it?

"I'm not racist," is the only thing I can come up with to defend my stupidity after several minutes of page flipping.

He chuckles, a deep, throaty sound that makes his entire chest shake. "I didn't think you were. Like I said, I'm probably just being overly sensitive. Being the poor little Afro-Cuban kid in a white-washed area must have left me with some sort of complex." He shrugs his shoulders and his lips tilt into a half-smile.

"No. You're right. I'm so sorry. You're not being sensitive, and you shouldn't ever discount your feelings like that. Realizing I imposed my own bias in my writing is a wake-up call. I've always tried to be diverse and inclusive, creating realistic characters for the area the story takes place, but this… this is not acceptable."

"Wow. Slow down. It's really not a big deal. You're right that the setting for the story is predominantly white… I guess… I just figured there are as many variations in white skin as there are black, so it seems worth mentioning."

"It is a big deal! My book is supposed to be funny and entertaining. Yet, I ended up making you feel less-than because of my own preconceived ideas. I hate that someone I love thinks I see him as some sort of after-market modification, different from the mass-produced models." The realization I did this makes me physically ill.

I don't give Theo time to reply to me before I hop off the couch and move to my computer. I'm going to fix this. Not just in my book, but fix things with Theo. I can't even imagine what he thinks of me now.

"Isla, it's fine. Let's eat and you can look at it later. I didn't mean to make you feel bad."

"Theo! You're being so nice about this, but *I* made *you* feel bad. I'm not going to make excuses for myself because I'm white and it never occurred to me. What kind of ignorant KKK mentality is that? Oh my gosh. I'm like… like Hitler!"

He laughs again, but I don't think he understands how awful this is. Part of my studies in University included assessing our biases in writing, and yet, something so obvious, me and everyone else has missed out on. Does that mean this is commonplace in other books too?

"You don't have a KKK mentality just because you didn't see things from another perspective. You're white. It's understandable that when you picture a character in your head, you don't pay attention to white skin. Someone different, they're bound to stand out."

I shuffle papers at my desk, readying myself to scour my document from start to finish and address this. I'm questioning what other biases I might have that I've unknowingly woven into the storyline. If I have to unravel this whole thing and stitch it back together, I will.

Before I can crack my knuckles and get to work, Theo leans over me with a hand on each of my shoulders, speaking in a baritone whisper, blowing his breath across my ear. "I'm only here for a few hours. Come spend time with me and you'll have all day tomorrow to fix whatever you want, but I really don't think it's a big deal."

It is. But, at the same time, he's right about only having a few hours with him. I desperately crave human interaction—no offence, Bond—so I should make the most of our time. I spin my white-leather desk-chair around and smile, but it's forced. Not because I don't want to smile at Theo, but because my insides are reeling from this revelation.

I pick at my food, and it's nothing to do with the fact it's Brussels sprouts—I love Brussels sprouts most days. My appetite is gone, and every time Theo tries to change the subject, I veer right back to his critique of my book.

"What about accents? Is it insensitive to point out someone's accent? Or do I mention everyone's accent?"

Theo rubs his thumb and forefinger back and forth across his tensed eyebrows. "I'm so sorry I brought it up. But I'd assume that if a story was set in a certain place, you'd mention accents that are different. Like if it were in Scotland, you wouldn't mention a Scottish accent, but you'd mention an American one. I think accents are different than skin tone because there is a default. Skin colour can be different everywhere."

I nod, accepting his explanation. That makes sense. After all of these years, analyzing and studying people, worrying about offending them when I speak, now I'm even more scared in my writing.

For the rest of the evening, it's as if a storm cloud is hanging over top of us, preventing either of us from enjoying ourselves. Despite Theo's constant reassurance that he's not upset with me and that he doesn't think his suggestion is a big deal, I don't see it the same way. How could he *not* be upset?

It's late by the time Theo leaves, and rather than go to sleep like a sane person, I ransack my bookshelf, wanting to start by pinpointing other potential biases.

What I discover chills my bones. It turns out, I'm not the only author to make this mistake. Nearly every book I look at has the same issue, but that doesn't make the situation any better. In fact, it makes things infinitely worse knowing a massive subsection of our population—scratch that, human beings—could potentially feel the way I made Theo feel.

I make it my personal mission to do something about it before finally drifting off to sleep as the sun rises.

In the five days since Theo's revelation about my writing, I've spent every waking moment tearing down and rebuilding each character in my book. I've become so hyper-aware of every aspect of my writing to the point I am driving myself insane. That's not a figure of speech. I haven't left my house for days and if Theo hadn't brought me food, I probably wouldn't have stopped to eat—because phoning for delivery and answering the door? No thanks.

Tonight, Theo insisted I join him to meet with his friends at the pub. I wanted to drive myself so I'd be able to escape if the need arises and he doesn't have to leave if I reach my limit. The parking lot is full when I pull in, which sets my nerves on edge before I step foot out of my car.

I spent the drive here repeating personal mantras to combat my anxiety. *It's okay to talk to as few or as many people as I want. I can contribute to conversation. I can laugh at myself if I do something stupid.* Somehow, I don't think any of those will help, but I'm trying.

Breathe.

When I walk inside, I'm hit with a burst of loud voices, laughter, and music. It's overwhelming. The air is thick and smells like alcohol; I'd rather smell wet dog. Safe to say, before I take two steps inside, I'm already planning my exit strategy, but for Theo's sake, I'll make an effort.

He catches my eye from across the room and doesn't wait for me to come to him. He strides toward me with his usual confidence, beaming. I relax slightly at the sight of him. That is, until he pulls me in for a knee-weakening kiss and people start whistling and cat calling.

*Everybody's watching.*

"Theo." My face flushes. "Stop. People are looking at us."

He smirks as he glances around the room. "Let them watch. They're just jealous I get to kiss you."

"That's definitely not true. They probably pity you. But regardless, I'm not interested in catering to people's voyeuristic fantasies." Shudder.

He chuckles but grabs my hand to lead me through the crowd. "Come say hi to everyone."

Once again, the same friends who were here months ago are divided up into groups. I have no idea why they come as a group then break off into cliques amongst themselves, but it works to my benefit. The fewer people I'm expected to interact with, the better.

After we say hi to everyone else, including my biggest fan, Clair, Theo pulls out a stool to the left of Shane, where he's seated with Dean. As soon as I sit down, I can't help but stress that my prejudice will come through in conversation like it did in my writing and I'll unintentionally say something offensive to Shane. From what Theo has said, they've dealt with enough ignorance regarding their skin tone in their lives.

*Safety first. Stay silent.*

After Dean and Shane greet me, they settle into comfortable—for them—conversation with Theo. I'm a reticent observer, following their conversation like a ping-pong ball. Their dynamic is so effortless and comfortable. Like how I used to be with Rory. Just like that, my shoulders slump, and the corners of my mouth drop, unable to force a polite smile any longer.

Theo takes notice because he places a hand on my jean-clad knee under the table and gives me a gentle squeeze paired with a questioning expression. I refuse to ruin his evening, so I excuse myself to the ladies' room.

I spend a few minutes secluded in a bathroom stall before I hear footsteps, giggling and laughing, friends happy to be in each other's company. That's my initial focus, bringing Rory back to the forefront of my mind, realizing how much I miss her.

"I know, right? He's way too good for her. He'll figure it out sooner or later."

That voice sounds familiar.

"Who dyes their hair pink, anyway? Attention seeker much?"

Both women laugh and it's no longer a mystery who they're talking about. But they don't need to tell me that pink hair was a magnet for attention. I confirmed that the second I walked out of the salon. Part of me wants to chime in and tell them that's the last thing I was aiming for.

*Nobody likes you.*

A crowded pub might appear as a companionable place to be, but sitting silently on a toilet seat, locked in a bathroom stall, is the loneliest place I've ever been. These two giggling and laughing with each other, even if I don't appreciate their topic of conversation, rips open my aching heart even more and I choke back a sob. At this moment, the pain missing Rory is just as much physical as it is emotional.

Confrontation is not my forte, so I stay quiet, stifling my cries, as Shawna and Clair continue to badmouth me and voice their opinions of all the ways I'm wrong for Theo. It stings to know how they really feel and to think that I'll never be friends with them, but I don't respect women who talk about others like that enough to let them come between what Theo and I have.

An eternity passes before they vacate the ladies' room, but I still don't want to drag myself out.

Moments later, a knock at the door startles me, and I hear it open, letting the noise from the pub flood in.

"Isla? Are you okay?" Theo's voice, firm but concerned, echoes off the bathroom walls.

"I'm fine. I'll be out in a second." Please don't come in. Please don't come in.

How long have I been in here that he felt the need to come check on me? Oh gosh, who knows what he thought I was doing. Why else does one get stuck in a bathroom for long periods of time? This is mortifying.

"Okay. I'll wait right here."

That settles my internal debate. Time to toughen up and leave the safety of the bathroom stall. I wash my hands for appearance's sake because last thing I need is for Theo to assume I was in here dealing with intestinal distress and walked out without washing my hands—plus I touched public bathroom things—and step back into the noise-polluted hallway.

Theo gives me a tentative smile. "Are you okay?"

I figure there's no sense in bringing up the conversation between Shawna and Clair because I don't want to drive a wedge between Theo and his friends, so I let it slide. I'll just replay their words every night as I try to fall asleep for the next twelve years. But nope. Not going to bother me one bit.

*Yeah, right.*

"I am just being stupid. Don't worry about me."

"I always worry about you."

Well, that's awful. Of course, he'll worry about me because I'm hopeless and pathetic. Poor complicated Isla can't listen to people talk without having a freak out. I'd roll my eyes at myself, but Theo would no doubt assume I was rolling them at him.

"I'm sorry, Theo. Can I just go? You can hang out with your friends and not waste time worrying about me. This keeps happening." I close my eyes because if I look at him, I'll start crying. He startles me by backing me into the wall, pinning me with his body and capturing my lips with a kiss. I try to stay in the moment—try to be here with him—but my mind is racing. When he pulls away, I can't stop the words from spilling out. "I miss Rory."

"Isla, look at me."

I open my eyes but can't look in his.

"What happened?" His brows are stitched together, and he's cradling my cheek in his palm.

I huff an exhale. "Everything. Your friends. How effortless you guys talk to each other. I don't fit in with your crowd and the girls hate me. I could probably win awards for world's worst girlfriend. Conversing with anyone but you is impossible because I'm paranoid I'll say something offensive, making socializing even harder than it was before. And the ONE thing I was good at, writing, I've failed miserably."

To his credit, he doesn't interrupt me on my rant. I didn't say any of it because I wanted to start an argument. I said it because it's all true.

It's somewhat alarming when he laughs. Is he drunk? Oh gosh, I can't leave now because I need to make sure he gets home safely. What if all his friends are drunk and I have to drive a bunch of giants home in my Honda Civic?

*Why is he still laughing?*

"You're cute, you know?"

"I'm sorry. What?"

"You get worked up like a chihuahua picking a fight with its own reflection. I don't know what makes you think you're a terrible girlfriend, but since I'm the only person who calls you that, I think that's my decision to make, and I love you. So freaking much, *Mi Alma*. And you don't have to talk to anyone here if you don't want to. Just having you here makes me happy, but I don't want you to be afraid of saying anything. And, I'm sorry I made you doubt your writing, but you're remarkably talented and if I have to get a megaphone to tell everyone in here to make you believe it, I will."

Of everything he just said, I focus on one. "What does *Mi Alma* mean? You never told me."

If I'm not mistaken, Theo has a fleeting moment of shyness and clenches his lips together. He takes twenty seconds to reply. I counted. "It means 'my soul'. Because I might be in control of my mind and body, but you, Isla Haynes, are my soul."

After Theo's confession about his nickname for me, we spent the rest of the evening with Shane and Dean. I struggled to converse because I couldn't get past my fear of saying something offensive, but Theo was a master at directing the conversation away from me when he could tell I was overwhelmed. His ability and willingness to support me when I find situations difficult makes me love him even more.

The rest of the weekend passes with nothing eventful happening, but my book launch is approaching at warp speed, so it's time to complete my manuscript by sending it off to a proofreader, then have it formatted. In my capacity as an editor, I've been fortunate to connect with a few freelance professionals over the years, so finding people I trust wasn't hard. Building relationships via email is a lot easier than in person.

The second I click the blue arrow, sending my manuscript through cyberspace to the next set of eyes destined to read it, I feel like I've lost 100 pounds, but also like I'm going to vomit. This is a huge step toward officially publishing my book and I still can't wrap my head around that moment arriving. Life is so much easier when I'm helping other people with their work. Putting my own into the world makes me vulnerable and exposed.

When the document comes back to me in about two weeks, I can send it to my advance readers, and that's when things get real. These people are not friends or family. They're legitimate book reviewers who will analyze and question everything. They aren't obligated to be nice about it because we share a last name or address—they'll be honest, no matter what. I want feedback, but once it's at that stage, it's past the point of no return.

My phone lights up with a call from Theo and knowing he was thinking of me in that moment and called brings a smile to my face, slowing my heart rate.

"Hey. Aren't you at work?"

"I am, but I had a minute and wanted to say hi since I didn't call this morning."

It was odd he didn't call on his way to work, but he prevented me from panicking by sending me a text to tell me he was fine. That didn't stop me from worrying that I upset him, so I'm happy to hear his voice. "Was everything okay? It was weird not hearing from you."

"Everything's fine. Mom was having a tough morning because her and Dad's anniversary is this weekend. I was trying to comfort her, but there's nothing I can do to make it easier."

"Oh, your poor mom. I remember that coming up in the grief support group; about how the firsts always seem harder after losing someone. For myself, even though any other year I've never given a second thought to New Years, starting a new year without Rory hurt. It felt as if I was leaving her behind."

*You always have to make things about yourself.*

"But your mom's situation is different, and I can't even imagine how hard it is for her. Is there something we can do to make it better? I can make dinner and you guys can come here to get out of the house. We can put something together to celebrate your dad and have an entire night dedicated to crying and eating cake."

This is an instance of my mouth moving faster than my brain. I blurted out a tentative solution without considering the implications or expectations.

"I'm not sure what she'll be up for, but I can suggest it to her."

*Please say no, please say no.*

"Okay. Let me know."

"That's really sweet of you to offer. I'm sure that alone will make her happy. She hasn't stopped talking about you since last time you were over."

I went to Theo's last week for dinner and his mom asked so many questions about my family, schooling, and writing. She was fascinated by the concept of homeschooling and by my sister's triplets. Theo was telling her about his interaction with the boys, which made Carlota laugh and start calling him a giant.

Our time together was enjoyable, and my departure was not in haste as it was the time before, so the evening was a better representation of me, and not my anxiety—even though my anxiety is always hanging around. We're a two-for-one deal.

Still, even after a nice visit, hearing that she's been talking about me makes me nervous.

"What does she say about me?" *You can't ask that. It's not your place. If she wanted you to know, she'd say it to you. Don't make things awkward for Theo.* "Sorry, never mind. Forget I asked."

Theo snickers through the phone. "You worry too much. She tells me how great you are, but I don't need reminding."

Now it's my turn to laugh. "Ha! Theo, seriously. You don't have to tell me, but don't make things up. No greatness to be found here."

"You're wrong there. But listen, I'm sorry to cut this short. I have to get back to work and complete some stuff. We can finish your cover design when I come over tonight, okay?"

I had no idea when I agreed to let Theo handle my marketing that I was also hiring a talented graphic designer. He's been studying different cover designs, creating one masterpiece after the next, but so far, none of them has been perfect. We're getting close, though.

"Okay. I'll make dinner and see you when you get here."

"*Mi Alma*, I love you." I can hear his smile through his voice, and it adds one to my face, too.

"I love you too."

By five-thirty, Theo is walking across my patio just as I finish making a pot of chili. He's surprised me by tolerating the vegetarian food I make without complaint. I'm convinced there's nothing he complains about, ever. He just goes with the flow and makes the best of every situation.

Bond and I welcome Theo, each with our own standard greeting; Bond with his ear scratches, me with a kiss.

Theo holds me in his arms and whispers in my ear, "Do you have any idea how much I love coming home to you?"

His words send a delicious shiver down my spine. I know my condo isn't his home, technically, but he comes here most days after work, and it feels more like a home with him here. For a moment, I allow myself to imagine a time in the future when we will share a home, a life, a bed. That jolts me from his arms before I travel down that path any further and allow things to get out of hand.

"What's wrong?"

"Nothing." Nothing at all, Theo. Just imagining taking you to bed. I roll my eyes at myself.

He notices. "Do you not want me coming here?"

Ah, shoot. Now he's misunderstanding my reaction and assumes the complete opposite of what I was thinking. "Of course I do. I was rolling my eyes at myself for something stupid. I love having you here."

He tilts himself back to get a better view of my face. "If you need more time alone, just tell me  I don't want to invade your space."

"No, Theo. That's not what I was thinking at all."

He steadies me with one hand on each shoulder. "What was it, then? Because it looks like you're annoyed with me."

I take a long exhale, leaning my head back until I'm looking at the ceiling, and close my eyes. "Ugh. That's not it." I bring my head back to face him for a second, but look away, embarrassed to admit where my mind was focused. "I was imaging what it would be like to share a home with you." My eyes flick back to meet his. "And a bed."

His eyes widen. "Oh."

Crickets.

"See. I told you I wasn't annoyed. Now I had to make things awkward." I pull my hands up to cover my face.

Theo gently removes them before leaning in to give me a kiss. "*Mi Alma*, I've thought about both of those things. A lot. *A lot*, a lot." He kisses me again with an intensity like never before. His hands rake through my hair, pulling me closer, kissing me deeper. When he pulls away, resting his forehead on mine, he smiles. "We'll get there one day. For now, your man's gotta eat."

I chuckle, grateful he broke some tension that was crackling through the air. "This way. Sit. I'll get you food."

We walk to the dining table, me leading him by the hand. Chili is not a couch meal, so he takes a seat and I return with two bowls and a plate of garlic bread.

"Yep. I could get used to this." His wide smile showcases his white teeth and wrinkles around his eyes.

"Me too."

The rest of our dinner conversation is less serious, talking about his grand ideas for my book launch and telling me about the new cover tweaks he's made.

Once I finish the dishes, we settle in the family room, where he pulls out his laptop to show me the new cover ideas. As soon as he pulls up one image, I exclaim, "That's the one!"

"Yeah? This was my favourite, too. You were right about adding the silhouette in the background."

"Theo, this is amazing. It's a perfect mix of quirky and funny, but still has a spy element to it. I love everything about it."

"I guess it's settled then." He closes the laptop as fast as he opened it, tosses it on the coffee table, and tackles me back on the couch. His body is pressed against mine and his weight on me should feel suffocating, but it's possibly the most at ease I've ever been. In between short, sweet kisses, he tells me, "I love you so much. You know that, right?"

"I do." The moment of serenity feels like pure bliss.

"Is the invitation to have us over this weekend still on the table? Because my mom said she'd love to."

Bliss is cut short. Time to panic.

Solana and Carlota arrive alongside Theo at 6pm on the dot. Charley has also been invited, and I'm curious how he and Bond will get along. We've been wanting to introduce them for a while but waited for the snow to melt and temperatures to warm so if they aren't automatic best friends, we could take one or both outside to sort out their differences.

I have no idea what to expect out of tonight, but ready or not, it's happening. The food is prepared, and I've sufficiently doubted my cooking skills for the past three hours. I'd be devastated if it was all awful and I ruined the evening. I added some personal touches to my living room for tonight and as I see the foursome walk toward my door, I have a ball of anxiety in my stomach, fearing I've overstepped. Just as I decide I shouldn't take the chance and want to hide everything, a knock and a smile comes from the other side of the patio door.

Bond is eager to meet his new friend, disregarding the humans and taking to Charley as soon as I open the door. The four of us laugh at their eager introduction, Bond keen on letting Charley into his home. I greet Carlota first, and she thanks me for having them with tears in her eyes. This is going to be an emotional evening. Solana pulls me in for a hug next, and despite me being as huggable as a cactus, she embraces me just the same as the first few times we met.

I welcome Theo with a quick peck after his mom and sister turned to face the dogs in a not-so-covert attempt at giving us a second of privacy. Every time I see Theo, I feel a flutter in my stomach, but not from nervous energy. There's a level of comfort, familiarity, and acceptance in our relationship now, and I'm just happy to have him around.

He lifts his head to scan the room and his eyes lock on the item I wanted to rush to hide.

"I'm sorry. I wanted to put it away, but you guys were already on the patio, so I didn't have time." My teeth bite into my bottom lip, and I'm afraid of how his mom will respond. She doesn't hesitate to go over and inspect my added touch. Now the butterflies in my stomach are on account of nerves.

"Did you make these, *hija*?" Carlota asks, staring at the decor.

"I did, and I overstepped. I'm so sorry."

She spins and walks toward me as I'm still standing by the front door, and I assume she's headed my way to slap me. My body goes rigid, waiting for the assault.

*Idiot.*

When Carlota is mere inches away, I wince, anticipating a sting on my cheek, but instead, she embraces me, squeezing me tight enough I can't take a deep breath.

"*Mami*, you're not an anaconda. Give Isla some room to breathe, yeah?"

"I'm sorry, *hija*. This is beautiful. Thank you for including my Lloyd tonight. I can't tell you how much this means to me."

I glance up at Theo, looking for an indication of whether I heard her correctly. He's smiling and I'm confused.

Carlota leads me by the hand across the room, stopping in front of the collage I assembled from Theo and Solana's Facebook photos of their dad. In every single image, he's smiling. The picture I saw of him in their living room is included and aside from the family photos of the four of them, that one is my favourite.

"The first thing that attracted me to my husband was his smile. He smiled all day long, even toward the end when he was sick."

Theo has his dad's smile, so I can empathize with her. Each time he smiles at me, my breath hitches. I'll never tire of seeing it.

"He was such a wonderful man and I'm grateful I had as much time as I did with him, but my heart feels empty without him here."

Theo walks up behind us, wrapping one arm around each of us. "We all feel a little empty without him, *Mami*, because he filled up so much."

That's all it takes for the real tears to start. I thought we'd at least make it to dessert, but I had to ruin everything by making my guests emotional. This is why I can't trust myself to make new friends or host family gatherings. I'm always bound to misjudge situations and make a mess of everything.

My body is tense, my fists and jaw clench. I can't find words and I have an overwhelming urge to run away, but this is my house. That's not an option.

"Are you guys ready to eat?" I slide out from under Theo's arm, needing to get some space. There's not a lot of space to be had, but I have to distract myself from the crushing weight of disappointment before my switch flips and there's no returning. "I'll get everything set up. Make yourselves at home," I add as I scramble across the room, bumping into furniture I've navigated around for years.

The dogs are both in the kitchen sniffing around. Can't say I blame them, but they'll have to wait for leftovers. At least if the food is awful, it won't go to waste, because Bond will eat anything.

After a few moments of solitude in the kitchen, my social battery is recharging, and I try to put any expectations for the evening out of my mind. Everyone takes a seat around the dining table, Theo and his mom on the opposite side from Solana and me, and we feast on a variety of South African dishes inspired by Lloyd, including bobotie, couscous, and egg chutney. Aside from the egg dish, everything else was new to me, but it was important to me to include Lloyd in the evening every way I could. He might not physically be here, but his impact on the trio at my dining table is obvious.

"*Hija*, this is all delicious. I know my Lloyd would have been impressed. He would have loved you." Her eyes well up with tears again, but they don't get a chance to fall.

"I know I do." Theo looks directly at me with a subtle smile that makes it clear his declaration is genuine.

Admitting our love for each other to our families seems like a level up in our relationship. That's not even a conversation I've broached with my family because they'll be planning our wedding and naming our babies. It's a serious step getting others emotionally invested.

Regardless, Carlota's tears dried up at hearing Theo's words and her expression turned from sad to elated. "*Mijo*, I'm so happy. There's nothing I want more for my children than to find the love of someone wonderful."

"Too bad he found me," I blurt before clapping my hand over my mouth.

Theo looks hurt and Carlota pins me with a terrifying, yet compassionate glare.

"I couldn't imagine anyone more wonderful for my son. This year has been hard on us, but you've given him something no one else could." She pauses for a moment as if she's waiting for me to complete her sentence myself, but I've got nothing. "Happiness. You've made him happy when we had little to be happy about, *hija*."

Maybe that's true, but is happiness all he needs? Am I enough for Theo? Can I be everything he deserves? I don't know, and I'm not sure how to measure that. If love were enough—if happiness were enough—things would never be complicated. It's the whole range of emotions that complicate dynamics, and I'm not sure Theo is processing the rest of his *beyond* happiness when he's around me. Or when he's around his family, for that matter.

Watching him tonight, each time any of us became emotional, he swooped in to offer comfort. His mind is forever in "fix it" mode, and he jumped in to repair broken hearts however he could. Perhaps that's his way of dealing with losing his dad—trying his best to heal everyone else.

I spend the rest of the evening lost in my head, as per usual, and Theo plays his part as the supportive son, brother, and boyfriend. I question every time his expression changes, because sometimes there's a split second of sadness before he switches back to strong, resilient Theo.

When everyone gathers to leave, his mother thanks me for a lovely evening, before she and Solana walk out onto the patio. It's a nice night out, so I take a moment to speak to Theo in private.

"Are you okay?"

"Of course, I'm okay. I'm always okay with you. More than okay."

"That's not what I mean. You know you can talk to me, right?"

"I do talk to you." He leans in, gives me a quick kiss, and turns to grab the door handle. "Thank you for this. It meant a lot to all of us. But don't worry about me. I'm fine."

Fine. The universal word that almost always means the opposite of its definition.

Now that the cover for my book is settled, Theo has really started pushing the marketing. I don't know where he's even found the time with his work and volunteer schedule, but there's never been a day when I haven't been his priority.

He encouraged me to approach a few of my favourite bookstores on my own with the press release he already created, so after five days of stressing over it, I finally made the move. I was disappointed when none of them were interested in buying copies of my books, claiming as a first-time author, there was no way for them to promote it. I walked out feeling like a nobody and cried for two solid hours when I got home. Theo called to check how I made out later that day, and when I told him the outcome, he was equally gutted as I was.

The infuriating thing is that he called the same places the following day, and each store agreed to buy at least a few copies. Whether it was the repeat request that wore them down, or if he talked to different people, I'm not sure, but I can't help but think it was because they didn't take me seriously.

Whatever their reasoning, I'll let it go, but I have to admit, it hurts. I put so much into this book and have spent more than a decade of my life honing my craft in anticipation of this moment. I've read thousands of books, and never just for entertainment; I study them, noting things I like or don't, highlighting sections that are particularly beautiful or memorable, and now, assessing every potential bias I can find. I've worked for this, and their response made me feel like none of it mattered.

So, yeah, I will let it go—someday. That day's not today. I woke up this morning defeated and discouraged, so I didn't have the energy to cook. The last thing I want to do is talk to someone, though, so I got in my car to head to the fast-food restaurant a kilometre away with the touch screen ordering system.

I stand there staring at my options and recall reading an article about how these screens were swabbed and tested for different germs, and it was determined most of them had fecal matter on them. Gross, but still a better option than speaking to people. At least I can wash my hands afterward, but if I say something stupid, that'll stay with me for months. It's a risk I'm willing to take.

I return home with a bag of food big enough to feed four people, but I wasn't sure if I'd want lunch too, so I stocked up.

Theo is seated on the resin sofa on my patio with Bond patiently waiting on the other side of the door.

"Hey. What are you doing here?" His presence surprises me, but immediately my mood lightens.

He stands, reaching forward to take my food from my hands, making it easier for me to find my keys. "I had nothing to do at work, so I thought I'd drop by."

I stand on my tiptoes to welcome him with a kiss. "Sorry. I didn't want to cook, so I got food."

"You went through drive-thru?"

I laugh. "No. I used the touch screen thing."

He glances down at the bag. "Were you expecting someone else, or are you starving?"

We walk through the door and are greeted by my waggly tailed boy.

"I wasn't sure what I'd want and didn't know if I'd be up for making lunch, so I got a bit of everything."

After setting the food on the table and placating Bond, Theo asks, "Why? What's wrong?"

"No, nothing. I just didn't want to cook." I try to brush off his question, moving to unload the bag of food onto the kitchen island.

"Isla," he says in a calm but stern voice. "Tell me."

I tilt my head and look back at him. "Nothing."

He steps around the island, wrapping his arms around me from behind, resting his chin on my shoulder. "Something is bothering you. Is it something with Rory?"

My stomach flips at the mention of her name. I've been pushing past my grief and focusing on my book launch because this book is just as much a part of her as it is me, but I'd be lying if I said my latest bookstore encounter didn't make me feel like I'm failing her.

"Not really. I mean, kind of, I guess. Really, it's nothing."

He kisses my cheek and speaks, blowing his breath across my ear. The sensation makes me shiver and is very distracting. "Talk to me."

"Ugh. Fine." On one hand, I appreciate that he wants me to talk so badly, but part of me is irritated because he doesn't reciprocate, and I can't push him. I also hate constantly unloading my stupidity on him because I'm afraid I'll drive him away. "I walked into that bookstore, dressed the part, practiced what I was going to say, faced my fears and I tried, Theo. It was so freaking hard for me, and I really put myself out there."

"I know you did."

"And what did they tell me? They said exactly what Nancy did. I'm not enough. I'm a nobody and they're not interested in nobodies."

"You are enough. They did agree to buy your books."

"Yeah, they did. Once *you* called. A simple phone call was all it took for you to accomplish what I stressed about for days. I probably would have felt better if they said no to you too, and I assumed it was the book they weren't interested in. But it was me. Me, they had the problem with."

"Isla, that's not true. You know what I think?"

I'm getting more irritated by the second now that I've opened up this conversation and he seems to brush the reality under a rug. "Please, Theo. Mansplain it to me. Tell me what you think."

He releases me from his hold and walks to the other side of the island, putting space between us. The reaction makes my anger shrink. I have no right being frustrated with him, yet he's being supportive and still gets the brunt of my anger. Some girlfriend I am.

His hardened face looks back at me, pinning me with his eyes. "I *think* you faced your fears, and that took a lot of guts, but maybe you were too in your head. It's possible that you were thinking too much and selling yourself instead of your book."

"Sell myself?" I shriek. "Like I'm a prostitute? Thanks. Yeah, thanks a lot for that." I stomp off into the family room wanting some space, but Theo trails behind, backpedalling.

"That's not what I meant, and you know it. I'd never say something like that."

Probably true, but now I'm so stuck in my head I can't think straight.

"What I'm saying is that because of your anxiety, you focus too much on what people think of you. When I approached them, I only told them about the book and how great it is. For me, even though I take the success of your book seriously, it's not personal. I didn't pour my soul into it."

Maybe he's right. I'm taking it too personally because I have an ingrained fear of people disliking me or of disappointing them. I close my hands over my face, leaning forward for my elbows to rest on my knees. Why do I have to make everything so complicated? Why can't I just be happy Theo sold my books after all?

"I'm sorry. This isn't your fault, and this is why I didn't want to talk about it. I knew I was being stupid."

"You're not being stupid. I get it. I've had situations at work when I tried to approach someone and they turned me down flat, but then as soon as the white guy next to me asked, it was approved. But I've learned that most of those times it was my approach, and not because of my skin colour. The few times it *was* because I'm black, I realized they weren't worth my time anyway, so I don't waste any more on them."

"That's awful."

"It is awful, but it's the world. Other people's reactions are out of our hands, but we can keep trying to be the best we can and finding good people who accept our skills and talents without prejudice over something we can't control."

He disappears for a second and returns with a plastic tray of pancakes. "Eat and then we can go do something that will make you smile, because this sad Isla"—he circles his hand around the air in front of me—"makes me want to punch someone and we can't have that."

Just then, my phone rings, making me jump. I glance down to see a familiar photo and answer with a smile, already feeling tension leave my body. "Hey, Chels. What's up?"

I listen to her request for a moment before replying, "Oh, yeah. Sure. I'll check with him, but five should be fine."

Some of the tension returns when I end the call, facing Theo. "Are you up for dinner at my sister's?"

When the door to Chelsea and Liam's house swings open, the soothing sounds of the outdoors are drowned out by utter chaos. I'm used to this reception, but Theo looks like his flight mode has activated. I squeeze his hand before releasing it to hug my sister and brother-in-law.

"Theo, so glad you could make it. We've wanted to invite you guys for a while, but Miss Big-Time-Author over here kept brushing us off." Liam issues me a knowing smirk because he loves embarrassing me.

"There's not even a little truth in that statement. Don't listen to him." Chelsea swats Liam on the shoulder and gives him a side-eye glare.

The boys finally look up from their intense wrestling match and notice company arrived. Linco n and Hudson run directly for me, but Lenox beelines for Theo.

"Giant guy!" He wraps his arms around Theo's leg, and I'm a little jealous because Lenox was always the first to welcome me. "I been eating aww of my dinner and sweeping wike you told me."

"I can tell. You're getting big! I hardly recognized you."

Lenox's smile is so wide, his chubby cheeks turn his eyes into slits. I've never seen him so happy.

Once the boys detach themselves, we move into the living room, where Lenox firmly plants himself on Theo's lap. I give Theo a questioning look to make sure he's okay with the attention, but his beaming face tells me he's not just okay with it, he's enjoying it.

Lenox tells Theo all about school life and the ins and outs of preschool. He recites his alphabet, counts to twenty, and reads a shapes and colours book cover to cover, then floors me with his declaration about his girlfriend, Melody. He's so caught up in proving to Theo how grown up he is, I realize how grown up they *are* getting. I've spent the past five months isolating myself and not visiting as frequently as I should have been, that I missed these huge milestones. My baby nephews turned into little boys.

Life doesn't stop moving because you're grieving.

"So, only a couple of weeks until the big day. How are you feeling?" Liam asks me from his perch on the arm of the sofa, his arm draped behind Chelsea's head.

"Excited." That's a lie. "Nervous. I sent the book out to advance readers two weeks ago and reviews have started coming in. So far everyone has had good things to say, but I'm waiting for the critics to speak up and deflate my ego."

"Or, it really is amazing, and everyone will love it," Chelsea adds.

"Chels, be realistic. I'm a brand-new author that no one has ever heard of. Even the all-time greats have haters. I'm expecting some of my own."

"This may be the first thing you've published, but you've been working towards this your entire life. Don't get so caught up in expecting the negative that you forget to enjoy all the positive feedback you're getting. It takes a lot of guts to put yourself out there and you deserve to lap up the praise you get." My sister, just like my mom, is always full of these nuggets of wisdom, wanting everyone else to be their own biggest fan, yet they doubt themselves as much as I do. Sure, she has a point, but that doesn't mean I can switch my brain from dwelling on potential one-star reviews to embracing the five-stars.

"Dis my fabourite book," Lenox interjects, holding up a book with a rainbow-haired penguin.

"*Spike, the Penguin with Rainbow Hair*," Theo reads aloud. "That sounds like a great one."

Lenox nods, leafing through the worn pages. I stare at him in awe and for a moment allow myself to imagine my writing having that kind of impact on someone. Maybe one day a random reader will clutch one of my books to their chest and reminisce about how the words inside the pages touched a part of them.

It's unlikely, but it's a nice thought.

"How's work going for you, Theo?" Liam redirects the conversation and I'm brought back to reality.

"Same old. Doing a job I care nothing about just to pay the bills. Marketing for Isla's book has been the one thing I've been excited about. I shouldn't complain because I'm grateful to be employed, but I wish I had as much excitement about all aspects of work, you know?"

"Yeah, man. I get it. I've had times when I resented my job, but we have to stick it out sometimes to survive." He stands and gestures with his hand for Theo to follow him. "Come with me."

Theo looks at me and I give him a nod of encouragement. Liam is probably leading him to the man cave in the basement. A home gym, a big screen TV, and a wet bar.

"I'll be the designated driver," I call after Theo as he strides to catch up to Liam.

"Love you," he shouts in reply.

Chelsea gives me a "big-sister stare" with a smile playing at her lips. Much like the situation with Theo's mom, I have hesitations about involving family in our relationship yet. It's been two months since Theo and I first declared our love for each other, but I enjoyed that time when it was just the two of us. Things get more complex when other people are welcomed into that love bubble. Suddenly he goes from being my boyfriend to being part of the family because that's how my family works. They just love without barriers—without expectations.

"The L-word, huh? That's big."

My face flushes. "I guess. It feels big, but it doesn't. Like he's got the potential to hurt me more than anyone but loving him is the most natural thing to do. I don't know how to explain it."

Chelsea's Cheshire Cat smile tells me she knows what I mean. "You explained it perfectly. You know how hard it was for me to let my guard down and trust people. It took me a lot longer to come to the same realization, but once I did, there was no stopping it. Liam could crush me like a grape, but I trust him not to." She leans forward to the table, popping a literal grape in her mouth from the appetizer tray. "If my opinion means anything, I think Theo is a good catch."

"I think so too. Lenox seems to like him."

With a laugh bordering on a cackle, Chelsea agrees. "After our anniversary party, he talked about 'the giant man' for days. I kept thinking he'd forget about him, but every night he ate his dinner and went to bed without complaint, which made the other boys follow suit. He's a low-key super nanny without being present."

I can hear the boys down in the basement and it sounds like they've got a game of monster happening. There's a lot of roaring and screaming. Picturing Theo and Liam running around pretending to be mean creatures makes me laugh because they couldn't be more opposite.

"Can I tell you something without you getting mad at me?" Chelsea asks.

"Have we not learned *not* to approach questions this way?"

"Sorry. It's just..." She grabs another few grapes, eating each one before she continues, leaving my anxiety to grow exponentially. "You and Rory, you were two peas in a pod."

I nod. This is not news.

"And I think you got so comfortable being in that pod, you got stuck there."

"What do you mean?"

"Don't take this the wrong way because I'm torn up about Rory too. All I'm saying is that you got trapped in your comfort zone being 'Rory's best friend' instead of being Isla. The past few months, you've grown more as Isla than you have since you were a pre-teen. You've taken charge of your career instead of letting yourself be pushed around. You've gone out and done things you never would have done. You're even living alone, which you never would have considered before. All I'm saying is that I'm proud of you."

Is she right? Did I get so consumed by being Rory's best friend that I lost sight of myself? Does letting go of that attachment mean I'm glad she's gone? I can't accept that. I refuse to relegate her to my memories and keep her locked away there as I blossom into a new version of Isla.

Rory encouraged me to chase my dreams and cheered me on when I made an effort. She had confidence in me that I didn't, and I in her. Is that why we became so co-dependent? We fuelled each other in ways we couldn't fuel ourselves?

Chelsea's words were well meaning, and, to some extent, she is right, but I can't help guilt from pouring on with the thought of how I've left Rory in my past. Her things may be gone from my home and her physical presence from my life, but her impact will be felt forever. If I change too much, there's a risk of that disappearing.

I realize I've been staring off into space, running my internal monologue when Chelsea says, "I'm sorry if I upset you. You know how much we loved Rory, so I don't want you to misunderstand what I'm saying. All I wanted to say is that I'm proud of you for not letting losing her break you."

Then why do I feel so broken right now?

After a short while, giving me time to come to terms with Chelsea's comments, she asks me to help her get dinner ready. It doesn't take long since she prepared everything in advance, so thirty minutes later, she calls up the boys to eat. The little ones come charging upstairs, jockeying for position amongst each other to be the first to the kitchen. A stern warning from Chelsea reduces the clamouring to murmurs and hushed shouts.

"I'm sitting beside Uncle Teo," Lenox declares as Liam and Theo arrive at the top of the stairs.

He climbs up in the seat beside Theo with no clue how his acceptance of the man I love warms my heart and terrifies me all at the same time. The same fears I had when Theo declared his love for me in front of his mom come flooding back with a paralyzing force. Our love is no longer just about the two of us. There are other hearts on the line too.

As if it's the most natural thing to do, Theo reaches over to help Lenox cut up his food and encourages him to eat everything on his plate. Lenox complies, talking with mouthfuls of food, despite Liam's repeated reminders about table manners. None of us can be bothered though because he's so happy, it's impossible not to smile at him as he babbles on.

I glance up behind Liam where he's seated at the head of the table and notice Theo's anniversary gift with a prominent place in their dining room. I smile and can't help but draw attention to it. "Nice artwork."

Everyone turns to look; even Liam, who spins around to peek before turning back to face Theo.

"It's my favourite part of the dining room," Chelsea adds.

"It's okay if you hang it just to make me feel better but take it down when I leave." Theo chuckles, and it's the first time I recall a self-deprecating comment from his mouth.

"Are you kidding? I made Liam hang it as soon as we got home that night and it hasn't budged. We really love it." She leans toward Theo but she's still a few feet away, so she whisper-shouts, "Don't tell Isla, but it was my favourite gift of the day."

I giggle. "Gee thanks. Five-hundred-dollar camera is no match for Brendon Urie."

"The man is a legend," Liam adds.

"And legends never die," Chelsea replies, and they both laugh over the lyrics from another *Panic! At the Disco* song.

We fall back into comfortable conversation and having Theo as part of the family seems right. Like no one else could ever walk in these doors and fit as well as he does. Everything is going so well.

Too well.

"Uncle Teo, did you know…" Lincoln shovels a heaping spoonful of potatoes in his mouth. "My dad is the bestest eber?" His eyes widen, waiting for Theo's reply.

"I did know that, buddy. He's pretty awesome."

Liam's reaction is priceless as he sits with a toothy grin, watching the conversation in his honour take place.

"Is your daddy a giant too?" Hudson asks.

I freeze, dropping my fork onto my plate with a clank.

Theo's smile falters for the first time all day. "He was a giant, yeah. And you know what else?"

Hudson nods, waiting for the answer.

"He was the bestest, too."

My heart is tight in my chest. Theo's bright smile is reduced to a thin line as he stares at his plate, pushing his food around. I know that grief-induced loss of appetite well. Chelsea shoots me an apologetic look, but there's nothing to be sorry for. The boys were just curious about "Uncle Teo" and wanted to learn more about him.

However, looking at Theo's face, my spot on the opposite side of the table might as well be a thousand miles away. I want to reach out to him, comfort him, encourage him, in the ways he's done for me, but before I have the chance, he schools his expression and picks up conversation as if his heart didn't just shatter into a thousand shards.

He reroutes the topic, getting the boys talking about their favourite TV shows and superheroes, which ends up in a shouting match, each of them trying to talk over the other, until Liam settles them down and establishes a system for taking turns.

When dinner is finished, Theo is smiling and laughing, but I recognize that pained expression when his smile doesn't reach his eyes. He's putting on a good front, but that question about his dad rattled him. I don't want to call him out in front of everyone, so I decide to wait until we drive home.

He and Liam go back downstairs and talk about who-knows-what. There's bound to be some whisky poured, but I hope it will help Theo relax. Maybe he'll open up to Liam. His dad nearly died years ago from a heart attack and Liam took it really hard. I'm sure if anyone can understand the dynamic between father and son, it's him.

Chelsea and I sit in the living room talking about everything and nothing. She doesn't bring up any more emotional subjects, so we just cuddle the boys, listen to them yammer on about whatever their heart's desire, and digest the insane amount of food we ate.

When Liam and Theo return upstairs, Theo's eyes are bloodshot, and I'm not sure if it's from alcohol or tears. Either way, he looks like he's ready to go. I stand from my spot on the couch, kissing each of my nephews on the forehead and encouraging them to be good for their parents.

Chelsea and Liam walk us to the door, where we thank them for a nice evening. Chelsea apologizes to Theo for Hudson's curiosity, but Theo assures her it's fine. No one can be upset with the child for asking an innocent question.

During the drive to Theo's, he's quiet—too quiet. A few times, I open my mouth to speak but decide not to in order to avoid upsetting him. He's always so perceptive with my needs, he often knows before I do, and here I am floundering, not knowing how to formulate a simple sentence.

I think back to when his mom called me wonderful and can't help but feel a stab of contempt for myself knowing I'm anything but.

Two-hundred yards before we turn onto Theo's Street, I ask, "Are you okay?"

"I'm fine," he answers, staring out the passenger window.

Maybe he's just quiet because he had a few drinks, but fine doesn't sound fine.

"Are you sure?"

He turns to me with a straight face. "I'm fine. Promise." He clears his throat as we pull into his driveway. His emotional suit of armour is back on, prepared for life at home. I wish he'd try talking to his mom instead of bottling everything up, but there's nothing I can do to change his mind. He's a grown man and I can't force him to talk if he's not ready. There are so many things I want to encourage him to do, like pick up his guitar again, but I'm so afraid of upsetting him, I never mention it.

He's pushed me to move past things I wouldn't have without him, or at least not for a lot longer, and no doubt he's helped his mom with the same. She's sleeping in the master bedroom again, which I know was a huge step for her. She sorted through and donated her husband's clothing, short of a few things she wanted to keep. They spent an afternoon searching through pictures, and Theo designed a special photo book for her with her most precious memories.

"Thanks for today," he says as he opens the door.

No goodbye kiss? No "I love you"?

I could chase after him and demand he open up to me, but I don't.

My drive home is riddled with unshed tears and tension in my body. There's nothing more I want than to talk to Rory and ask her what to do. She might not have known, but she would have listened. Often rambling to her without interruption was exactly what I needed to figure things out for myself.

So, that's what I do. For the first time since she died, I pretend Rory is seated beside me in the passenger seat and I pour out my heart. I tell her about her song I found that feels like a secret part of her only I got to see. I talk about Theo and how in love with him I am, and I tell her how much I miss her. By the time I get home, it's as if I ran a marathon because the emotional toll that one-sided conversation took was heavy.

But for a moment, I felt like I had my best friend here, and when the realization hits when I walk into my condo to find she's not there, my grief consumes me more viciously than ever before, because I know she's never coming back.

The day after I dropped Theo home from Chelsea and Liam's, he called me as if nothing happened. He didn't acknowledge that he hopped out of my car without a backwards glance. He didn't mention why he was so distant, nor try to explain why he pushed me away. It didn't sit right with me, but I didn't know what else to do.

We're two weeks out from my book launch and he's been all business. The past three nights he hasn't come by after work, claiming he had stuff to do at home. That's fine, but until that day at the Davis household, he'd always made time for me. I'm not sure what I did wrong, or how to fix it, and I'm not sure how to approach him about it.

My phone dings and I look down to see a text from Theo. That's another new thing; instead of calling, he's been texting, and I never thought I'd miss phone calls so much.

**Theo: Want to go to open mic night at Mad Dog on Saturday?**

Not really. That sounds like a miserable evening, but I don't want to upset him more.

**Isla: Sure. What time?**

He doesn't reply for a while, so I busy myself checking emails, reading a few more reviews that have trickled in, trying to get excited about the responses I've received, but nothing feels good right now.

A full hour passes before my phone dings again.

**Theo: Meet me there at 8.**

Meet him there? So, we're not even going together? He knows how I feel about showing up at places alone. *Isla, you idiot.* I asked to drive myself last time, so now I'm getting upset over situations I asked for. *What do you expect from him when you can't make up your own mind?*

With no work for me to do, I whistle for Bond and ask if he wants to go for a walk. His wagging tail tells me it's a brilliant idea. The weather is warm, but not hot right now, so it's a perfect time to take advantage of the outdoors.

I pull on my sneakers and leash Bond, then walk outside to a breeze cooler than I expected. It'll be fine. Bond can't walk far, so we won't be long.

I peek around the patio to make sure no one is in the parking lot. The last thing I want is to be caught up in small talk with one of my many elderly neighbours. Most of the people living in this building are in their sixties or older—a feature my dad probably chose on purpose. The coast is clear, so Bond and I venture off through the parking lot, onto a walking trail that runs past the waterfalls.

We're about a mile from home, admiring the falls, when a mist lands on my face. I assume it's spray from the raging waters, but that doesn't make sense. Realization hits me as the sky opens up and a downpour starts. I try to run, but my old dog is tired and unfazed by the water.

I pull the back of my thin yoga jacket over my head to stop my hair from getting wet, but within minutes, my clothes are soaked through. Bond is dawdling along despite my pleas to pick up the pace, but I can't be upset with the poor guy. I pick him up to carry him home, thinking that would be faster, but a ninety-pound German shepherd is a lot different from a couple of eight-pound chihuahuas. I don't make it more than fifteen feet, and I'm impressed I made it that far.

With no choice but to drag my tired dog home or wait out the storm, we seek shelter under a stranger's awning. We stand on a random porch belonging to a house with no vehicles in the driveway and pray no one shows up while I'm standing here. I'm panicked someone will be angry with me, but my clothes are drenched, I'm shivering, and my dog can't budge.

For Bond's sake, I pull out my phone, drying it as best I can with my t-shirt, and dial.

"Hey." He doesn't sound excited to be hearing from me.

"Theo, I need your help."

I hear a loud noise in the background and guess it was his chair falling over. "Are you okay? What's wrong?"

As soon as he asks, I babble an emotional run-on sentence. "I'm fine. I… I wanted to get out of the house, so I took Bond for a walk, but I didn't know it was going to rain, and now he's too tired so he can't walk anymore, and I'm soaked, and I'm standing on a stranger's porch hiding from the rain, and I'm afraid they're going to come home and find me here…"

"Tell me the address, and I'll come get you."

"I don't want you to get in trouble with work. I'm so sorry. Never mind."

"Send me the address. I won't get in trouble, okay?"

"Okay. I'll text you."

Seven minutes later, Theo pulls into the driveway of the house I'm seeking shelter at and jumps out of his SUV holding an umbrella. He passes the umbrella to me, greets Bond, and scoops him up like he's a chihuahua. I swear it's not that easy. Once we're safely in the car, he turns the heat on full blast.

"Are you cold?"

"I'm fr... freezing." My entire body is convulsing from the cold dampness.

Theo notches the car into reverse and directs his car toward my condo. He doesn't speak until we're a few hundred yards away. Déjà vu. "I'm sorry for the past few days. I really have been busy, but I should have made time for you."

"It's fine." It's not, but I have nothing else to say until he does.

He pulls into the guest parking spot, and I press unlock, hop out into the cold rain, and open the back door for Bond to get out. My poor boy is soaked too and looks disappointed in his short car ride.

Before Bond hops out, Theo is standing beside me. "Let me carry him in. He's tired."

I don't argue. As much as I'm upset, I'd do anything for my dog. I never should have taken him out.

We walk into my condo, where I toe off my shoes and rush to grab a towel for Bond. Theo grabs my hand before I can go anywhere and pins me against the door with a kiss. Every illogical part of me wants to melt into him and forget how distant he's been the past few days, but the miniscule bit of logic I have pushes him away.

He looks dejected, as if he thought one kiss could make me ignore the past few days. This isn't *Sleeping Beauty*. Kisses don't fix things.

"I'll see you Saturday?" he asks, without acknowledging the widening gap between us.

"Yeah. Thanks."

I never expected that going to my sister's house would result in the emotional distance created between Theo and me. Between Chelsea's revelation about my dependence on Rory and Hudson's questions about Lloyd, it seems Theo and I are spiraling into renewed waves of grief, unable to reach solid land together.

When I wake up the next morning with a raging head cold, I couldn't be happier. Who in their right mind would be happy for excess snot and a pounding headache? Someone who wants a legitimate excuse to avoid social interaction. AKA, me.

I text Theo to let him know I won't make it to open mic night, but judging by how he ran out of here yesterday, I doubt he'll be bothered.

It's not long after my text that I hear a knock at the door. I'm not expecting anyone, and I look like the Ghost of Christmas Past, so I'm not answering.

The relentless knocking continues for a minute, then my phone rings. Nope, not answering that either. My head hurts. Final straw is a text message notification.

**Theo: Can I come in?**

Oh great. I've been the bottom of his priority list all week and now he wants to come see me?

I drag myself to the door with a furry grey blanket draped over my head. The last thing I want to be doing is getting out of my bed.

Theo steps inside. "Oh, *Mi Alma*." He places a hand on my forehead and pulls it back like I burned him. "You've got a fever. Do you have any medicine? Soup? What do you need?"

"Sleep." I turn and walk back to my bedroom, unsure why he's here, but without enough energy to converse, I don't ask.

My head is so stuffy, I don't even hear his footsteps behind me until I climb into my bed and see him a few feet away in my bedroom doorway.

"I've got the plague. You should hide somewhere it's safe."

He chuckles. "I'll take my chances. I can work from here today, so I'll be around if you need anything."

"Theo."

"Yes?"

"Why *are* you here?"

He walks into my room and sits on the bed beside me, pulling my duvet up to my chin. "I love you and I want to take care of you."

"It hasn't felt like you love me."

He winces, hearing my words. "Isla..."

"No, it's find, Theo."

"Find?" His eyes light up and he smirks. The nerve. I have half a mind to cough on him.

"I'm stuffy. Sue me. Point is, I'm sick and miserable. Now isn't a great time for heart-to-hearts."

"Get some sleep." He leans over to kiss my burning forehead. "I'll be in the living room if you need me."

I always need him, and that scares me.

**M**y eyes flutter open hours later and I'm feeling better than I did. I'm still congested and my body aches in places I didn't know I had, but rest helped. Before leaving my room, I step into a steaming hot shower, hoping it will open up my sinuses. The steaming water beats down over my head and I remember Theo said he'd be around if I needed him, but I haven't heard him for hours.

I towel off and put on a fresh pair of pyjamas, unconcerned with my appearance right now. We might only be dating, but now's as good a time as any to test out the whole "in sickness and in health" bit.

Me and my red nose amble our way to the kitchen but spot Theo's laptop on the coffee table in the family room as I walk by. I guess he's still here.

"Theo?"

"Here, *Mi Alma*."

I find Bond's wagging tail before I see Theo standing at the kitchen island, chopping an onion. He scrapes at his eyes with the back of his hand, greeting me with a smile.

"How are you feeling?"

Ignoring the question, I ask, "What's all this?" I take in the scene of my kitchen, and it appears a tornado has ripped through. There is onion skin, carrot peels, garlic cloves, herbs, and empty containers strewn about the space.

"I'm making you Mediterranean white bean soup. Bear with me though because I don't know what I'm doing."

He's making me soup? From scratch? That's an automatic pass on the "in sickness and in health" test.

"Theo, this is amazing. Can I help?"

"You can help by going to lie on the couch and pick a movie for us to watch when I'm done. You're not lifting a finger until you're cured."

My lips curve into a smile. "Is your mom this bossy when you get sick?"

He gives a one-sided grin and a raised eyebrow from his position at the stove. "You have no idea."

I chuckle-snort, imagining Carlota Malinga being intense when loving her children.

I settle on the sectional sofa in my family room with Bond on the chaise and navigate the Netflix menu. Once I scroll to an option, it's an easy decision what we'll be watching.

Theo peeks his head around the corner. "Let me clean up and I'll be there in a second."

I could get used to house-boyfriend Theo.

Moments later, he's placing a steaming cup of tea on the table in front of me and settling in beside me. "I went to the store and got this special tea for colds. It's a mix of peppermint and some other magical stuff."

"I must have been unconscious because I didn't hear you leave."

"I took Bond for a walk too, but he didn't make it far. He planted himself in the grass about a kilometre away and refused to walk any more. I had to carry him home. That was before I left for the store, so I stopped at *Mullin's Pet Market* to pick up some glucosamine treats. Maybe that will help."

Making soup and going to the store for me is one thing, and I'm beyond grateful for that, but stopping at the pet store to pick up something to help my dog brings me to tears.

"Hey, what's wrong?"

"Noth… nothing." Sniffle. "I just appreciate you so much." Even if I am confused over the past few days.

He rubs his thumb across the back of my hand. "I wish I could kiss you right now. I'm tempted to take my chances with the plague."

A snot-tastic snort sounds from my nose. "Stay there and stay safe." I turn my hand over to clutch his massive hand in my clammy grip. "Ready to see a cinematic masterpiece?"

"I didn't peg you for a Schwarzenegger fan."

"*True Lies* was part of the inspiration for my book."

"Really? I didn't think you were a movie watcher."

"Not normally, no. But one night Rory and I were babysitting for Chelsea and Liam, so we raided Liam's old DVD collection. We watched *True Lies*, and I laughed so hard. It's so cheesy, and Harry apologizes so much. I joked that's what it would be like to have a Canadian spy. My friendship with Rory struck me with more inspiration and I knew I wanted to write something about two best friends, and there you have it." By the time I get all of that out, I'm out of breath.

Theo stares at me for a beat. "You can really find inspiration anywhere, huh?"

"No, it's not that easy. I mean, I write because I'm an observer. When people speak around me, I watch for things they don't say as much as the things they do. Their shifts in body language, micro-expressions, gestures. I'm not good at speaking to people, so writing is my way of communicating. Being able to craft a character's growth is pretty cool and understanding people's motivations and emotions is why the book is always better than the movie."

"How so?"

"When you watch a movie, you are seeing what the director wants you to see. Sure, everyone has their own perspective and takes away different things, but for the most part, it's the same. With a book, every reader is creating their own unique version of the story in their head. They're picturing characters in their own way, forming their own opinions on motivations and emotions. They're envisioning a story shaped by their imagination. Books make you think. Movies are entertainment."

"I never thought about it like that. I always just saw books as words, pages. Something that was forced on me to evaluate and be tested on. Books never seemed like entertainment."

I offer Theo a sympathetic smile because I know many people feel the same way. "I think that's an unfortunate side-effect of a lot of education models. Students read things to be tested on instead of enjoying it. As much as I love to read, if I'm told I *have* to read something, it takes the fun out of it." Now I'm really breathing heavy from talking and feeling exhausted. This is ridiculous. I just had a five-hour nap.

Theo hops off of the sofa and runs to the kitchen. He returns a minute later with a steaming bowl of soup. He sets it down in front of me, warning me it's "piping hot." Seeing how willing he is to care for me makes my heart soar and clench at the same time. I love him for wanting to look after me, but I want him to accept it in return. He still hasn't addressed why he's been so distant the past few days, but I can't force him to tell me. Now that he's so close again, I don't want to push him away by asking.

We cuddle together for the movie, and I laugh just as much this time around. I might be a book lover, but I can see the appeal in movies.

Part way through, Theo sweeps my hair from my forehead. "Your temperature has gone down."

"I think your soup and tea have cured me. I feel better already."

"Good thing because I really want to kiss you again." His tender smile makes me feel so loved. "I guess we're skipping open mic night this week, but they're doing it again next Saturday. We can catch that one instead."

Oh, great. Just when I thought a wicked head cold was my ticket out of the torture chamber known as *The Mad Dog Pub*, he goes and drops that on me.

"Do you not want to go?"

My expression must have given me away. "No, it's not that. Just… ugh."

"What is it?"

"Last time we were there, Shawna and Clair were talking crap about me in the bathroom, not knowing I was in there. Being around groups of people when I *assume* they hate me is hard enough but knowing they do makes it worse."

"They what? What did they say?"

"Never mind that. I know petty girls when I see them, but that doesn't mean I want to interact with them."

"You don't have to. If it makes any difference, those girls mean nothing to me. I know Clair has a thing for me, and it turns my stomach knowing she's dating my friend. They make no difference to me, though. You're the one for me, Isla Haynes, and it would mean a lot to me if you'd come with me next weekend."

After days of distance growing between us and having him here to look after me today, I can't say no. More importantly, I don't want to. He doesn't ask me for much, so if stepping out of my comfort zone to show up for him is what he wants, then I'll toughen up and show up.

"Okay, I'll go. As long as I don't have to sing." Even Bond's ears quirk at that comment because he's suffered through my singing voice more than anyone.

Theo's response, though, holds a hint of mischief, and I can't help but wonder what that's about.

When we walk into *The Mad Dog*, we find Theo's entire group of friends in the crowd. Shane is the first to greet us as we walk through the door, with Dean next in line. Randy and Shawna are cuddled together in a booth across from Mitchell, Brent, Clair, and a new face I don't recognize. The moment Clair makes eye contact with me, her gaze is intense enough to light me on fire. I'm used to being hyper-aware of people's eyes on me, but I've never felt outright despised.

"Theo," I whisper once there's a lull in greetings.

"Yeah?"

"Clair hates me. She's staring at me like I'm her mortal enemy."

He spins to face me, blocking me from Clair's view. "You are. I told you, she's had a thing for me forever and didn't make it a secret. She hates you because she can tell how much I love you. That's jealousy… it's got nothing to do with you and only tells me I made the right choice." With a quick kiss, he turns to face his table of friends and greets the rest of them, Clair included. He puts his arm around me, pulling me into view of everyone and adds, "You guys remember my girlfriend, Isla?"

"Yeah, the author, right?" Mitchell replies.

I issue a meek wave to everyone, avoiding the death-glare from Clair.

"This is my friend, Dominic," Mitchell adds, gesturing toward the newcomer at the end of the table whose back is toward us.

Dominic? Dominic and Mitchell?

"D-Dominic McKay?" I ask, but the words taste like chalk.

"Yeah. How'd you know that?" Dominic asks. His golden blond hair and sun-kissed skin make him look like a business-man surfer. When Rory described him, she always talked about his piercing blue eyes, so when he turns to face me and I see exactly what she was talking about, there's no doubt in my mind.

My knees buckle, but Theo still has an arm around me, so he squeezes my waist, keeping me from falling.

"Woah. Are you okay? What's wrong?"

"Dominic and Mitchell... Domi—" And my tears start. "Dominic and Mitchell were the guys Rory and I were supposed to meet for a date the day she died." I mean to whisper, but my emotions make my voice louder than expected. The whole table hears me.

*Everybody's watching.*

Dominic mutters a curse word before he pushes his chair out to stand. He places a hand on my shoulder. "Isla, I'm so sorry about Rory. I felt like a schmuck because I liked her for so long, but I was too chicken to ask her out. Then when I finally did..."

"Yeah."

He doesn't need to explain to me how that story ends. I was there; I watched how it played out. She bled out in front of me.

"She liked you too. For a year, all I heard about was Dominic this, and Dominic that." I snicker, but it sounds like a snot bubble. Cute.

"Hey, Theo. Could you imagine if I was here with your girl instead of you?" Mitchell adds. Not helpful.

Theo stares at him with an intensity he must have learned from Clair, who has been silent this entire time, but not taken her eyes off of me.

"*Mi Alma*, we can leave. If you're not up for tonight, we can go."

I shake my head, knowing how excited Theo was about watching the performances, and I need to push myself. Sure, I'm emotional, but Dominic is no more a reminder of what I lost than anything else that brings her to mind. I can get through this—as long as I don't cry any more in public. "It's fine. Just give me a minute."

I enter the bathroom, reminded of the last time I was here but push that memory away. Clair has no bearing on mine and Theo's relationship. I splash cold water on my face and freshen up, trying to mitigate the effects of my tears. Splotchy and red is not a cute look. Once I take a few breaths, I exit the ladies' room to find Theo, once again, waiting outside the door.

We walk hand-in-hand to our table with Shane and Dean, who are much more receptive to my company. Dean spends twenty minutes asking me about my book and the latest updates. I inform him my launch is a few days away and tell him about the event Theo has arranged at a bookstore. He surprises me by saying he'll attend, as does Shane.

Our conversation is tedious on account of me questioning every look, breath, or change in tone, but I keep it together. The bar owner makes his way to the stage to inform us the performances are about to start.

My mouth gapes open when the first performer is announced: my ol' buddy Death-Glare Clair.

She puts on a raunchy display, singing a shameless rendition of *The Boy is Mine* by Brandy and Monica—A cappella. The three men at my table chuckle as she pours her heart and soul into the song, but she's no Brandy. She's more like Fran Drescher with sinusitis. Still, I admire her tenacity.

Mercifully, the next few singers are skilled, and play passable covers of *Lean on Me* by Bill Withers, *Mr. Jones* by The Counting Crows, and *Tequila Sunrise* by The Eagles.

As the final lyrics of *Tequila Sunrise* blast through the speakers, Shane slides out his chair and I stare at him, wondering if he's going up on stage. That's surprise enough, but seconds later, Theo gets up to follow, only stopping to kiss my cheek on his way toward the stage.

What is he doing?

Shane and Theo both strap on acoustic guitars and strum a few chords from the stools on stage. I guess he didn't need me to push him to play again.

Theo leans into the microphone and speaks while looking at me, like no one else is in the room. "You'll have to bear with me tonight because I've never sung in front of anyone other than Shane here, and I think he's tone deaf."

"Hey!" Shane says in mock outrage.

Theo chuckles, but continues, "I'm stepping out of my comfort zone because I want to play a song on behalf of a woman I owe a debt of gratitude to."

Oh, please don't draw attention to me. Please, no.

"Rory, this one's for you."

That's not what I expected.

The duo strums along together in perfect unison, playing a melody I don't recognize, but as soon as Theo sings the first line, tears pour from my eyes. Again.

*"We were both shy when I first met you..."*

He's playing Rory's song. He's not only playing her song, he's playing a melody for her lyrics—lyrics she never shared.

Before he finishes the first bridge, I'm sobbing, and Dean moves to the chair beside me, placing an arm around my shoulders. "I didn't think he'd pick up a guitar again after his old man died."

I glance at Dean, but his eyes are fixed on his friends. Theo's smooth, breathy, effortless voice glides across the room, and everyone is captivated. It's like watching a rapture, and everyone is unknowingly gravitating toward him.

As I listen to the lyrics, knowing my best friend wrote them for me but she never shared them, this feels like a major invasion of Rory's privacy. She shared everything with me, and perhaps, if she didn't share this, it's because she wasn't ready for anyone to hear it. Or maybe she changed her mind about the lyrics and stuffed the scribbled-on paper in a drawer, never giving it a second thought.

There has to be a good reason I never heard her version.

As the song ends—which I am painfully aware of because I read Rory's lyrics at least a thousand times—I need to be alone. The crowd is closing in on me and I can't breathe.

Dean senses my distress and asks if I'm okay.

I shake my head. "Tell Theo I had to go, please?"

Dean's face looks sickened by my request.

*He hates you.*

That thought only makes me walk faster. I barely get a breath of fresh air when Theo calls behind me, "Isla, wait."

I stutter step, trying to regain the rhythm of a normal walking adult, but my entire body is vibrating with emotion. There's so much pent up everything in each cell, I'm struggling to tell up from down.

"That wasn't your place to sing her song. That was Rory's song." My words are muffled by renewed sobbing.

"It is. It will always be Rory's song, no matter who sings it." He braces himself against the wall, and the gesture has me nervous about what he's going to say next. "I know it hurts, but she's not here to share it with the world, and I thought she'd want everyone to know how amazing you are. That's why she wrote it. I wasn't taking it from her; I was sharing it *for* her. To thank her."

"It wasn't your place," I repeat, staring at my feet through the pooled water in my eyes.

"Okay, I'm sorry. It was a mistake for me to ambush you with that. It was my failed attempt at showing both her and my dad that they'll always have a place in our lives. I thought you'd like it." He scrubs his face with his hands. "After that day Hudson asked about my dad, I had an overwhelming urge to do something for him, and for Rory. That's why I seemed distant, because I was practicing every spare moment with Shane to do this for you."

Really, he was amazing, and I see his point, but I can't negate the sick feeling I have knowing Rory's words were shared and she may not have wanted them to be. Knowing that I can't ask her for clarification makes it so much worse.

Pushing himself off the wall, Theo adds, "I just thought lyrics from one person who loved you paired with the melody of someone else who loves you would be a beautiful song."

"*Gesundheit*." That's all I can say before I turn and walk away.

Like a coward.

I'm clacking away at my laptop with headphones in, listening to whatever doesn't remind me of Rory. Heavy metal, reggae, even a little polka; anything unlikely to feature an acoustic guitar solo. My book launch is only a few days away, and since I've successfully driven Theo from my personal life, our professional relationship has all but disintegrated.

There's supposed to be a book launch in my honour, but I'm not worthy of anything short of a kick in the teeth. Yeah, grief makes people do stupid things, but I must be approaching all-time stupidity levels.

I feel a presence in my room and turn to see my dad's head peeking in the door, so I remove my headphones to hear what he's saying.

"Can I come in for a second, Kiddo?"

I spin my desk chair around and gesture for him to sit on the bench at the end of my bed. He assumes his position and stares at me. The kind of look when you just know you're going to be called out.

"So, do you want to tell me why you are pushing Theo away?"

And there it is. He isn't playing around. "What makes you think I am?" Avoidance, denial. Either are solid options right now.

"The fact you've been hiding in here for four days instead of your condo. And also the fact that Liam called and told me Theo looks like he hasn't slept for a week."

"How would Liam know?"

"They're workout buddies. I'm not sure what's going on with you two, but Liam has adopted him as a little brother, so if you don't work things out, they're both going to be heartbroken."

More guilt. Part of me wants to chuckle, but a majority of me wants to cry. I'm hurting Theo because I can't process the loss of my best friend and after eight years attached at the hip, doing anything without her seems unfair. Chelsea's words replay in my head that I've busted out of my role as Rory's best friend, and I can't stop the hurt that comes along with leaving her behind. "I don't even know what's wrong with me. Theo did something that should have been sweet, but I made an issue out of it and it didn't need to be. I'm scared I'll keep doing it again and again because I can't move on from losing Rory."

"We're all a little scared, Kiddo. There's always a chance we'll get hurt or hurt people we love but choosing to not love them at all isn't saving you from anything; it's only stopping you from being happy. And I know Rory wouldn't want your life to end when hers did."

"How did you get over losing Leo… and your parents?" I hate bringing up his brother and parents. His twin, Leo, was his best friend and losing him to a drunk driver when they were only fourteen abruptly altered the course of my dad's life.

"I never have; it's not something you get over. But I know they would have encouraged me to do what made me happy. When Leo died, I thought my life was over. I felt guilty that he was gone, and I was given a second chance; it didn't seem fair. It took me years to realize something, so I'll tell you now and hope it saves you from wasting years of your life." He adjusts his position on the bench to settle in better and places his elbows on his knees. "If I could have traded places with him, I would have. If there was some way I could have sacrificed myself so he could have a chance at a happy life, I wouldn't have hesitated."

"That's how I feel about Rory," I interrupt.

"I know you do. So that's why what I'm going to say applies just as much to you as it has to me. Trust that she loved you as much as you love her, and don't let her sacrifice be in vain. Your happiness does not come at the expense of hers. So choose happiness. Even if sometimes it's only for a moment, if you're chasing happiness with a good heart and the right intentions, it's never something to feel guilty about. Find enough happiness for you *and* for her. Chase it, embrace it, and spread it around. You've got light to shine on this dark world, and everyone who loves you sees it. Theo included."

Of everything he just said, my mind focuses on that final bit about Theo loving me. "Did he tell you?"

"He didn't need to. I saw it the first time I met him. He'd be stupid not to love you."

Maybe he loved me, but after how I treated him, I'm not so sure anymore. I love him, but that's what has kept me away for the past few days. I'm afraid I'm not enough—that I'll never be able to move beyond my fears and it will prevent me from being who he deserves.

"Imagine the world we'd live in if everyone stopped loving because they lost someone. What would it look like if everyone stopped trying to be happy? It's hard but moving on from losing someone and being happy isn't a betrayal of Rory. If anything, it's taking all the love she gave you and growing it."

He has a point. Being married to a counsellor for fourteen years has rubbed off on him too, because he has a very analytical way of approaching things, but never brushes over the emotional challenges. He's never steered me wrong in the past, and the logical part of my brain says he isn't now. I just can't wrap my head around everything. Love, grief, anxiety, fear. It's all too much.

Even when I thought Theo was being distant, turns out, he was still doing something to help me process my grief by playing Rory's song. I'm scared that his dedication to me and helping me work through the grieving process is stopping him from doing so himself. But what if I never heal from this and his efforts are not only wasted, but he's neglected his own emotions along the way? How can I see myself as adding any value to his life if all I keep doing is hurting him? No matter how much he loves me, nothing is worth that.

"I'm not saying you should run over there and patch things up if that's not what you want." My dad rubs his palms across his thighs and stares out the window before turning back to peer at me. "But I love you enough to tell you…"

A pause far longer than I'm comfortable with passes. "Tell me what?"

"If you don't make things right with Theo, Liam *will* adopt him."

I burst out laughing and it's the first time I've laughed since I ran away from *The Mad Dog*.

"Seriously, Isla. I'm not going to push you into the arms of someone just because you love each other. Sometimes love isn't enough, and if that's the case, I'll respect that. But I can't sit back and let you throw good things in your life away because you're being destroyed by guilt that's not yours to carry."

"Do you… um… do you feel less guilty now after all these years?"

He stares blankly at my bedroom floor, not responding for a minute. "No. What happened wasn't my fault and no matter how many scenarios I play out in my head, it won't change anything. That doesn't make me miss Leo or my parents any less, though, and I always will. But now, instead of that guilt eating away at me and ruling my life, I use it to remind myself to be happy enough for all of us. My love for you, your mom, your sister, my grandsons, it's everything Leo and my parents could have ever wanted for me." His voice becomes hoarse, and his eyes are glistening. My dad is not a crier, but I can imagine how hard it is to talk about his family. "You guys gave me more than I ever could've dreamed and made my life worth living again. Please, don't pass up that chance. Not allowing yourself to love is just going to leave you grieving for a different kind of loss. Don't put yourself through that."

Before I hesitate, I'm seated on the bench beside my dad and we're crying together. He's stroking his hand across my back and Bond places his head on my lap.

The last time I cried in my dad's arms was at Rory's funeral, and this moment is like coming full circle. In no way am I "over" losing my best friend, but I think I am finally accepting the truth: it's okay for me to be happy again.

I owe Theo an explanation, but I hate making excuses for my behaviour. My reaction was immature and that doesn't change because I rationalize my reaction. He deserves so much more than me pushing him away and hurting him because I'm emotional. He can't dedicate his life to someone who runs away every time things get hard. It's time for me to stop running.

The past several years of my life have been leading to this day and facing the reality of what it all means has left me paralyzed by panic. What if people hate my writing? Or if the only people who buy it are family members who pity me? I wouldn't put it past my dad to buy 10,000 copies just to make me feel better, but that's the last thing I want. This book has to sell. It's the final thing Rory contributed to before she died, and I need this to honour her.

My reflection is taunting me as I will myself to put one foot in front of the other to get out the door. My long-sleeve beaded champagne mini-dress is modest on the top half, but it ends around mid-thigh. I don't think it's supposed to be mini, but with my body type, I can't really help it. I've paired it with strappy gold stilettos and pray I won't have to be on my feet all night. It's so unlike me to choose style over practicality, but I have a long list of other things or my mind. One, my mother chose this outfit and I want to make her happy, but I'm terrified people will be looking at me. Two, I feel sick knowing Theo might not show up because he hasn't answered my calls the past two days. Three through ninety-nine, I have no idea what or who I am after tonight.

Am I still Theo's girlfriend? Am I still an author if I don't sell any books? If people hate it, do I still pursue a career as a writer? If I'm no longer a writer, who will I be?

I blow out a long, shaky breath before giving Bond a goodbye scratch and walking to my car. The few people in the parking lot stare as I walk past, which sets the few remaining deactivated nerves in my body on alert. My nervous system is in overdrive, and my heart is practicing for marching band tryouts. I'm going to pass out before I even get my car in reverse.

The entire thirty-five-minute drive, I sit in silence. No pump-up music or last-minute podcasts on book launches or speaking in front of a crowd. Just my own thoughts, reeling, questioning everything about my past, present, and future.

As I pull into the parking lot of the bookstore hosting me this evening, I don't see Theo's car, or anyone I recognize.

What do I do? I don't know who I'm supposed to speak to or what I'm supposed to do. Theo arranged everything, and all I knew to do was show up on this day at this time. Maybe he's not coming after all, and my entire career is going belly up before it even starts. This is exactly what Chelsea warned me about, putting too much stock in his role in my life.

It takes a solid ten minutes to convince myself to go inside and speak to an employee. If they don't know anything, I'm going back home. There's no way I'm sticking around to make a fool of myself.

I step through the automatic sliding doors, staring at the ground in front of me. I lift my gaze to scan the room and halt when I see the space before me. Theo's back is to me as he sets up a display table. He's created banners with my book cover and my author photo—that's embarrassing—various merchandise like coffee cups, bookmarks, and pens. It looks amazing, and he's so caught up in doing a good job, he doesn't hear me approach.

"Hi."

He glances back, still arranging items on the table, but once he notices me, he turns around. "Hey. You're early."

My stomach plummets when he doesn't reach out to hug me or show any sign of affection. I can't say I blame him, but tears sting the corners of my eyes before I get a grip. It's my fault I pushed him away, but I owe him a proper conversation and I intend to make this right between us.

"Can we talk for a minute?"

"Isla... now isn't the best time. I... maybe later?"

"Right. Yeah. Sure. Okay," I stammer. The familiar sting returning. "Thank you for being here tonight."

He raises one eyebrow and cocks his head, making him look ultra-adorable. "Of course, I'd be here. This is business, and I take my job seriously."

Ouch. This is going to be so much worse than I thought.

"What can I do to help?" I try to play off his comment as if it didn't hurt like open-heart surgery without anesthetic.

He's facing the table again, adjusting things that don't need to be adjusted, so I can't help but feel like he's avoiding me. "Nothing. This is what you've paid me for."

So that's it then? We're just supposed to slide into a comfortable business relationship and pretend like he doesn't light my world on fire?

"Theo—"

"Please, not now, Isla. I can't do this with you." His body goes stiff, and he halts his movements, but the harshness in his words has already inflicted a fatal blow to our fragile relationship. He turns back toward me, but before I allow his eyes to meet mine, I walk back out the door.

I'm not running, but I'm going to sit in my car to have a good cry away from prying eyes.

If my career and my family are all I have left, I'll be damned if I'm going to let my success hinge on Theo's feelings for me, but that doesn't make the reality of losing him any easier in the moment. Convincing myself we're over before we really began leaves me choking out sobs in the silence of my car. If I were Rory, I'd be able to turn this heartbreak into beautiful music, but I'm not, and she's not here.

A knock on my window startles me, but I can tell by the shape that it's Theo without turning to look.

"Isla. Can you open the door?"

"No. I can't do this with you." It's immature. I'm not proud of it, but I throw his words back at him.

"That's not what I meant. Please, can you open the door?"

I wait. Unsure whether I want to open this can of worms here and now, on what's supposed to be the biggest day of my life.

"All right then. I'll just talk through the door so everyone can hear what I need to say." He clears his throat in dramatic fashion. "I love you, Isla Haynes. So much that the past few days I've been on autopilot, trying to give you space, but wanting nothing more than your presence."

This isn't going how I thought it was going to go. I reach down and pull the handle to open my door and get out. Once I'm face-to-face with Theo, I look in his glassy eyes and I can tell he's being honest.

"Thank you. I didn't mean I couldn't do *this* with you, and I felt like garbage as soon as the words came out. The truth is, I'm drowning. I wanted to focus on tonight to make this successful for you, but beyond my focus on that, I'm a mess."

Drowning? A mess? His eyes look so pained right now. I want to kiss him, but I don't understand what he's telling me. If he wanted my presence, why didn't he answer my calls?

"Let's just get through tonight, then we can talk, okay? We both have things we need to say, and your launch is supposed to start in twelve minutes."

I swallow the lump in my throat and nod. Like I'm going to be able to focus on anything else.

Once the event is in full swing, there are around thirty people waiting to buy a signed copy of my book. There have been entire years of my life when I spoke to fewer people than I have tonight. I'm not cut out for this.

As much as possible, I try to keep my head down and exchange as few words as possible without appearing rude.

*Everybody's watching.*

"Can you make this out to Barbara?" a familiar voice asks.

I look up to find Barbara and Mark Anderson smiling down at me. My brain doesn't have time to catch up with my body before I leap up to greet them both with a hug. Before they release me, I'm consumed by guilt. It's been over six months since Rory died and even though I promised they wouldn't lose me too, I haven't attempted to see them once.

"How are you, Isla?" Barbara asks.

I swipe a rogue tear from my eye, looking back at the line of people waiting for me. "You guys didn't have to come, but I'm happy to see you."

"It's good to see you too." Barbara smiles in a way that communicates her hurt that I haven't made an effort for them. "You've got quite the fan club already. We won't keep you, but we'll stick around for a bit if you have time to come talk later." She reaches out to place a hand over mine. "Otherwise, you can stop by the house sometime."

I nod and try to shake the emotions off. Easier said than done.

Once I take a seat back behind the table, I get through as many autographs as possible. Theo works quickly and efficiently to keep people moving and despite a few people giving up and leaving, I'm surprised most of them wait.

My hand is cramped and stuck in an awkward claw by the time I'm done, and I scan the room for familiar faces. My entire family came to show their support, but Liam and Chelsea had to head home early with the boys. Even Liam's parents and my mom's friend Quinn made brief appearances. Shane and Dean stopped by, which was made more awkward by the unsaid words lingering between Theo and me, but Dean seemed excited about the book.

All in all, every single important person in my life showed up to support me tonight even though I didn't ask. Everyone except one.

I shelve thoughts of Rory until I have a minute to myself. Right now, I owe her parents my time. They took me in like a second daughter without hesitation and never made me feel anything but loved. I've been selfish to stay away just because I found it too difficult to go to their home. To say I'm disappointed in myself is a gross understatement.

"Barbara, Mark. Thank you for coming… you really didn't have to." I stare at my gold stiletto, watching as my clenched toes turn white.

"Of course, we wanted to come. You've been talking about this since you were a little girl." Barbara's eyes tear up and one droplet trickles down her pale cheek. "Now you're a young woman, living your dream, and we're so proud of you."

I choke back my emotions hearing that statement, because I've all but left the Andersons in my past with no effort or intention to return. Rory's death was probably a million times harder for them, but they still came to support me when I didn't deserve it.

Pile on more guilt. Guilt if I move on, guilt if I don't.

"I'm so sorry I haven't been by." I really mean that, but I can't come up with anything else to say. Excuses don't serve a purpose and negate a genuine apology. Truth is, I'm just sorry but have no valid reason to ghost people who were like an extra set of parents. I was at the Anderson house when I got my first period, for goodness' sake. Barbara didn't even bat an eye, going into great detail about everything I needed to know. I spent my childhood afraid of anyone outside of my house, except for the people in Rory's.

Before I can spiral any further, Barbara surprises me. "Do you remember what I said the day of Rory's funeral?"

To be honest, I remember little from that day beyond freaking out and crying on the floor of the funeral parlour. Not my finest moment. I shake my head.

"I said, don't let your grief stop you from finding happiness, and that looks like a good start over there." She lifts her chin, directing my eyes toward Theo.

How she guessed there was anything going on between Theo and me, I have no idea.

"Before you ask, I can just tell. I've seen you grow from a little girl into a young woman. There are few things that have made your face light up the way looking at him does."

Theo is having an animated conversation with my dad. Not happy animated—he looks like he's had his heart stomped on, and I am responsible.

"I think I may have burned that bridge."

"So build a new one." Her words are so matter of fact, like it's a simple next step. "Isla, you are young, beautiful, talented, kind, generous, loving, and so many other things. But most importantly, you're alive." Her voice cracks and it's all I need as permission to start my waterworks. "You're alive, and there's nothing I want more than for you to be happy." She reaches for my hands, clasping them each in hers. "Don't let your happiness get away from you because you're sad sometimes."

I glance up at Mark, wanting to avoid Barbara's watery eyes, but he's no better. The two of them pull me in for a group hug.

"Now, go sell some books, and then think about what I said, okay?"

I nod. "Thank you."

As they turn to leave, Barbara adds, "And don't be a stranger."

I make a silent promise to myself to check in with the Andersons regularly.

After we clean up, my parents congratulate me on a stellar evening. My dad gives me a knowing look as his eyes bounce back and forth between Theo and me. Theo's packing up banners and the few remaining book swag items fifteen feet away, so he's not out of earshot. Mercifully, my father says nothing embarrassing, but his eyes express a sadness that say more than words could. I give him a tight-lipped nod as they leave.

I amble over to Theo, my shoes killing my feet, but they're the least of my concerns. "You did such an amazing job tonight. Thank you."

He speaks again without turning to face me, and this new habit might as well be a kick to the face. "It was all you. People came because your book is amazing."

"No. It doesn't matter how good a book is. Without good marketing, it's bound to collect dust. So this was all you."

He doesn't reply. He finishes tossing the remaining books in a box, which he tucks under his arm before turning around. "I'm happy for you. You deserve it all."

There might as well be a solid brick wall between us.

"Can we go talk somewhere? Please?" I beg.

His eyes flick around the room, everywhere except at me. "I don't want to ruin your night."

Why would talking ruin my night unless he was going to break up with me? No, Isla. You're not going down that trail of assumptions and guesses. You love Theo, so you will listen to what he has to say, giving him the attention he deserves.

"The only thing that will ruin my night is not knowing what you're thinking. I'm liable to come up with sixty-four different, irrational scenarios and drive myself crazy analyzing each one." I step toward him, hoping against all hope that if our spark is still alive, he'll feel it too. "But I don't want to talk for me. I want to talk for you, because I can see you're hurting, and I hate that I caused that."

His eyes soften, but he doesn't respond.

"If you want to break up with—"

"I don't," he interrupts and, while it brings me a wave of relief, it also has me confused.

"Okay. Good, because I don't want to break up with you either. I'm so sorry. You have no idea how sorry I am for overreacting. For being selfish. For everything."

"Let me load this stuff in my car, then I'll meet you at your place in an hour."

For the first time all night, I smile genuinely. Theo leans down to kiss my cheek and his lips turn up into a grin. It's a start.

Once I arrive home, I change out of my dress and into a pair of silk sleep shorts with a tank top. Then I wrap myself in a thin cotton robe and venture out to the patio with Bond. His tail thumps against the back of my rattan sofa just as a tall, devastatingly handsome man steps out of the shadows in the parking lot.

My heart has a visceral reaction to his presence. Earlier it was fear of losing him. Now I have hope again and my body's response adjusts accordingly.

He greets me with a "hey" and pulls me in for the first kiss we've shared in a week. I want to cry tears of relief, but his smile encourages one of my own.

We settle inside on the sectional in my family room once Bond finishes outside. It's late, and I'm a confusing combination of wired and exhausted from today, but my focus is on Theo.

"I missed—"

"I don't know—"

We talk over each other, both stopping abruptly.

"You don't know what?" I ask, encouraging him to say what's on his mind.

He smirks at me, displaying his long-lost dimples. "I missed you too."

Heat creeps up my cheeks and I realize how much I crave sentimental Theo. "What were you going to say?"

"I don't know how to explain everything going on in my head." He looks down at the ice water in his left hand as he absent-mindedly strokes Bond's ears with his right.

"Okay. One thing at a time, I guess? You said you were drowning. What did you mean?"

He huffs a sigh. "That's the thing. I'm not sure. I spent months with you, and every time I was around you, I was happy. Then when I wasn't, I couldn't function. Like you were my life source, and I became addicted to you."

My face falls. In some circumstances, that might sound romantic, but not in this one.

"When you took off the other night, I wanted to make sure I gave you space, and decided to take some for myself. It nearly killed me to not answer your calls, but we both needed time. I understood I upset you with the song, and I'm sorry for that. My intentions were good, but obviously my execution was trash."

"No. I overreacted. I see how stupid I was being."

"Regardless, that's not the point. We started talking before my dad was buried and, honestly, I was just looking for someone who understood what I was going through. For all I knew, you were a forty-eight-year-old divorcee with a beard and bad breath."

I chuckle. "Did you want me to be?"

"I didn't know what I wanted. That's the problem. I started out wanting an escape from being the strong one in my family, but…"

"But you ended up having to be strong for me too." I feel sick. Properly sick, like I'm going to hurl.

"Yeah. And I don't regret that." He leans forward to place his glass on the coffee table and takes my hand in his icy grip. "Not even a little. I love you and nothing can change that. I started falling for you and the last thing I wanted to do was add to your pain, so I stopped talking about my own. This past week just shed some light on things."

Trying not to vomit, I ask, "What things?"

"Things I'm still figuring out."

s this what happens when two people bond over their grief instead of processing it? They block it out by chasing the endorphins they get from each other's presence? I suppose so. I understand that happiness is the cure for sadness, but that doesn't mean that you can neglect the sad feelings and hope they get swallowed up by pleasant ones.

From the first time Theo and I started talking, he told me he didn't have anyone to turn to because he was trying to be strong for his mom and sister. I started out wanting to be that person for him, hoping we could support each other. Somewhere along the line, I became so self-absorbec, I didn't notice the depth of his pain. Thinking back on our interactions, I recognize signs of that now, but is it too late?

I don't regret falling in love with Theo, but I resent myself for not being the person he needed me to be; for not being who he deserved. All those occasions where I assumed he was being silent because he had nothing to say, I was respecting his wishes. But what if he had something to say, and I didn't clarify that I was willing to listen if he did? What if it was me who was so absorbed in my grief that I didn't tell him I was a listening ear—a shoulder to cry on—or that I'd be his support the way he has been for me?

I choke back my emotions, determined to make this right. "How do we go about figuring these things out?"

He fidgets with his glass of ice water, using his thumb like a windshield wiper, clearing away the condensation. He's stalling.

"Just talk to me. I'm sorry for this past week. My dad knocked some sense into me and it helped ease some guilt I was carrying around. Then tonight, Rory's mom shovelled off some more. It all made me realize how important you are to me, Theo, and I don't want to lose you… I can't." I pause for a second, willing myself not to cry. This is supposed to be about him.

"You won't lose me. It might seem like an easy thing for some people to say, but when I told you I loved you, I meant it. That's not something I can walk away from, and I don't want to."

I breathe a sigh of relief but prepare myself for this conversation to switch direction.

"Everything will be fine. I'm fine."

That's not the direction I expected, and I'm not thrilled about him dismissing his feelings, but how far is too far to push? My inability to read social situations is causing a major hurdle right now.

"I'm not going to push you if you don't want to talk to me, but I want you to know that you can. It was so stupid and immature of me to get upset last week and I can never tell you how sorry I am, but I'm here now. I'm here, and I'm not going anywhere. Whenever you're ready to talk, I'll listen."

"Actually, there is something I need to say." He props himself up in his seat; his posture is tense.

"Oh… okay."

"I know you deal with anxiety and I'm understanding of that; I get some things are harder for you and sometimes you need to be alone to recharge."

A bout of nausea returns as I nod for him to continue.

"When I came up with the idea for the safe word, I thought it would be a way to let me know when you're at your limit and we could address it together. Instead, you've used it to run off on me and it freakin' sucks."

I'm speechless; partly because I don't think he understands being at your limit, and partly because I can tell my actions hurt him. More than once.

"The first time you ran out on me at the coffee shop, I thought it was a onetime thing. But each time it's happened after that... well, I don't know if you've ever seen *Dumb and Dumber*, but there's a scene where the main character has a dream that he punches a guy in the chest, rips out his heart, and puts it in a doggy bag. That's an accurate representation of how you left me."

"Theo... I..." I stare off into space, still unsure how to respond.

"It hurt, Isla. Each time I wanted nothing more than to support you and help you, you didn't give me the chance. It wasn't just that you left me. It was the realization that you didn't trust me enough to fight alongside you. I could have sat next to you in silence or brought you home if you wanted to be alone. Whatever you needed, I was willing to do it."

"It's nothing you can fight. Whatever goes on in my brain is mine to deal with and I don't want to make it your problem."

"See. You get it." His tight-lipped smile gives pause to his words and suddenly what he's saying makes sense. "I want to help you with those things, but you think it's not mine to deal with. That's how I feel too."

I thought he hadn't opened up to me because I hadn't made it clear that I'd listen. In reality, we've both been stubborn and not let the other in. Not completely. It's a hard balance to strike when you love someone, wanting to be the best person you can be for them, but not wanting to burden them with your baggage. But what's love without trust? Without reciprocity? Without mutual support? It's not long lasting, that's for sure.

"I'm sorry." I shake my head to break my stare and refocus on Theo. "Can you promise me something?"

"Anything."

"In the future if a similar situation happens and I try to run away, don't let me."

"Isla, I'm not going to stop you if you want to go. I just wish you trusted me enough you didn't want to run away."

"No, that's the thing. When my switch flips and I get overwhelmed, my instinct is to hide away. I don't want to run or hide from you. I do trust you, and I don't want to add my problems to your plate, but if you don't let me run, I have to deal with it. Just force me to face it and let me be strong enough to."

It's time for me to get myself back on track. My anxiety was minimal for years because my parents always pushed me to face things they knew I was strong enough to handle. Mom would repeat mantras to me I could tell myself when my world was closing in, and I was doing really well.

*People are not waiting for me to fail. I can contribute valuable things to conversations. It's okay to take a break if I need to. Focus on what other people are saying and be a good listener rather than focusing on what I'll say next.*

Then Rory died, and every wound from my childhood was ripped back open and compounded by her loss. My mantras were drowned out by grief, and I lost myself and my strength in the process. I'm done making excuses for myself, though.

"So you're telling me not to let you get into the pumpkin carriage?"

I chuckle. "I guess I am. You are my Prince Charming, after all."

"It's a deal."

I hoped Theo would be inspired to open up to me after this breakthrough, but he tells me it's late and he should go home. Having him walk away does sting, and that hurts even more knowing how I made him feel all the times I took off. I have to give him time, though. We had a long day with a lot of emotions.

Sleep is calling me once he leaves, so I breeze through my nighttime routine and climb into bed. I lie there, staring at my spinning ceiling fan, coming up with ways I can show my support for Theo without pushing him too far. That balance again—it's tricky. How do I know what will encourage him and what will set him back? There is no way to until I try, and that's terrifying because I don't want to hurt him more.

As a couple, we keep moving in these waves where one minute we're solid, strong, and united, but then the tides shift and we're distant, awkward, and uncomfortable. I'm sure the awkward and uncomfortable is entirely on me, but it's not a good feeling. The last thing I want to do is to contribute to any reason for distance between us—again.

My ceiling fan provides a surge in clarity though, because before I drift off to sleep, I make a plan.

The tombstones we walk past are a wide range, from large and ornate to small and simple. The cemetery itself is well kept, the grass lush, now that the weather is warmer, but what catches my eye is the pre-dug hole off in the distance. It's hard to be at ease standing in a place that represents the worst days of people's lives, but it also serves as a reminder of all the love shared. The hard part is focusing on that love, and not the pain.

I give Theo's hand a squeeze as his pace slows. His car is only 100 feet behind us, so it's not as if it's been an arduous journey, but it's an emotionally taxing one.

We stop in front of a granite place-marker with the name Lloyd Theodore Malinga etched into its surface. It's tasteful and reserved, much how I imagine Theo's father was.

The silence extends for several minutes because I want Theo to steer this interaction. I know it's hard for him, so I'm not going to push, and I don't want to upset him more than this situation already does.

"Isn't it weird how everything you are and all you leave behind comes down to that one little dash? They write when you were born and when you died like those are the most important milestones, but everything else—your passion, your voice, your impact on the world—it all gets condensed into that little dash."

That's a really profound place to start this visit, and it catches me off guard. "Wow... I never considered that before. All these"—I wave my hand around at the other tombstones in our immediate area—"dashes tell a lot of different stories."

Theo reaches his hand out to take hold of mine without needing to search for it. He has a sixth sense—Isla sense. "I spent so much time thinking about my dad's dash, and everything that I'd include in it. How he was always smiling, even after a full day at work. How he never let anyone make him feel less-than because he was a blue-collar worker. How he took pride in everything he started and didn't settle for anything less than his best, even if that didn't translate to success. How he loved my mom like she was his own atmosphere keeping him alive."

I stare at Theo with a tight-lipped smile, listening to his voice crack as he talks about his dad. I can't help but tear up, hearing the pain in his voice over missing his father. When I glance up to meet his eyes, Theo has tears running down his cheeks. As soon as he sees my tears, he pulls me in for a hug. For a second, I worry he's trying to comfort me, but for the first time in the six months since Theo's dad died and the entire time I've known him, he cries. Sobs tear through him and I force myself to get it together so I can hold him up. I feel his pain as if it were my own and not because I can relate after losing Rory, but because I love him so much; his hurt is my hurt.

Theo straightens himself after a minute and apologizes for being so emotional. When I realize he thought he had to apologize, it hurts differently than seeing him upset. His assumption that he isn't *allowed* to be emotional makes me sad and angry. No, not angry with him—angry with society for making men feel inadequate for discussing things that are bothering them. Angry with our entertainment industry, glamorizing the man always being the knight in shining armour when he, in fact, needs saving too. Angry with myself for spending the last six months consumed in my grief, I didn't offer Theo a safe place to address his.

Now is the time to fix that.

"Theo, look at me."

He swipes his eyes with his sleeve, looking at my face for a split second before returning his gaze to his dad's tombstone.

"Please, I need you to listen to what I'm going to say."

He tilts his head back, looking up at the sky, then settles his eyes on mine.

"You do not need to apologize for hurting. You do not need to apologize for having emotions. In fact, you having emotions makes me love you more."

"Oh yeah. I'm a real catch, sobbing like a little girl."

My stomach twists again at his words and that same anger boils up inside of me. "You're not sobbing like a little girl. You're sobbing like a man. A man who has experienced a painful loss and is feeling that pain. I need to get one thing straight with you."

"Fierce Isla is a little intimidating."

"Well, buckle up," I reply with a chuckle, deflating my anger. "I haven't been a good support for you; I see that now and I'm sorry it took me so long—"

"Isla, you—"

"Please, let me finish because I know you're going to make excuses for me and that's not going to help us move forward. I need to take responsibility for where I failed you so we can be better—stronger." I take an intentional breath and square my shoulders to appear as determined as I can. "In the future, when you are hurting, I need you to trust that I love you enough to help you through whatever it may be. I *need* you to remember that there's no time limit on grief, and at some point, eight years down the road, you might think of your dad and be sad all over again. When that time comes, please be honest with me. And before you argue with me or tell me you'll be *fine*, know that I'm only happy when you're happy, and I can only move forward when you're moving with me. Processing my grief doesn't matter if you're holding back yours. If we're going to do this— be together—we need to pick each other up when the other is down. That's not your job, it's ours."

My little speech is the longest I've held eye contact in my life, but I wasn't itching to avert my gaze. I want Theo to know I mean every word.

His only response is a nod.

"Theo, promise me you won't hold in whatever it is you're feeling. You don't have to be strong all the time, and to be honest, I think tackling hard feelings takes incredible strength. Just like you encouraged me to open Rory's bedroom door, it was impossible until you were there with me. Let me do that for you."

"*Mi Alma*, look where we're standing. You already are."

"I love you, Theo."

He leans in, planting a kiss on my lips and his abrasive stubble is a welcome sensation. It would be so easy to get lost in him, trying to kiss away his pain, but now is not the time and this is definitely not the place.

I step back, maintaining my hold on his hand. "Tell me about your dad."

"What do you want to know?"

"I want to know what you want to tell me."

A beat of silence passes before Theo speaks. "All this time, I thought my dad wasted his life working and giving every spare minute to help anyone who needed it. He was always the first guy to offer to help someone move or repair something. We used to have this old neighbour before he moved to a long-term care facility, Mr. Whitcomb. He slipped and fell shovelling his snow a few years back and broke his collar bone." Theo's lips curve into a smile, and I'm confused what about the situation is cause for smiling. "He was in his eighties and struggled to do anything on his own while he healed. My dad was over there every day after work, making sure he ate, shovelling his driveway, even giving him sponge baths."

Now I understand. "Your dad sounds like an amazing man. That's really sweet of him."

"After your book launch, when I said I realized some things, I think I've finally figured it out."

I try not to cringe as my stomach turns sour. "What... what did you realize?"

"My dad didn't waste his life. He made the most of it. I wish he had more time to do things he enjoyed, but I thought because he didn't have any hobbies other than work and his family, that he was missing out on the good things in life. Now I see, that's not the case at all. To him, living for other people *was* living. Being someone other people could count on and making a difference in small ways, that's what made him happy. Being a father and husband, that gave him purpose, but he didn't stop there." Theo's eyes are watering, but his face is lit up with enthusiasm. "I want to carry on my dad's legacy. Honour him by being the type of man that lives for others. Volunteering at Carter's is a good start, but I want something more than marketing mortgages. I need to merge my skill-set and my passion."

"I think that would make your dad really proud."

Theo smiles as an idea strikes me that could offer us both a way to chase our dreams.

253

Theo noticed the spark in my eyes while we stood in the cemetery and questioned me relentlessly until I pacified him with a request to discuss it elsewhere. I wanted him to focus his time on coming to terms with his dad's death and understanding that it's okay to have grief-stricken setbacks sometimes.

So, we stood at his father's tombstone for nearly an hour as he told me all about his childhood memories and funny stories about his dad. Theo now knows that I want him to talk about his dad, and when a memory occurs to him, I want to hear it.

The discussion we tabled for another time is ready to be served up now, five days later, as Theo shows up at my condo after his day at the office. We haven't seen each other since our visit to the cemetery because he's been so busy. Since my book launch, he hasn't let up on marketing and I've sold more copies than I ever imagined. I owe it all to his hard work. That makes this idea of mine even more exciting.

Bond welcomes Theo in the door, but instead of his regular head scratch routine, Bond tilts his head around Theo's legs to look behind him.

"I think he's looking for Charley," I point out, standing behind my kitchen island, washing the last of my dishes.

"Ah, sorry, buddy. Charley couldn't come today, but I'll bring him tomorrow."

Bond seems to understand and prances off to return to his dog bed in the corner of the living room.

"I ordered food, but it hasn't arrived yet. I was waiting for you to get here so you can answer the door."

Theo chuckles. "You called in a food order?"

"Are you kidding? No. I used an app. Otherwise we would starve." I pull a dish towel from the front of the oven to dry my hands just as Theo enters the kitchen. He lifts me onto the counter and kisses me with an urgency I haven't felt for weeks. Aside from the physical reactions to his touch, a sense of calm washes over me because we're whole again.

"I missed you."

"You're kind of obsessed with me, huh? Good thing I'm obsessed with you too. I always miss you." I giggle.

"If I were ever going to have a stalker, I'd pick you." He laughs in response.

"How romantic. Don't forget I wrote a spy novel, so I'm practically a CIA agent."

His face-splitting smile is everything. My Theo is back, better than ever. We're better than ever.

I rub my thumb along the scar on his cheek that I've been curious about since we met.

"Little league accident. Shane clocked me in the face with a bat." He's still smiling, relaying the memory and I can't help but grin, imagining the antics little Shane and Theo would have gotten into.

He kisses me again, but we're interrupted by a knock at the door.

I give Theo a pleading smile, asking him to answer the door without actually asking. Before he arrives at the door, he looks back at me with a concerned expression.

"Hey, Clair," he says in a flat tone.

"Theo, I didn't know you lived here. I thought you lived in Gravenhurst."

"Yeah, I do. This is my girlfriend's place." He reaches out to accept the food, placing the bag on a small table inside the entrance.

"Oh, the pink-haired chick? You guys are still together?" she asks, her voice dripping with disdain.

"Yep. Very much together, and very much in love." He grabs the final package, and all but shoos Clair away. "Thanks for the delivery, Clair. See you around."

I gawk at him from my spot on the kitchen counter, having frozen in place to watch the interaction. Thankfully she didn't start singing *"You Belong With Me,"* or some Mariah Carey power ballad. The poor girl needs to move on, especially considering she's dating one of Theo's friends.

We both chuckle together, not bothered by Clair's petty interference in our relationship. We're solid. I would thrust— not the right word—place Theo in a room full of naked models and trust him fully. He's never given me the impression he has eyes for anyone but me. *Mi Alma*.

We get comfortable with our plates of food and sit on the couch for a casual dinner. Theo wastes no more time before he asks, "So, you promised we'd talk about whatever this idea was. Start talking."

I laugh at his bluntness because when someone else is privy to information I am not, it stays on my mind until I'm in the know. "When you were talking about your dad, and how you want to carry on his legacy by merging your passion and your skills, it got me thinking."

Theo is practically buzzing—his leg bouncing and his hands fidgeting with his fork. His anticipation is making me nervous.

I take a steadying breath to continue. "You did such an incredible job marketing my book, and your insight into the storyline brought a lot of things to my attention. At the cemetery, I was angry with mainstream media for promoting the mindset that men need to be tough and being emotional makes them weak."

"I'm sorry."

"No, Theo. That's my point. You keep apologizing, but you shouldn't. That's what I'm talking about. From the moment your dad died, you felt the need to be the man of the house, and I love you for that and for wanting to take care of your mom and sister, but you need support, too. You're allowed to have feelings." I shake my head because I'm getting off track. "My point is, there's so much in mainstream publishing that you shed light on when you called me out for my bias."

"I'm sorry for that too."

"Theo, stop apologizing. I *neeaed* to be called out. What I'm suggesting now is that we work together to call out everyone else."

"You want to start a riot? A book-club riot?"

I huff out a sigh because he's gone from feeling bad to joke-mode and I'm doing a terrible job relaying what I want to propose. "No. I want to start a publishing company. Somewhere that breaks down social constructs and promotes books that upset the status-quo. Books that change the way people look at things and make them question everything about their own pre-conceived notions and encourage them to grow. Books that make people *better* people because they don't ignore things that are inherently wrong."

"That sounds like an uphill battle, but I think it's amazing."

"I can't do it without you."

"Me? What do I know about books?"

I slide closer to Theo on the sofa and take his hand in mine. "I want you to join me and be in charge of marketing. We can hire out anyone else we need on a freelance basis, but you're already amazing at graphic design so you can do covers and all the marketing. I can do editing and the actual book stuff. We already proved we make a good team. We could really make a difference."

Theo stares wordlessly, not indicating what he thinks of my idea.

"You don't have to decide right away, and you don't need to say yes just because you're my boyfriend. I know business and personal relationships can get messy, so if you're hesitant about that, I understand. No hard feelings if you want to say no."

He still says nothing for another few seconds and I'm reassessing my entire explanation, questioning whether I relayed the important points and gave him an appropriate out.

"I'm trying to decide the most creative way to quit my job."

What? Did I black out for a minute and miss the part he agreed to this? "Quit your job?"

"Yeah. I mean, I'll keep working there for a while so I can make sure I have an income to support Mom and Solana, but I'm all in, *Mi Alma*. The question now is, what are we going to call ourselves?"

I dive the few inches forward and tackle Theo with an intensity even I wasn't expecting. I plant a kiss on him to thank him for considering taking this leap of faith with me. There's so much to sort out and plans to make, but for right now, I want to get lost in this excitement. Get lost in his kiss.

When we break apart, I can see the wide smile on Theo's face reflecting mine. Him being as excited about the prospect of this new business venture as I am gives me a confidence boost I didn't think was possible.

"What do you think of 'Paint the Town Read'? A play on words."

I snicker. "I do love a good pun, but I think the connotations of drunkenness might not relay our mission very well."

"You're right. Give me a second. I'll come up with something." He scrunches his face like he's thinking really hard and places his thumb and index finger on his stubbled chin. He looks adorable. "'Publication X', like Generation X."

I love that he's getting so into this. "That's an option."

"How about 'Publishing Schmublishing'?"

I quirk my brow in response.

"You know, like 'to hell with those other publishing companies'."

"'Publishing Schmublishing'? That's hilarious. It sounds catchy."

He pulls me toward him again as he leans back on the sofa, placing my head on his chest. We've abandoned our dinner plates on the coffee table, all thoughts of food gone. I could get lost in this moment with him, feeling real excitement for the first time in so long. Even my book launch didn't incite this kind of passion in me, and the future holds promise again. With Theo and a plan to change the world one book at a time, there's no stopping me.

I'm not the little girl who is too afraid to speak anymore. I'm a woman with a voice, and I *will* be heard.

Who knew that getting your own publishing business up and running would be such a challenge? Really, publishing a book has so many aspects, writing it is the easy part. I've been fortunate to establish good relationships with clients through editing and connected with other freelancers who I can keep on standby if I need to outsource work. Theo got us set up with a website and all the technical stuff like a business license and so on. My lawyer handled a contract so Theo and I can maintain separation from business and personal dealings, because as much as I'd hate to think about things between us going south, I don't want him or me to be at risk of losing everything.

My days have been so jam-packed with all things business-related, for the first time since Rory died—scratch that, since we met—I went a full forty-eight hours without remembering her. That, of course, made me feel guilty once I realized it, because if my memories of her fade, all that she was will be lost. If she's not on my mind, what's left? She's not here to create any more soul-touching masterpieces or ease my anxious mind with a song. Without my memories, does she finally cease to exist?

I've been struggling with these thoughts and find myself torn between talking to my mom or talking to Theo. Throughout my childhood, watching my parents and seeing how solid their relationship was, I saw how they've always gone to each other first; even when there was cause for complaint between them. If I'm going to model a relationship after anyone, they're a good couple to emulate.

So, I decide to talk to Theo first because if we are committing to each other, he should be my first point of contact whenever possible.

He's coming to pick me up in a few minutes so we can get a business account set up at the bank. The money from my book sales—minus what I had to pay out for breaking my contract with my original publisher—will be a small nest egg to build our business with. My parents bankrolled my college years, so everything I earned went into savings. Right now, I'm still using that to survive, but I'll need to earn a steady income soon. This business must succeed, but not only for financial reasons. I believe in what we're doing, and I want to make a difference.

I assume Theo will text me when he arrives, but like a gentleman, he comes to the door, knocks, and lets himself in. He's always giving me a hard time about leaving the door unlocked, even though I only unlock it when he's coming. Bond isn't much of a guard dog anymore, but I hope the "beware of dog" sign is a deterrent for anyone with nefarious intentions.

After our standard greeting kiss, which never fails to take my breath away, Theo takes my face in his hands. "Have I told you how amazing you are?"

My face warms and I wouldn't be surprised if it's burning his hands. "I didn't do anything amazing."

He shakes his head, offering an amused smile. "You have no idea how much you've changed my life, *Mi Alma*."

What has gotten into him today? "Were you watching rom-coms with your mom again?"

He throws his head back with a booming laugh. "No. I was thinking on the drive here about how you've pushed me and inspired me to do things I never would have done without you. I would have kept going in a job I hated, just trying to make ends meet. But you've helped me see there's so much more to life. You've given me courage I didn't know I needed, so sue me if I think that's pretty amazing—that you're pretty amazing." He leans down and kisses me again. "And pretty."

Now it's my turn to laugh. "You'd make a good love interest someday, Mr. Malinga. Keep dishing up that inspiration and maybe I'll write a book about you."

"Only if you're my leading lady."

"Always."

We arrive at the bank, paperwork in hand, ready to take this last step in our business set-up. Theo distracted me with his sappy lines when he got to my place and I didn't get to address my concerns with him, so I told him on the drive over I wanted to talk when we got back home. I appreciate that he didn't push or fish for more and agreed we could discuss whatever it was after we deal with the bank.

The process is uneventful. Sign here, date here. Blah, blah, blah, these are your terms. Nothing exciting, as per usual with adult responsibilities, but as soon as we clear the doors to outside, Theo picks me up and spins me in circles, eliciting a squeal from me and glares from passersby.

*Everybody's watching.*

"Theo, put me down, you goof. People are looking at us."

"Let them look. I'm happy." He reconnects my feet to the sidewalk, and I straighten my shirt, avoiding looks from strangers.

"You're happy for another bank account? I'd say you need more excitement in your life."

"Downplay it if you want, but this is a huge step. This is the last item on our checklist before we start changing the world. The fact I get to do that with you by my side, yeah, that makes me pretty dang happy."

I grin at him. His enthusiasm is infectious and seeing happy Theo is the best thing I could ask for. "Let's go home."

His smile grows wider. "I like the sound of that."

Today has been a whirlwind already, and again there were long periods of time that I didn't think about Rory. By the time we return to my condo, I feel more guilt over moving on. Theo notices my change in demeanour because the smile I was wearing outside of the bank has long since disappeared.

"Okay, hit me."

I glance at him, my forehead wrinkled in confusion. "Hit you?"

"I mean, time to talk. What's got that gorgeous face so worried?"

"Oh. Are you sure you wouldn't rather I hit you?" I huff a weak laugh.

Theo grabs a hold of me, lifts me up, and drops himself down on the couch with me in his lap. "You can hit me if that would help, but let's try sorting out whatever's bothering you first."

I focus my eyes on the dusting of chest hair peaking out the top of his V-neck t-shirt. "Do you ever go days without thinking about your dad, and then realize you haven't thought about him, so you feel terrible?"

"Uh… no."

"No, you don't feel terrible, or no, you don't go days without thinking about him?"

Theo tilts my head up to focus on him. "No, I don't go days without thinking about him, but he was a part of my life every day for twenty-five years. My mom talks about him constantly because he was the love of her life. If you've gone days without thinking about Rory, that's nothing to feel terrible about."

I understand there's a difference between my friendship with Rory and Theo's relationship with his father, but that doesn't make me feel better. "I've been so caught up in getting our business started, Rory didn't cross my mind for two days—at least that's how long I think it was, but I can't recall how long I went without thinking about her because I *wasn't* thinking about her. Ugh. And not thinking about her makes me feel guilty."

"Why do you feel guilty? Is there some kind of memory quota you have to meet to honour her?"

"Well, when you put it that way, it sounds stupid, but yeah. It's up to me to keep her memory alive."

"*Mi Alma*, her memory will be alive whether or not you're thinking about her. She's not going to fade into obscurity because she's not on your mind every minute of the day. And beyond that, you're not solely responsible for remembering her."

"But what if I stop thinking about her completely? That's not fair to her." My eyes well up with tears, so I wipe them with the back of my hand. I can have a conversation about Rory without crying.

"You won't. There will always be things that remind you of her. Remember this: there was happiness in your life with her. Right?"

"Of course."

"And there has been happiness after her, right?"

"There has. But—"

"No buts." He kisses the corner of my mouth. "Both scenarios are possible, and it's okay. As much as you want her to be a part of everything going forward, you can't torture yourself, feeling guilty you can't bring her along. Your mission now, which Rory would want, is for you to live the life she knew you were capable of. That's how you bring her with you."

I swallow the lump in my throat. "How did you get so good at this grief talk?"

"Well, you see, my future mother-in-law is a counsellor, so sometimes when I'm having a bad day, I call her."

My jaw drops. "You what?" I'm not sure what part of that is more surprising; the fact he calls my mother, the fact she never mentioned it to me, or the mother-in-law bit.

"I should have told you, but she was at Chelsea and Liam's while I was there to workout. It was after the song disaster, and I was trying to give you space. I couldn't help myself, so I asked her how you were doing, and our conversation went from there. She gave me her phone number and told me to call if I ever needed to."

"And you have? You do?"

"Twice. It was my way of finding a balance. I needed someone to talk to, but I couldn't get past the idea of adding to your grief, so the day we went to the cemetery to see my dad, I needed help wrapping my head around everything."

"And did she... did she help?"

He nods. "She listened while I talked, and I didn't even realize half of what I was feeling until it started pouring out. I don't know how she does it, but she had me open up like a gutted fish."

It makes sense now. I thought our trip to the cemetery was the reason his demeanour changed, but I should have known it would take more than that.

"Are you upset I went behind your back?"

"Upset? No! Theo, I think it's great that you recognized you needed someone to talk to. Even though it wasn't me, I understand why you made that choice and I'm happy you spoke with someone."

"I'm sorry I didn't tell you sooner."

It's my turn to kiss the corner of his mouth, brushing my lips against the stubble on his cheek.

Knowing Theo spoke to my mom instead of me doesn't bother me, despite my decision to speak to him instead of her. I understand now that sometimes the choice to seek someone else isn't to the detriment of a relationship, nor an indication of its strength.

I'm proud of him and I love him. This year has taught us some hard lessons, but we're here, together, stronger than ever.

'**ve kept my promise to the Andersons to stay in touch and make it a point to visit them often. They saw Theo at my book launch, but this is the first time I've introduced them officially. Barbara has been begging me to bring him over, so earlier today when she called, asking if we could meet at a coffee shop, I couldn't say no. Theo is a good sport, allowing me to parade him around, introducing him to all twelve people I know. Considering he met my family five months ago, meeting Barbara and Mark shouldn't scare him off now. Not that Barbara and Mark are scary.

It's been eight months since Rory died and judging by my regular visits, Barbara, Mark, and Marcus are all coping okay. We still cry every time I'm there, but it's transitioned from sad to happy tears. Our conversations are a mix between funny stories about Rory to random things happening in each of our lives. Marcus has a girlfriend named Lydia—something Rory no doubt would have teased him about, so I took on the role of big sister and gave him a hard time.

We're all still dealing with the heartbreak surrounding her loss in our own ways, but everything is easier when you're surrounded and supported by people who love you. I was selfish for not seeing that I could have provided that for the Andersons in the months after Rory's death, but we can only move forward, so I attempt to remedy that.

Theo and I walk into the café, hand in hand, and spot Barbara and Mark sitting on one side of a booth. They both stand to greet us, so I introduce Theo. Barbara embraces him in a tight hug, and he doesn't so much as flinch. He hugs her back.

"Isla has told us so much about you, young man. Please, take a seat." Barbara gestures to the red vinyl bench opposite to where they were sitting.

Mark takes everyone's drink order and darts off to the cashier. Theo and I slide in across from Barbara. Her smile reminds me of my mom.

"So, Theo. Tell me about yourself."

He grins back at Barbara, undeterred by her forwardness. "What would you like to know?"

"Everything. Where did you grow up? Go to school? What do you do for work? What are your hobbies? Any criminal record?"

I never thought to ask that, but I hope Theo realizes she's only asking because Mark is a prosecutor.

Theo throws his head back with a laugh. "No criminal record. My mom would beat some sense into me if I ever called her from the police station. Jail would be a safer option, actually."

"I like her."

"She's a tough lady." He glances at me, giving a reassuring smile. "My family and I have lived in Gravenhurst my whole life.

I have a degree in marketing. I've worked at a place in Bracebridge the last two years until I quit last week."

"Oh, yes. I heard about your joint business venture. That's very exciting."

Mark rejoins us with drinks in hand, distributing them out to each of us. I can smell the sweetness of my French vanilla cappuccino and can't wait to taste it, but I'm not a masochist. I'll wait for it to cool.

"Thank you, Mr. Anderson," Theo says.

"Mark, please. What did I miss?"

"Theo was just telling me about his degree in marketing and confirmed he doesn't have a criminal record."

Mark laughs. "Twenty-five years married to a lawyer; she can't help herself."

"It's fine. Isla has told me you guys were a bonus set of parents for her, so that's nothing I wouldn't expect from a father." Theo's hand squeezing mine under the table reassures me that he's taking their interrogation in stride.

The mood turns sombre, and I know it wasn't intentional, bringing up Mark's role as a father, but I panic the evening will get off track before we sip our drinks.

Mark replies, "So, you played a rendition of one of our daughter's songs."

Theo, who is taking a sip of his piping hot coffee, chokes, eliciting a coughing fit.

I reach my hand to rub his back as if that's doing any good at all. Last time I visited the Andersons, I mentioned that Theo wrote music to accompany unfinished lyrics Rory wrote. They were both elated, which made me feel more stupid than I already did for my reaction.

"I'm sorry if I overstepped. I was trying to do something nice for Isla, but—"

"Don't think for one second you have to apologize, son. Honestly, Barb and I were touched that someone was out there keeping our daughter's music going. That was one thing she never lacked passion for. Since she was a little girl…" Mark's voice cracks, so he stops a second to clear his throat. "She always knew she wanted to be a song writer. We told her she could have been a singer, but that part wasn't important to her. All she wanted was for other people to perform her songs. Knowing that's happening, witnessing her dreams come true even when she's no longer with us, that means everything. We'd both really love it if you could play it for us sometime."

Why didn't I see it that way? I was so blinded by emotion after seeing Dominic that night, I failed to recognize that Theo was doing exactly what Rory dreamed of. He got up on the stage and played a song she wrote. He was achieving her dreams and that, no doubt, would have made her happy. Happier than her music sitting unfinished in a drawer because I felt like it was some secret for my eyes only.

"I'd love to, sir. Though my voice doesn't do it justice."

"He's being modest. He's a beautiful singer." Now my voice is cracking. "Rory would have loved it."

The rest of the evening passes with idle conversation, hearing about Marcus' antics with Lydia and the struggles of young love. I'm happy to see them finding their own versions of happiness again. I'm reminded of Theo's point from a few months ago that happiness can exist *with* Rory and *after*, but that doesn't mean she's not with each of us.

"So, when should we expect a wedding invitation?" Barbara blurts, eliciting my own coughing fit.

"Soon." Theo replies, and I'm not sure which part of this conversation has surprised me more.

Soon? After all the difficulties these past several months, is he ready to make that commitment? Am I?

Yeah, I think I am. If there's one thing eight months of grieving my best friend has taught me, it's that happiness doesn't just happen. Reach for it, work for it, and don't let it slip through your fingers when you find it.

I smile at Theo in silent acceptance of his declaration, which has Barbara and Mark beaming from across the table.

"Well, young man, not that my opinion has any bearing on Isla's decisions, but you certainly have my stamp of approval." High praise, coming from Mark. "I consider myself a good judge of character, but beyond that, I've watched Isla blossom from an awkward, shy teenager into a beautiful young woman. I can confidently say, I've never seen her so happy." The four of us are swiping tears from our eyes, but Mark continues, undeterred. "I might not get to walk my daughter down the aisle, but make no mistake, seeing you achieve your dreams, succeeding as an author, finding love, and hopefully one day, having a family, that brings us as much joy as it would have for Rory."

Now Mark, Barbara and I are blubbering messes, holding hands across the table. Theo's hand reaches out, placing it overtop of ours, and it's possibly the most perfect moment we've had.

In the past eight months, I was scared of love, fearing that it only ended in heartbreak when it was ripped away. But now I see how love grows and blooms… and heals. Happiness can cure sadness if you allow it to.

Time has a funny way of healing if you put the effort into helping it along. A year has passed since Rory's death and most days, she's not far from my mind, but those thoughts get easier as time goes on. Instead of overwhelming guilt about having happy moments without her, I celebrate them for her. Instead of only dwelling on the things I miss about her and feeling sad, I often laugh at memories we shared and inside jokes only we understood. Rather than force back tears and avoid things that remind me of her, I embrace them. I've started dancing in my kitchen again, and badly singing along to songs on the radio. I appreciate the sun on my skin, and the sound of my nephews' laughter. Grief isn't an easy road to navigate and there are waves that come and go without any logic, but as hard as it is, there are lessons to be learned along the way.

Time has been kind to Theo, too. As the anniversary of his dad's death approaches, he's accepted that it's okay to be sad, and beyond that, it's okay to talk about it when he feels that way. He still feels vulnerable and sometimes requires a little prompting to open up, but I'm proud of him for attempting to share his feelings.

Liam and Theo have forged a full-fledged bromance, but my brother-in-law is one of the most wonderful people I know, so I couldn't have chosen a better friend for him to bond with.

Speaking of Bond, Theo asked Bond and me to meet him and Charley at Centennial Gardens in Bracebridge to go for a walk and let the dogs play together. Despite Bond's age, he still has moments when you'd think he's a puppy, and Charley brings that out in him. It always brings a smile to my face watching him play. Theo's glucosamine purchase has done wonders for my old boy's joints.

Once I park and equip myself with a hat and a warm coat, Bond and I set off to wait in the pavilion for Theo to arrive. I don't see his SUV in the parking lot, and I assume he's not here yet. It's been a long time since I came to this park; probably since my time in college when I would come here to read. There's beauty to be had at any time of year, and I've learned to appreciate that again.

I round the curve of the walking path and stutter step when my eyes lock on my dad. He disappears from view, and I wonder if I'm hallucinating. Theo steps out from behind the brick surround on the leg of the pavilion, smiling, but he looks nervous. His dark teal bomber jacket makes his skin radiant. He looks incredible in anything, but I love when he wears brighter colours.

I'm losing my mind if I thought I saw my dad, and it was actually Theo. I shake my head and drop Bond's leash, giving him permission to go greet Theo and Charley. Bond gets his mandatory ear scratches before he and Charley dance around each other. When I step onto the concrete slab of the pavilion,

Theo wastes no time pulling me in for a hug. He's warm, smells like citrus and ginger, and where I belong.

I stand on my tiptoes for a kiss, but Theo steps back.

"Wait. I want to give you something first." He reaches under his coat and pulls out a nondescript black book. It has no title, so my first assumption is that it's a journal.

"Uh… Thank you." I furrow my brows as I look at him because I'm confused why he wouldn't kiss me until he gave me a journal.

"Read it."

Oh. It didn't occur to me he'd write in it.

"Make sure you start on the first page." He's rocking back and forth on his feet with his hands in his jacket pockets and his uncertainty is unnerving. Theo wears confidence like skin.

I open to the first page and see a quote from Paulo Coelho's book *Aleph*. "Love is just a word until someone comes along and gives it meaning." I look up at Theo, surprised he'd include a literary quote, knowing he isn't a big reader.

The next page, and several pages after, are more of the same with quotes from Jane Austen, Emily Bronte, Margaret Atwood, and A. A. Milne, amongst others. Each quote is paired with a photo of us, which are mostly silly selfies of us sitting on my living room sofa. They sum us up so well, though, because we don't need elaborate dates or fanfare to enjoy each other's company. Quiet nights alone have always been my favourite times with him.

"Theo, this is beautiful."

He steps forward, placing one hand on each of my elbows so I can still flip through the pages. "You're beautiful. You've taught me so much, *Mi Alma*, about life, about love. Because of you, I understand how precious the love of a dog is. Because of you, I know the book *is* always better than the movie. Because of you, I realize I don't have to be strong all the time and that

I'm stronger with you by my side. And because of you, I know how important it is to pursue things that make my heart sing."

"You're going to make me cry. You know you've done all that for me and more, Theo. We make a good team." I flip the next page of the book and the last hundred pages have a hole in the centre. Sitting in the opening is a stunning ring with a vivid pink stone. I almost let go the book when I clap my hand over my mouth. Theo takes hold of the book as he drops to one knee.

That very second, a bunch of curious onlookers stand from behind their hiding places and I see Mom, Dad, Chelsea, Liam, Solana, Carlota, Barbara, Mark, Shane, and Dean. Clearly, my dog is not a suitable guard dog because he looks just as surprised as I am. I mimic a goldfish as I stare at their smiling faces.

"It was important for me to have everyone we love here for this—except your nephews because Chelsea said they'd behave like wild animals, and we'd never be able to keep them quiet. I've known from the moment you came into my life with your highlighter head and weird eating habits that we'd end up here."

His highlighter-head comment and the truth about my nephews' absence make me chuckle. Pink hair really wasn't a good choice for someone who abhors attention, but I can't argue with the results after all.

"I wasn't searching for love when we met, but there was no stopping it. You're my other half, Isla. I have no doubt that we could take on the world together, but what I want more than anything is to make you happy. If you give me the chance, I promise I'll never stop trying. I'm an idiot, so I'll fail sometimes, but all I can ask is that you let me keep trying."

I giggle again through my tears which are now trickling down my face.

"*Mi Alma*, my soul, will you do me the great honour of becoming my wife?"

I scan our surroundings, looking back at our loved ones gawking, awaiting my answer with bated breath. For the first time in my life, something that used to terrify me is now a source of comfort—a feeling of love.

Everybody's watching.

"Yes. Yes, Theo."

He slides the ring on my finger, and I finally get my kiss. It's better than anything I've ever experienced.

He pulls back, staring at me with a face-splitting smile. *"Puede que no sea tu primera cita, beso, o amor, pero quiero ser el último."*

"What does that mean?"

"It means I may not be your first date, kiss, or love, but I want to be your last."

"You'll always be my first and last love."

"I love you."

When I look down at the oval-cut stone on my finger, I ask him, "Pink?"

"Did you know pink diamonds are formed by adding enormous amounts of pressure?"

"I did not."

"It seemed fitting for us and how we got here. Plus, I really love pink." He winks at me as our family and friends charge toward us.

I'm not the only one with tears of joy.

Theo and I were married sixteen months ago, after an eight-month engagement. We had a small ceremony with only our family and closest friends, and it was perfect. I didn't want a big crowd of people who were only acquaintances—ahem, Clair—showing up to take advantage of the open bar. Nor did I want excess attention.

Our publishing endeavour has been going great, and I published a successful sequel to *Double Double Agent*, called *Flat White Lies*. We've also helped thirty-one other authors to publish their books, scouring every manuscript to ensure well-rounded and diverse characters. We may be a teeny-tiny fish in a massive ocean in publishing, but I love what we're doing. I'm proud of all we've accomplished together and being able to work with the love of my life, each of us pursuing things we are passionate about, it's my fairy-tale.

My parents surprised us when we opened our gifts at their house the morning after our wedding and found a set of keys. Theo and I were both confused, staring at their smiling faces.

Dad told us they were gifting us their house in exchange for my condo. Since he technically bought them both, I didn't feel right arguing, but I questioned them just the same. They said they were ready to retire and wanted to travel a little. They no longer needed a big house and condo life would be easier to manage if they went on any extended vacations.

It made sense, but it's still an excessive gift to accept. Theo and I both struggled with the lavish present, but after all was said and done, we moved in a month after our wedding. It's cathartic being back in a home where I gave and received so much love, knowing we'll keep that trend going. The curse of tragic pasts were broken in this home, and going forward, we hope there will be a lot less healing, and more loving.

Once Solana goes to college next month, Carlota will move in with us so she can sell her home and have some financial freedom. It's important to Theo that his mom not work herself to death like his father did. Plus, it will be nice to have her around.

I don't want to say the gift of a house was conditional on certain terms, but Mom didn't hesitate to tell us she expected a house full of more grandbabies.

So, that's where we're at. Thirty-nine weeks pregnant with our first child. Theo is zooming around like a crazed lunatic, loading my hospital bag in the car because my water broke. I'm terrified but try to calm him by reminding him labour usually takes hours, and my contractions are still five minutes apart.

I don't think he has any capacity for logic right now though, because he's covered in a sheen of sweat, panting like the dogs, and tripping over his own feet. Nothing about his movements is graceful as he crashes into furniture and struggles to string together a sentence. He's getting a glimpse into life with anxiety.

"I'll call our parents on the way to the hospital. Do you need me to carry you to the car? Can you walk? Do we have everything?"

He's been spending far too much time with Liam.

"I'm fine. As long as I make a break for it in between contractions, I can walk. I just need you to stick close in case one hits me while I'm walking."

Theo holds my hands, walking backwards with more efficiency than he's done anything else since I told him my water broke thirty minutes ago, and leads me to the passenger door of our cherry-red Hyundai Santa Fe. He's lined the seats with towels, which makes me laugh. This is his first new car, and he's not taking the chance of any bodily fluids ruining the upholstery. Good luck maintaining that streak with a baby in the back.

Just as I ease into my seat, a contraction hits and I throw my head back with a scream.

"Oh, *Mi Alma*. Just hold on." He gives me a peck on my temple before closing the door and running to the driver's side.

We arrive at the hospital thirty-one minutes and nine contractions later, and Theo parks outside the emergency entrance before he disappears inside. He reappears seconds later with a wheelchair and a petite, olive-skinned brunette nurse dressed in mint-green scrubs. Theo opens the passenger door, helping me out of the car and into the wheelchair.

"The nurse is going to take you inside while I park. Don't have our baby without me."

"If it could be over that fast, I'd be too happy to check if you were in the room."

He glares at me in response.

I throw my hands up, chuckling at his reaction. "I promise."

He nods at the nurse and races around to go park the car as I get wheeled inside.

"Is this your first?" the nurse asks.

"It is."

"I can usually tell the first-time dads from a mile away. Every bit of sense goes out the window as soon as the first contraction starts."

I chuckle right as my stomach tenses and the pain radiating through my body has me gripping the wheelchair arms with white knuckles.

The nurse pauses, waiting for the pain to subside. Before we're through the first hallway, Theo is back at my side, holding my hand in his.

"Are you ready for this?" Theo's face is etched with worry lines.

My uterus releases its death grip, and my body relaxes. "Let's get this show on the road."

By some miracle, by the time I make it through triage, I find out I am seven centimetres dilated with contractions less than a minute apart. Twenty minutes later, I'm in the delivery room with three labour and delivery nurses, but no doctor.

Our impatient child can't wait. Sixteen minutes of pushing, I hear the first cries from our baby as Theo declares, "It's a girl. *Mi* Alma, we have a girl."

Our daughter enters the world weighing eight pounds, four ounces. She has a head of fine, dark blonde hair, deep blue eyes, and her skin is the same ivory colour as mine.

I look up at Theo with tears in my eyes and say, "I swear she's yours."

He kisses our daughter on the forehead before doing the same to mine. "She's so beautiful. She's perfect."

I stare down at this tiny human who was born from our love and agree. "She is."

Hours later, when we're settled in a private recovery room, our family members make their way in. Having the room to ourselves means we're able to have everyone here at once, which is overwhelming, but I can't pick who gets to meet our baby girl first. They're excited and just as important to both Theo and me, so it only feels right to have them all here.

Mom, Dad, Chelsea—who is eight months pregnant with her own baby girl—Liam, Carlota, and Solana are all crowded around my hospital bed as I hold my daughter. Mom and Chelsea are crying, and if I'm not mistaken, so is my dad. Liam has an arm wrapped around Theo's shoulder, beaming at his "adopted" brother. Solana and Carlota are smiling wide, glancing back and forth between me, Theo, and the baby.

With the all-too-familiar tears in my eyes, I look up at my family. "Everyone, this is Rory."

THE END

If you enjoyed Isla's story, please consider leaving a review on Amazon and/or Goodreads. Your reviews help give me feedback so I can continue to learn, and also helps my books garner more attention from other readers. I would greatly appreciate your thoughts!

And there we have it. I'd be lying if I said finishing this book didn't bring me to tears, because it totally did. I've come to love these characters so much, and each one was inspired by someone or something in my life.

A lot of Zach, Liam, and Theo's personalities were based off of my husband. Even when Theo talked about his dad giving the 80-year-old neighbour sponge baths, my husband really did that. I never would have completed this series without his support, because obviously, he is amazing.

This story, as a whole, was based largely on my journey through grieving the loss of my mom in 2018. Like many people, I had a lot of guilt and struggled to "move on." I was drowning in my own grief so much, I then felt guilty for not being a support for my husband, knowing he was grieving too. Those unrelenting thoughts of wanting to be a support, but not wanting to push can be exhausting, and I hope someone, somewhere, finds comfort through their hard journey from Isla's experience.

Don't forget, sometimes the men in our lives need saving too.

I owe a debt of gratitude to my girls, who laughed along with me when writing this series, and listened to me talk about them incessantly.

Thank you to my ARC readers, Sara, Barbara, Tara, Lucia, Elaine, Carly, Charli, Celine, Hayley, Harriet, and Michelle. I appreciate each one of you for taking the time to read Isla's story and giving me your feedback.

I have plenty more planned, which you can catch a sneak peak of in the "Also By This Author" section! Stay tuned to my social media or sign up for my newsletter to keep in touch.

Linktr.ee/burdenofproofreading always has my latest links.

Needless to say, I'll be busy writing for the next few years, so I hope you enjoy reading!

Lastly, always remember, You Are Enough.


Much love,
Tiffany

You may have noticed the Taylor Swift influence throughout this book. My last novel, We're All a Little Guarded, was greatly inspired by Panic! At the Disco, and when I set out to create Isla's story, I wanted to find a musical influence that was the singer-songwriter type because of Rory's character. Given that Brendon Urie and Taylor Swift have a song together, she naturally became my choice. Beyond that, when I saw photos of Taylor with Pink hair, I knew she was the perfect fit for the story!

Some songs it was the message as a whole, others it was a single line, or even the title that provided inspiration for a specific scene.

So, here is the ultimate, We're All a Little Scared, Taylor Swift playlist that coordinates with the chapter titles, and any mentions in the story.

(All music Copyrights belong to Taylor Swift or other artists listed, and I do not make claims to any of the songs below. This list is merely to share my influences for the story.)

Hold On
Bad Blood
Eyes Open
Breathe
Come Back, Be Here
All You Had to do Was Stay
Crazier
Everything Has Changed
Long Story Short
Perfectly Good Heart
It's Nice to Have a Friend
The Lucky One
Safe and Sound
Only the Young
Delicate
King Of My Heart
All Too Well
Both Of Us
Sparks Fly
Cardigan
The Best Day
Beautiful Eyes
All of Me – John Legend
Soon You'll Get Better
I Almost Do
Jump Then Fall
I Think He Knows
Me – (Featuring Brendon Urie)
The Moment I Knew
Sweeter Than Fiction
Tell Me Why

You Are In Love
Our Song
Loser – Beck
Loser – Julian Moon
Call It What You Want
This Is Me Trying
Shake It Off
Two Is Better Than One
The Man
The Other Side Of The Door
Ours (This Love is Ours)
Emperor's New Clothes – Panic! At the Disco
Half of my Heart – John Mayer (featuring Taylor Swift)
Change
You Need to Calm Down
The Boy is Mine – Brandy and Monica
Tequila Sunrise – The Eagles
Mr. Jones – The Counting Crows
Lean On Me – Bill Withers
Happiness
Mr. Perfectly Fine
Renegade
How You Get the Girl
I'm Only Me When I'm With You
Right Where You Left Me (Write Where You Left Me)
You Belong With Me
I Forgot That You Existed
Begin Again
Invisible String
Closure

You can find the link to the entire playlist on Spotify through my LinkTree at linktr.ee/burdenofproofreading

# Also By This Author:

### You Are Enough Series:
**We're All a Little Broken: Book 1** (Zara's story)
**We're All a Little Overwhelmed: Book 1.5** (Zara's extended epilogue)
**We're All a Little Guarded: Book 2** (Chelsea's story)
**We're All a Little Tired: Book 2.5** (Chelsea's extended epilogue)
**We're All a Little Scared: Book 3**

This women's fiction series focuses on various aspects of mental health and overcoming trauma. It addresses anxiety, depression, panic disorders, miscarriage, adoption, grief and loss, racism, descrimination, and more, but in a light hearted way that will also make you laugh. The entire series is set in Muskoka/Bracebridge, Ontario.

**Suburban Watchdogs:** Long-time friends, Justin, Morrie, Brendon, and Josh, live in a small farming town north of the big city. When crime starts making its way onto their streets, the group of men brought together by circumstance, rather than choice, band together to keep their town safe. One movie night watching a good ol' gangster film is all they need to motivate them to take action, thereby forming the Suburban Watchdogs. If criminals think they can just waltz into the Suburban Watchdogs' territory without resistance, they are mistaken.

Justin takes matters one step further by adopting Karma. Karma is a... female dog, and she'll make sure you get what's coming to you.

Join the group of unlikely friends and their canine companion on their hilarious vigilante mission and laugh at the chaos and mayhem that ensues.

### A New Leash on Life Series:
**Coming Spring, 2022**
This series will consist of sixteen interconnected standalone romantic comedies. Some characters from Suburban Watchdogs and

the You Are Enough series will have cameos or their own starring role!

Sign up for my newsletter or follow me on social media to learn more.

Linktr.ee/burdenofproofreading